THE ALGORITHM WILL SEE YOU NOW

JL LYCETTE

Black Rose Writing | Texas

ISBN: 978-1-68513-149-4
PUBLISHED BY BLACK ROSE WRITING
www.blackrosewriting.com

Printed in the United States of America
Suggested Retail Price (SRP) $21.95

The Algorithm Will See You Now is printed in Garamond Premier

*As a planet-friendly publisher, Black Rose Writing does its best to eliminate unnecessary waste to reduce paper usage and energy costs, while never compromising the reading experience. As a result, the final word count vs. page count may not meet common expectations.

To E., N., and S.

PRAISE FOR
THE ALGORITH WILL SEE YOU NOW

"I've been waiting for a book like this: a full-frontal assault on the dangers of artificial intelligence and the failures of our mangled health care system, all wrapped up in a clever, ripping thriller. Jennifer Lycette is an author to watch."
–Rob Hart, author of *THE PARADOX HOTEL*

"In her debut, Lycette explores the darkest realities about the healthcare system and what generations of the near future could potentially face if power shifts to the wrong hands. Perhaps even more gripping is how she delves into the ways grief can shape someone, causing them to make questionable decisions in the name of redemption. With nuanced characters and a truly terrifying premise, *THE ALGORITHM WILL SEE YOU NOW* is an ambitious debut that delivers. "
–Heather Levy, author of Anthony nominated *WALKING THROUGH NEEDLES*

"Both tense and topical, The Algorithm Will See You Now is a meticulously researched and deeply informed novel about the perils of where healthcare is likely heading, and the agonizing human costs involved. There are no easy decisions here, and Lycette paints a wonderfully complex portrait in an exciting debut."
–E.A. Aymar, author of *NO HOME FOR KILLERS*

Full of intrigue and smart thrills, The Algorithm Will See You Now is a incisive vision of a tech-driven future, amping up the contemporary horrors of our healthcare system to the extreme. Lycette's mastery of the medical field shines through, and her empathetic storytelling invites us to examine where we are headed and how we treat each other as human beings.
–Victor Manibo, author of *THE SLEEPLESS*

This book contains plot elements surrounding cancer, cancer death, pregnancy loss, and sexual harassment in the workplace.

THE ALGORITHM WILL SEE YOU NOW

PART ONE: *DIAGNOSIS*

*May I never see in the patient anything but
a fellow creature in pain.*
—The Oath of Maimonides

CHAPTER ONE

MONDAY *08 OCTOBER 2035*
7:15 AM
PRIMA, *Prognostic Intelligent Medical Algorithms*
Main Campus, Seattle

Dr. Hope Kestrel was the only person who knew the patient in Room 132 wasn't responding to the algorithm-selected treatment.

She shuffled forward in the hospital security line, wanting to get her day started already yet dreading how she'd tell her patient the unexpected and devastating news. The straps from her work bag dug into her right shoulder as she shifted the trays of coffee and scones in her arms, her usual Monday morning offering to the staff. From PRIMA's lofty location at the top of "Pill Hill," the floor-to-ceiling windows framed downtown Seattle's skyline, lit up by the early morning sun—its first appearance in over a week. In the distance, a ribbon of pink sky silhouetted the Space Needle, the tip poking out of the murky blue of the cloud bank. She frowned down at her pale hands, unable to recall the last time her skin had seen the sun. Even her freckles were fading.

Her heart lifted when she spotted Bear, the Security Force service dog, rounding the corner. The German shepherd dashed for her, pulling Kyle, his Security Force guard, with him. The people next to her in line stepped back.

Bear nosed at her lab coat, and she lifted the pastry box in one hand higher while shielding the cardboard carrier of coffee in the other. Hot liquid sloshed onto her wrist, the sting on her skin not far off from the burn in her chest that had been present all morning, triggered by the impending meeting in Room 132. One where she'd need to engage on an interpersonal level without the usual buffering layer of technology.

Her gaze shifted from Bear to the familiar logo on the wall behind Kyle's head—*Prognostic Intelligent Medical Algorithms*—and she shut out the searing pain in her chest. They were so close to the breakthrough to enhance the artificial intelligence even further. To render tumors like her mom's curable. Because to rely on only *hopefulness* promised everything and got you nothing. No matter her damn name.

She had to focus on the big picture. All she needed was to maintain her top ranking for a few more months. Then the coveted post-residency position at PRIMA would be hers—complete with her own research lab. Soon, she'd work side-by-side with her mentor Cecilia, no longer an underling.

Bear gave a muffled woof and sat down obediently at her feet. Although Kyle would probably deny it if asked, she strongly suspected the guard went out of his way each morning to find her, knowing how much she loved Bear. It had been their unofficial routine for five years now.

Hope gestured with her elbow. "Kyle, could you take this for a sec?"

The burly, middle-aged man accepted the breakfast offerings with a flash of white teeth gleaming in contrast to his warm brown skin. "You got it, High Resident Kestrel."

"For the millionth time, you can call me Hope."

His eyes twinkled. "Whatever you say, oh most High One."

Heat flamed Hope's cheeks, and she tried to cover it with an eye roll. Three months into her final year, she still wasn't used to her lofty title. She'd be called the Chief Resident—not the High Resident—at any other program, but PRIMA had its own language.

The loyal dog emitted another stifled woof from his barely contained seated position.

Hope fished in the front pocket of her white scrubs for one of the dog biscuits she always carried and tossed the treat to Bear, who snapped it up.

Kyle returned the pastries, then spoke in the deep, rumbling voice that Hope had come to learn only masked his kindly nature. "He sure loves you,

Dr. K. He'd follow you anywhere. Have you reconsidered about one of the puppies?"

She shifted her grip and gave a wistful shake of her head. "It wouldn't be fair. I'm never home."

"So? You'd figure it out. Hire a dog walking service—and doggie daycare, too. You don't have to do it on your own."

"I'd be nothing more than a familiar stranger who provides shelter and food."

Kyle bent down to rub Bear behind his ears, only to glance up and hastily straighten into a military posture, shoulders back. He tugged Bear to heel, his gaze fixed over Hope's head.

The dog sensed his handler's shift in mood, the fur on his neck bristling upward.

Hope swiveled, following the direction of Kyle's eyes. More coffee dribbled on her hand, but she barely felt it this time. A man and woman in matching black suits and pressed white shirts were staring in their direction. Hope couldn't help but stare back. The man was tall and broad-shouldered, mid-thirties, with angular cheekbones and deep-set eyes, his striking features set off by his onyx black hair. The woman appeared to be of similar age and height, equally imposing, with skin paler than Hope's, commanding eyebrows, and white-blonde hair in an identical short haircut to her partner.

Hope's eyes darted to Kyle, who flashed another smile, but it didn't reach his eyes.

"Are those two—?"

"Not regular Security Forces. They'll notice me deviating from my route." Kyle grimaced. "And letting Bear interact with civilians."

"But—"

Kyle dropped his voice. "Last week, another disgruntled non-responder tried to get in."

A *non-responder*. A patient the algorithm had identified as refractory—resistant to all known therapeutics—and therefore wouldn't be offered treatment at PRIMA. Or *shouldn't*, at least.

Hope went cold all over. All patient volunteers agreed to abide by the algorithm's determinations in exchange for free healthcare. What would the guards do if they discovered another non-responder already here, admitted by mistake? On Hope's service, no less.

But that wasn't her fault—

"You're a busy doctor, and we shouldn't be holding you up." Kyle tugged Bear away before she could ask him anything more. "We'll see you again soon, Dr. K."

Before the dog was out of reach, Hope hurried to transfer the pastry box to the crook of her elbow, bracing it against her side enough to allow her to extend a hand to trail her fingers in Bear's soft fur. The brief comfort the touch provided would have to last until tomorrow. She re-joined the line to watch the man and woman cut through the security checkpoint.

Her muscles tightened, and she forced them to relax. She needed to focus. At least medical training had made her a champion at putting extraneous thoughts out of her mind. Compartmentalization for the win.

A few moments later, she passed through the checkpoint and stepped onto OASIS—the *Oncologic and Surgical Intervention Success Unit*—and its familiar buzz of activity.

Patients strolled the oval hallway in the sunshine-yellow robes and plush slippers allocated upon admission. If not for the slim IV poles, they might be in a luxury hotel. The hidden panels in the walls and ceiling secured all medical equipment out of sight.

Abbie Fuentes, the charge nurse on OASIS for as long as Hope or anyone else could remember, spotted her arrival and trailed her into the break room. Hope wordlessly handed her one of the coffees, and she took a noisy sip while scanning Hope up and down, her impeccably bobbed hair not moving an inch. "What's going on with you today? You're late."

Hope shrugged. The nurses hadn't yet seen her patient's latest test results, and the part of Hope that feared being perceived a failure planned to wait until the last possible moment to tell them. "Line at security. You know, it's getting slower every day."

Abbie grunted in assent, taking another greedy gulp and releasing a satisfied sigh. With the other hand, she jerked a thumb at the tall, young woman who'd slipped in behind her, wearing the deer-in-the-headlights expression of a fresh intern. "Found you a present, too."

The intern took a nervous step forward, twisting her slender hands, the standard-issue white scrubs highlighting her dark complexion. She hunched her shoulders as if out of habit, although it didn't disguise her striking height, a good half a foot over Hope's five foot five. "Dr. Kestrel? I'm Jacie Stone. Your new intern."

She'd artfully draped a bright purple scarf around her neck, making her stand out from the conformity of the other residents. The color matched her glasses and complimented her skin tone. Behind the glasses, a fervor shone out of her eyes. She had a restless manner that made Hope think of a coiled spring—filled with potential energy ready to explode.

Before Hope had the chance to greet her, Abbie interjected. "You forgot, didn't you?"

"What? Of course I didn't."

Abbie arched her eyebrows at Hope and then turned to Jacie. "She forgot. But don't worry, she'll still take good care of you."

"Don't listen to her." Hope steered Jacie by the elbow. Even though truth be told, she'd prefer to leave the intern there. But if she left Jacie in the break room, Abbie would ask why. So, no, she couldn't leave Jacie behind. She'd have to bring her along to witness her failure.

She stopped at the workstation in front of Room 132 and pulled out her tablet. Out of habit, she did a quick scroll to first check her ranking. She stifled a breath of relief to find she remained at the top, with Leach—her main rival—second. Too bad her High Resident position didn't give her any advantage in PRIMA's resident physician ranking system, but she wouldn't want it even if it did. She'd earned her top place.

Jacie cleared her throat. "Would you like me to activate *Osler* for you?"

Osler was OSLR, the Online Speech and Language Recognition assistant. But the residents had long since dubbed it Osler—after Sir William Osler, the so-called Father of Modern Medicine—and like most, Hope thought of it as a him. He—or it—could be called on from anywhere in the hospital.

"No, I've got it."

Each workstation came equipped with a large flatscreen that would sync to their tablets and an optional keyboard—rarely used since OSLR responded to voice commands. Hope spoke briskly in the monitor's direction. "*Osler*, open the chart for patient last name Medrano, first name Sean."

The AI's masculine voice, with its hint of nonspecific accent, floated down from the ceiling.

"Good morning, Doctor Kestrel. Opening chart for Patron 564."

Jacie cleared her throat again. "Did you know PRIMA decided against a female-coded AI assistant? Because supposedly doctors of all genders are more responsive to a male voice?"

Hope gave her an appraising glance. She did know.

Jacie interpreted it as permission to keep the questions coming. "And why are we calling patients 'Patrons' now?"

"Part of PRIMA's new marketing plan. Personalized, precision care." Hope channeled her High Resident persona, imbuing her words with confidence. At twenty-nine, she was probably only a few years older than Jacie, but most days, her own internship faded into the distant past. Even though inside, a part of her remained that young woman who'd arrived five years ago in awe of the AI technology. Apparently, these new interns were harder to impress. She returned her attention to the monitor. "Osler, bring up this morning's CT scan."

The images appeared. Hope used her thumb and index finger to pinch and magnify one in particular. "The largest tumor in the liver is blocking the bile duct. Obstructing the normal outflow of bile, which causes?"

Jacie glanced from the images to Hope. "Jaundice. But can't you stent it?"

"You're asking the wrong question. Can I? Yes—I'm a pro at endoscopic stenting. However, *should we* stent it? That's the more relevant question." Hope addressed the workstation. "Osler, what's the prognosis after stenting the biliary obstruction?"

"The stent would relieve the obstruction but would not add survival time. Primary resistance to this targeted therapy is a predictor of refractory disease. Estimated time to death is three weeks. No available intervention can change the prognosis."

Jacie's eyes darted over the images on the monitor. "But shouldn't we try? To stent it anyway?"

Hope shut off the workstation. "You heard Osler. It would be futile."

"But what if it's wrong?"

Hope forced herself to take a slow breath. The interns never got it at first. "Look, it's normal to want to save everyone. But the AI ensures we're using the right treatments on the right people, not ineffective treatments on refractory disease."

Jacie's face fell. "Oh... what do we do then?"

Hope studied the monitor, where the PRIMA motto had appeared as the screensaver. *We Optimize so You can Flourish.*

She looked Jacie full in the eyes and forced herself to say the words she'd been dreading. "The recommendation is for transfer to HEARTH. There's nothing more to be done."

Jacie's head flinched back slightly. "Hearth?"

"The Hospice and Restful Transitions House—our hospice facility."

"I know, but... I don't understand." Jacie glanced around as if looking for answers before her gaze returned to Hope. "To become a Patron means PRIMA tagged him as a responder. The machine learner algorithm matched his data to a therapeutic protocol and assigned him Patron status, right?"

"Very good. That's a textbook recitation from your first-year curriculum."

"But he shouldn't be here at all."

The very problem that had Hope replaying his results in her head all morning. She told Jacie the same thing she'd been telling herself, although it hadn't helped. "This case is a one in ten thousand occurrence."

PRIMA was everything Hope had wanted, the healthcare system she'd dreamed of, the one she wished had existed for her mom. The AI kept doctors on track. It ensured she'd be the right kind of doctor and represented her life's work. She struggled to find the words to make Jacie understand. "I know it's difficult, but an individual with *no* chance of benefit from a particular treatment should be *spared* that treatment. Administering toxic therapies to a non-responder would be no better than torture."

Jacie's brows drew closer, her face tightening. "What if it's a mistake?"

"The algorithm re-examined all options for him. It determines which tumors respond to particular treatments and which don't—*at the DNA level.*" Hope paused, then continued in a softer voice. "His cancer is incurable."

She knew she sounded cold, even uncaring. But how else to keep back the empathy that made her job too difficult? She'd been the one to sign the orders on his treatment. *She'd* let this happen. Allowed him to believe he'd get better when he never would. Now, she'd have to deliver the worst news. He was dying.

Jacie stared at the floor.

Hope forced herself to speak slowly to portray a calm she didn't feel. "You don't know how lucky you are. Because of the algorithm, PRIMA has compressed your pre-clinical training, and you start internship sooner. But that means you've got a lot to learn."

Jacie cocked her head. "But if something like this happens, can we trust it?"

A flashback of her mom's chemotherapy-wracked body played in Hope's mind, and her vision clouded for a second. Jacie didn't yet understand. Identifying non-responders to spare them the needless suffering of ineffective treatments was a necessity—not only a practical imperative but a moral one.

She needed Jacie to understand. "Don't you see? The AI *frees* both patients and doctors from the fallacy of choice. The algorithms are more trustworthy than people. It's like DNA."

Jacie fiddled with her scarf. "I don't—"

"DNA doesn't waste its time over choice. *G* doesn't dither about partnering with *C*, and *T* doesn't debate endlessly over whether it should partner with *A*. There are rules to how it all works. It doesn't matter if we *want* it to be different. Some things we can't change."

Jacie's stance went rigid. "So, you would trust it with your family?"

If only her family had been afforded that chance. Because Hope had learned the hard way—relying on *hopefulness* promised everything and got you nothing. She spoke through clenched teeth. "Absolutely."

CHAPTER TWO

MONDAY 08 OCTOBER 2035
7:25 AM
OASIS Unit, PRIMA

The faint citrus scent from the automated sanitizer filled the room. Sean sat propped up in the hospital bed. Golden light streamed from the ceiling, highlighting the yellow cast of his jaundiced skin. His wife hovered by his bedside, her makeup not entirely hiding the bags under her eyes.

Hope's throat constricted at the light in Sean's eyes and the hopeful expression on his wife's face upon spotting her. But of course, they should be hopeful. He was here, at PRIMA, where they'd promised him a cure. Now, she would shatter their hope, the unexpected grim reaper in the room.

She stalled from disclosing the bad news, instead introducing Jacie. "This is my new intern, Dr. Stone."

Jacie said hello, and the Medranos gave her polite smiles before fixing their gazes back on Hope.

She drew in a few slow, steady breaths, needing to detach herself from the situation. A solution popped into her head—the new Patron terminology. Using patients' names only made this kind of thing harder.

Hope reset her thoughts.

Patron 564.

"I'm afraid I have difficult news." She held herself erect, her feet shoulder-width apart and her arms crossed behind her back. Her words came out distant and clinical. "Your scan this morning revealed the tumors in the liver are larger and causing obstructive jaundice."

Jacie looked at her askance.

Heat surged upward to Hope's head, and she had to remind herself that medical care determined by the algorithm ensured no single doctor could be responsible. So why did she somehow *feel* responsible? But everyone waited for her to say something else. "I'm sorry. The PRIMA analysis shows the cancer cells are resistant to the targeted therapy."

Sean's shoulders slumped. His wife's expression changed from hope to confusion to fear. A heavy silence followed, broken by a stifled whimper from Mrs. Medrano.

Jacie's eyebrows shot up to her hairline. Hope ignored her. Jacie didn't understand how difficult this was for Hope. She'd joined PRIMA to avoid precisely this kind of situation. *One of her patients was going to die.* He would die of his cancer, and Hope was powerless to stop it.

She reminded herself of what Cecilia always told her — "When something goes wrong, it isn't automatically your fault."

It's not your fault, it's not your fault...

But no matter how many times she repeated Cecilia's words to herself, another voice overpowered it. Her own.

It's all your fault, it's all your fault...

Mrs. Medrano crumbled, bending her head down over the union of her hand with her husband's. He reached up with his other hand to stroke the back of her head, her gray-blonde curls slipping through his fingers.

Hope pointed her body toward the door, her instinct to give them privacy in their grief, and signaled Jacie to follow.

But Jacie moved toward the bed.

The throbbing in Hope's temples accelerated with her pulse. What was Jacie doing?

Jacie crouched down to Sean's eye level. "What Dr. Kestrel means is the treatments aren't working... because this is a kind of cancer we can't fix. Your liver is failing. Going forward with more treatments would only risk causing you more harm and not change the cancer's growth in your body."

"What do you mean, can't fix?" Mrs. Medrano wiped her face with a shaky hand. "Isn't this PRIMA? Isn't that why he's here? Why we bought the fancy insurance? Mortgaged our house, used up our granddaughter's college fund..."

Something flashed in Jacie's eyes. "The algorithm isn't always righ—"

Hope stepped in front of her, cutting Jacie off. Her pulse raced. She needed to take control of the situation, not allow doubt to take hold because of Jacie's words. "What my intern means is that in rare circumstances, a Patron doesn't respond to PRIMA-directed therapy despite the initial algorithm's prediction. Perhaps only one in ten thousand times. It's in the paperwork you signed when you agreed to take part in the program. I'm sorry to tell you, as unlikely as the odds were, it appears you are that one."

In response, Sean did the last thing Hope expected. He gave her a warm smile, like the kind her mom used to give her. "It's okay, Dr. K. I know you did your best."

The acceptance in his words intensified her guilt. A great sense of relief flowed through her. He didn't blame her. No, that wasn't right. A doctor shouldn't feel relief at such a moment.

His wife's trembling voice interrupted Hope's cascade of thoughts. "What... what happens next?"

Hope didn't meet her eyes. "PRIMA recommends a transfer to HEARTH."

The words struck like a physical blow, and Mrs. Medrano appeared to collapse further. "No... please... isn't there anything else you can do?" Her voice dropped so low Hope strained to catch her words. "What if we refuse?"

Hope's breathing became shallow. She hadn't considered they might refuse. Nothing like that had ever happened before.

But she suspected he couldn't afford health insurance anywhere else— like most patients enrolled here. PRIMA offered the best plan the government subsidies could buy.

She had to make Sean and his wife see reason. She would hate for them to bankrupt themselves to chase down treatment somewhere else that didn't exist. Hope had seen how that road ended. The Medranos needed to see the tighter they clung, the worse it would be.

"That would be a mistake. The algorithm predicts a life expectancy of three weeks. At HEARTH, he'll be allowed opiate pain medications." Not an insignificant thing since Congress had passed the Opiate Ban in 2032.

Hope thought of her friend Poppy, a nurse now at HEARTH, where Sean would receive the best of care. "He'll be cared for by highly skilled nurses trained in the proper use of medications at the end of life—"

The door swung open, and a girl slipped in.

Hope guessed her to be about twelve, with reddish-brown hair in double braids, dressed in ripped jeans and a green t-shirt with the Seattle Aquarium logo. The girl hesitated upon seeing the full room.

Mrs. Medrano reached out to the girl in a quick motion. "Come here, sweetie, it's okay."

The girl sidled over. Hope watched her take in the scene.

"Chloe, our granddaughter," Sean said. "We've raised her since she was two—"

He pressed his hands to his face.

"What's wrong, Poppa?" Chloe pulled at his hands, shooting daggers at Hope with her eyes. Hope didn't wonder how she'd deduced Hope was responsible and not Jacie. Her guilt must be radiating off of her.

Sean's eyes traveled from his granddaughter to his wife. Somehow, his face shone with an inner light. "It's okay. Everything's going to be alright."

Hope flinched at his words after what she'd just told them. She'd tried to deliver the facts so they could prepare for reality. They needed something better than blind optimism, and because of PRIMA, they had it. Her nails bit into her palms again. They were *supposed* to have it.

He smiled at Chloe in a way that cracked something deep inside Hope.

No. She wouldn't let it.

She was doing the right thing. The necessary thing, heading off the false expectations that only made things worse.

But she found herself averting her gaze, unable to meet the girl's eyes. This small person who reminded her of... someone she hadn't allowed herself to be in a long time.

Chloe's determined voice rang out. "What's going on?"

Mrs. Medrano tried to shush her, but Chloe stepped away. She crossed her arms and faced Hope.

Memories flooded Hope. All the times her mom's doctors had treated her like she didn't have the right to know the truth, that her mom was dying.

All the times they'd gone silent in her presence. She'd deserved to have been told the truth sooner.

So that she could have said goodbye. But the last time Hope had seen her mom, she'd been too late. Eighteen years ago...

Damn it, she was supposed to have done better. *Her* patients weren't supposed to die. She studied Chloe and made a decision. "Your grandpa is very sick. He's—"

Mrs. Medrano made a clucking sound and shooed Chloe toward the door, putting herself between Hope and the girl. "Your grandpa needs his rest. We'll come back a little later."

The room became stifling after they exited.

Sean broke the silence. "It's alright, Dr. K. We'll tell her in our own time. Sometimes you've got to do what your gut tells you, even when the rest of the world's telling you something else."

But there won't *be* much time, Hope wanted to yell. Chloe deserved to be told. It would only hurt more later if they didn't tell her now.

Jacie gave an almost imperceptible shake of her head.

The walls pressed in. Hope needed to move, to escape. She'd later regret not saying more, but she strode out, pausing at the nurse's station only to deliver the order. "Patron 564. Transfer to HEARTH."

Abbie started to say something but stopped herself, acknowledging the order with a dip of her chin.

Hope didn't miss Abbie's reaction. She already knew what the nurses thought of her—that she was sometimes too *demanding*, too *driven*.

She believed in the mission of PRIMA. *To optimize.* To prevent the wrong treatment. Or *ineffective* treatment. She almost felt as if the algorithm had betrayed her. But that was ridiculous. The algorithm wasn't sentient—it was objective code.

From behind her, Jacie cleared her throat. "Um... what happened back there?"

Hope whirled. "Delivering bad news with soft words is not a kindness. It's best to be direct and never provide false hope."

Jacie stared at her. "It's just—if they were my parents—I mean... I thought about how I might want them to be told—or how they might want to be told... and I think kindness might be an important part of—"

"You think showing *empathy* would be better? Trust me. It's not." Empathy was something to keep inside.

Jacie crossed her arms. "But what about our moral obligation? The Hippocratic oath?"

"Exactly." Hope stepped closer. "First do no harm. What do you think we would accomplish by continuing to treat non-responders?"

Jacie remained silent.

"All the side effects." Hope gave her a measured stare. "And zero benefits."

"But—"

Hope clenched her fists to hide their shaking. "Have your parents ever had cancer? Either one?"

Jacie shrunk into herself. "No, but—"

Hope moved away before Jacie finished speaking, the constriction in the back of her throat demanding she find somewhere with more air.

Behind her, Jacie whispered, "—my sister..."

The words hung in the air. Hope didn't break stride. Far easier to pretend she'd been already out of earshot.

●　●　●

All Hope wanted was somewhere off OASIS, away from patients and interns and cancer, somewhere she could breathe. But a lanky, red-headed resident stood between her and the double doors. Leach.

He flashed a charismatic smile. "I heard you might need some help."

Hope had seen the smile too many times to trust the motive behind it. His styled hair and toned physique always made her think of one of those old 1990s medical show caricatures. Many of her colleagues—women and men—considered him attractive, but she didn't see it.

Now, it wasn't a coincidence he was here. He'd come to gloat, no doubt, over her misfortune of having a non-responder. Word traveled fast.

She whipped out her tablet, pretending to finish her documentation. "I've got it under control."

"Too bad about your patient, Kestrel. Let me know if you change your mind. I've got a meeting later with Maddox." He paused, but when she didn't respond, he swiveled and walked away.

It was so like him, name-dropping the Director. As if Hope cared. He was only trying to get under her skin and make her worry about him getting the faculty position over her. She muttered under her breath, "In your dreams."

If she was a different type of person, she might allow herself to get angry. But anger only led to the loss of control, and if she lost control, more memories would surge upward, and she couldn't afford that. Because remembering would be like losing her mom all over again.

It was the girl—the granddaughter. That's all. Her arrival had triggered the things Hope had worked so hard to forget. A chill passed through her, out of place on the climate-controlled unit, and more memories rose to the surface despite her effort to keep them suppressed...

Herself, at age eleven. Her dad staring down at her with red-rimmed eyes. *No, it won't hurt. They'll give her medicine so she won't get sick. This time it's going to work.* She recognized the lie in his eyes and voice. *Why don't you tell me the truth? She's dying, isn't she?* Hope had wanted to scream. But she'd understood the lies weren't only for her, but for her dad himself...

She forced her mind back to the present. Better to transfer Sean to HEARTH than subject him to more futile medical interventions.

So why did she feel so empty inside? Like somehow, something was missing. She focused on her charting. Better to be told the truth, nothing hidden, and say your goodbyes. So when death came, all were prepared.

Even the girl. Especially the girl.

If Hope didn't believe that, she was no different from the doctors who preceded her. The ones she swore she would never be like.

She would keep emotion out of this, go to Cecilia, and ask her what they could do to improve the algorithm even further, redoubling her DNA research efforts to provide even better source data for the machine learner. She would put Sean Medrano out of her mind, focus on her work, secure the post-residency position and earn her own lab. So she'd never have to have a conversation like the one with Sean and his family again.

CHAPTER THREE

Podcasts / Algorithm Anarchist Podcast / Why We Need to Keep Questioning PRIMA (and Why We Must Keep Talking About It)

Rachael: Hi everyone, I'm Rachael, and this is *Algorithm Anarchist.* **Where we remember, the most dangerous lies are the ones that use the truth to sell themselves.**

[music]

Today on the podcast, I'm sharing more of my thoughts on PRIMA. I mean, here's what I'm asking. These researchers at PRIMA, *Prognostic Intelligent Medical Algorithms,* **they want us to believe they've done it?** *They've* **developed the elusive "master algorithm?"**

For our listeners just tuning in, here's what we know so far:

First, they claim their neural network has accomplished what no other AI has done. It's a machine learner that can discover knowledge about any disease. A true "master algorithm" of healthcare.

Second, since 2029, they've offered free medical care to anyone who agrees to sign up for their program. Legions of

uninsured—thanks to the healthcare crisis—have flocked to them, hoping the neural network will tag them as responders so they'll receive free medical treatments.

Third, these 'volunteers' have all consented to PRIMA using their DNA data to hone the neural network further.

But here's what we don't know:

One, how does the neural network make its decisions? It's all a black box.

Two, what happens to those tagged as non-responders? They're not offered healthcare at PRIMA, that's for sure. And we're hearing reports that even non-PRIMA facilities are using the PRIMA predictive report to deny insurance coverage of medical treatments. But it's all buried behind confidentiality clauses.

Three, what else is PRIMA doing with its data?

Think about it, people. The algorithms are already everywhere in our society, multiplying and expanding over this past decade. They influence what we buy and when we buy it. Where we work, even where we live.

Here's where you need to listen up. Because the way I see it, it's not just about influence. It's about control.

They want to control not only who gets selected for which jobs but who gets offered the interviews that lead to the jobs. And now, they want to reach back even farther to determine who gets into the schools that afford the interview opportunities.

It's algorithms that decide if we can get a home loan and, if so, what the interest rate will be.

And don't get me started on what happens if you're unfortunate enough to come up against the police. The algorithms decide your bail or whether you're even lucky enough to get bail. How much time you serve and whether you're eligible for parole.

So now, they want to control your healthcare. Yeah, you heard me right. This isn't about the shiny, happy technology. This is about those same people who control more and more of our daily lives, now extending those powers to your body. Think about it. Everyone's talking about how great it will be, but the bigger question is, what's in it for them—?

• • •

Hope shut off the podcast and waited for the standstill on I-5 to move, releasing a frustrated huff. The streaming service's algorithm had definitely got her preferences wrong with that program. PRIMA's data was undeniable, and she was proud to have been a part of the research that proved it. But she knew some non-PRIMA physicians agreed with the podcaster.

So damn ridiculous. As far as Hope was concerned, any physician unwilling to embrace algorithm-directed care was as dangerous as nineteenth-century surgeons operating without sterile technique because they refused to believe in germ theory.

She twisted her necklace, fingering the pendant at the base of her neck. Today had been a challenging reminder the algorithm couldn't do everything yet. Sean Medrano was only fifty-five years old. *Fifty-five.* The same age her mom would have been this year. Not that old at all.

The technology should have prevented her from having to tell him his cancer had progressed.

She ripped off the scrub cap she was still wearing and tried to smooth her short hair. The hair she'd cropped and dyed black years ago, tired of the comments about the pale strands reminding everyone of her mom's. Of course, they always meant her mom's hair before she'd lost it to the chemo.

Who was this podcaster? And what would they say about Sean Medrano's case? They'd probably twist it out of proportion—take a rare instance and make it seem like a threat. That's what misinformation did.

Hope wanted to kick something—hard. But that was difficult while driving. All she wanted was to get home, but the Seattle traffic stood in her way.

The day had been a blur. After delivering the bad news to Sean, she'd had no time to find Cecilia, and by the time she'd finished her clinical duties, her mentor had gone home. Hope kept seeing the way Jacie had looked at her. But she'd had a duty to fulfill, a responsibility to her mom's memory. Jacie didn't understand yet. Sometimes, doing nothing *was* the right thing.

She groaned and double-checked the auto-drive was engaged, then closed her eyes and pressed her fingers to them. She had an early case tomorrow and planned to crawl into bed the minute she arrived home. All she needed was to forget about today and start over tomorrow.

CHAPTER FOUR

TUESDAY 09 OCTOBER 2035
6:55 AM
PRIMA Main Campus, Seattle

Hope scrubbed her fingernails faster, even though it wouldn't matter. The nurse anesthetist, Oliver, could glare all he wanted at her from his station at the AAU—the Automated Anesthesia Unit—but it wasn't her fault the attending wasn't here yet. She might be the High Resident, but she wasn't a miracle worker. She sighed behind her surgical mask.

Next to her, Jacie also scrubbed in, mimicking Hope's every motion, while Hope pretended not to notice the frequent glances she cast her way.

Hope concentrated on her breathing, reminding herself she'd resolved to put yesterday's events out of her mind until she could head to the lab to find Cecilia and talk it through.

"Not to worry, Baldy." Oliver's voice floated out to them from inside the O.R. He was speaking to Brayden, her young patient on the table. "We'll get started soon."

Hope squeezed the scrub brush until the bristles dug into her palm. Brayden *hated* his hair loss. Who says that to a ten-year-old? The brush clattered into the sink.

Jacie hesitated for a moment, then threw hers down too.

Lincoln, the scrub nurse watching over their sterile routine with an eagle eye, seemed to sense what was coming and put his hands up to placate her. "Dr. K., we're already getting a late start—"

Hope stepped around him and was at the boy's side before Lincoln could finish his sentence. "Hey, Brayden."

The boy peered up at her, his wide brown eyes suspicious until a light of recognition appeared. "Dr. K?"

She waggled her eyebrows at him above her mask. "Yep, it's me underneath all this."

Hope found his hand under the sheet. He needed a new port-a-cath. The current device under his skin for his chemo had clotted off, and they'd had to stop treatment, a delay he couldn't afford. She gave his hand an extra squeeze. "I'm going to give you the absolute best port, so you can get on being cured."

He grinned up at her.

"But I've got to finish getting ready first." She released his hand and gave him a wink. "Oliver here's going to take good care of you."

Brayden gave a small nod and closed his eyes.

She bent down to whisper in Oliver's ear. "Never call him Baldy again."

Oliver had the good grace to appear sheepish.

She returned to the scrub sink, ignoring Lincoln's pained expression, and started over from the beginning.

Lincoln had already provided Jacie with a new scrub brush.

Hope used the ritualistic motions to regain her focus. When finished, Lincoln assisted her in donning her sterile gown and gloves. She then bent forward, and he placed the sterilized smartglasses onto the bridge of her nose. The device scanned her retina and powered on.

She blinked and adjusted to the interface, welcoming the familiar adrenaline rush at the start of a case. The AR overlay showed her a 3-D map of Brayden's blood vessels, highlighting the malfunctioning port's location. Yesterday's events faded from her mind, replaced by a new augmented reality.

A soft whoosh of air behind her signaled the outer doors had swung open. Finally.

But it wasn't the attending, only another nurse, who Hope didn't recognize.

The new nurse glanced between her, Jacie, and Lincoln, clearly unsure who was who under the surgical attire, even though Hope wore the surgeon's smartglasses. The nurse's gaze settled on Lincoln. "Um, Dr. Kestrel?"

Hope rolled her eyes, then realized the nurse wouldn't be able to see her expression behind the glasses. She raised a gloved finger. "Here. What is it?"

The nurse hesitated, her glance darting back to Lincoln for a second, then waved behind her toward the door leading out of the O.R. "There's someone here for you."

"We're about to start the case." If the attending ever bothered to arrive.

The nurse shifted her feet. "But, it's Dr. Maddox. She said it can't wait."

Hope swore under her breath, then turned to Lincoln with a helpless shrug. If the Director said it couldn't wait, she didn't have a choice, even if she was fully scrubbed.

Lincoln sighed in resignation. "You've got to be kidding me."

He gestured to her face, and Hope leaned forward to allow him to remove the smartglasses. That was a waste. They'd have to be re-sterilized now.

She yanked off the gown and deposited it in the recycling. The gloves followed.

Jacie started to lower her hands to do the same, but Hope stopped her before she contaminated her gloves. "Don't. Stay scrubbed. When the attending comes, introduce yourself as the intern, and you'll observe the case."

"Without you?" Jacie squeaked.

"You'll be fine." Hope glanced back into the O.R., where the equipment around Brayden swallowed his slight form. She'd made a promise, damn it. "Keep an eye on him for me, okay?"

Not waiting for Jacie to answer, she exited the O.R. and crossed the red line painted on the floor to demarcate the sterile zone. A crowd of suits filled the hallway, and a half-dozen heads swiveled at her arrival, Maddox at the front of them.

Hope tried to cover her surprise at the entourage of VIPs, recognizing among them the CFO, COO, and a few of the various department heads. Behind them lurked an imposing, red-headed resident dressed in scrubs. *Leach,* again.

What was *he* doing here?

Just then, her attending finally showed. He slowed and gave the group a curious glance.

Before Hope could say anything, Maddox spoke. "I'm afraid I need to borrow Dr. Kestrel. If you can manage without her."

The attending nodded and hurried onward through the O.R. doors. Hope wondered how much of his rush was because he was late to start the case versus wanting to avoid Maddox.

Maddox's gaze swiveled to Hope.

On casual observation, an outsider might take PRIMA's Director for a schoolteacher or a librarian. Hope guessed Maddox to be in her mid-sixties but a very fit mid-sixties. She kept her silver hair in a stylish pixie cut, dressed in classic cardigans and tailored slacks, and accessorized with tasteful jewelry.

But upon a second glance, one noticed the details. The heels—designer, sable-black. The sweater—cashmere, pinot-red. Hope caught a whiff of perfume she couldn't quite place, not floral but sharp. Power, she decided. It smelled like Power, with a capital P.

Hope drew her posture up straighter. Out of the corner of her eye, she spotted several others doing the same.

She shifted her gaze past the group to the two people flanking them. The guards in the identical suits. She'd been right, then. They must be some new higher layer of security.

Maddox fixed a laser focus on Hope. "Quite a situation we had yesterday. Quite a goddamn situation. Wouldn't you say, Dr. Kestrel?"

Yesterday. Her heart hammered in her chest, and her eyes darted back to Leach, who now sported a snide grin.

"Is Cecilia with you?" Maddox demanded.

Hope gestured behind her in confusion. "I just came from the O.R."

Cecilia was a researcher, not a surgeon, and had a bad habit of forgetting things outside her lab, like meetings. But this hadn't been a prearranged meeting, had it?

Maddox tilted her head back and projected her voice upward. "*Osler*, begin recording."

"Yes, Doctor Maddox. Beginning recording now."

"Under the circumstances, I suppose it's understandable you forgot about the policy. But thankfully, others did not." Maddox directed a warm smile toward Leach.

He responded with a self-deprecating nod.

Wait, what? Hope's mind scrambled but came up with nothing. "Policy?"

"Surely, as High Resident, you're aware of the policy requiring any admitted non-responder to be reported to me immediately." Maddox crossed her arms, making it clear this was a statement, not a question.

The energy in the hallway shifted. Hope didn't think it her imagination that none of the others would meet her eye now. But despite the rarity of her patient yesterday, she knew PRIMA's regulations inside and out. She hadn't forgotten about any *policy*. A chill crept from her neck down her spine and out to her fingertips. Out loud, she stalled for time. "Um, which pol—"

"I find it hard to believe you've spent five years here, worked your way up to be our High Resident, and yet aren't aware of this." Maddox's tone was light, but she pulled down her glasses and examined Hope over the rims with a flat gaze. "Do you think you're some kind of exception?"

The hallway remained silent. Hope waited for someone, anyone else, to speak up. Of course she wouldn't think herself an exception to a PRIMA policy. Even one she didn't know existed. She stammered a reply. "No—"

"You *are* the High Resident." Maddox spoke the words as if she'd only now recalled something trivial that she'd forgotten. "An appointed position."

Hope's mouth went dry. This conversation had gone horribly wrong, and she needed to turn things around. She attempted to keep her face blank and speak in a professional tone.

"I apologize." The words choked her as they came out. "I should have reported to you immediately. It was an unfortunate turn of events for my patient—"

"*Patron*." Maddox cut her off. "Patrons belong to PRIMA, not to *you*. Patrons come here with an expectation—*cure*. We are to deliver on that expectation."

Heads nodded again around the group

Hope's heart raced, and her mind circled back to the question her brain wouldn't let go of since yesterday, allowing it to surface fully. She'd given a patient—a *Patron*—ineffective therapy. Treatment he would be destined to fail because he was a non-responder.

What she had sworn to herself she would never let happen again.

Because the algorithm directed her to.

Hope twisted her necklace. "I know the algorithm doesn't often make mistakes—"

"Mistakes?" Maddox cut her off a second time with a sharp wave of her hand. "You're right. *Our* AI doesn't make mistakes. People are a different story."

Somehow, the way Maddox said it gave Hope a sensation of a target on her back.

The corners of Maddox's mouth turned down in disapproval. "When's the last time we've had a non-responder?"

Hope opened and closed her mouth. Surely, Maddox and the others knew the answer to this already. But everyone appeared to be waiting for her to speak.

"Dalton—I mean, Dr. Fall." The name hung in the air between them— the former High Resident, Hope's predecessor. And at one time, perhaps something more. But that was in the past. Her cheeks warmed. "Last year. Not long before he..."

She trailed off, not coming up with the word she needed. Quit? Disappeared?

"Dr. Fall." Maddox drew out the name. "A shame the way he left us."

The CFO cleared his throat in the silence that followed.

Hope's heartbeat grew louder in her ears. *She* was now the High Resident, but Maddox was treating her like some screw-up intern. In front of all these people.

"It makes me wonder, Dr. Kestrel, what's your motivation?" Maddox's gaze bored into Hope. "Our technology is on the verge of changing the world, but if PRIMA is going to prove itself, *we have to use it*. No deviations. No hesitation. No questioning. I thought you understood that. Perhaps I was wrong, and it can be arranged for you to return to your old hospital—"

"I'm sure that's not necessary." The COO broke in. "Right, Dr. Kestrel?"

Hope's breathing became shallow, and she dropped her gaze to the floor. Maddox was right. She needed to put the technology first, and she *did*. The technology was the answer.

She couldn't meet any of their eyes. She'd wanted Maddox to notice her, but not like this. At this moment, she wanted nothing more than to restore her status in Maddox's view.

"Right." She squared her shoulders and lifted her gaze to meet Maddox's. "Absolutely."

Maddox gave her a sudden warm smile—the same one she'd given to Leach. "It's as Virchow said. 'Medical education doesn't exist to provide the student with a way of making a living, but to ensure the health of the community.'"

The smile fell away from her face, and she addressed the others. "I think we're done here. Those of you on the merger committee, remember our extra meeting this afternoon. *Osler*, end recording."

The others broke off. Hope turned back toward the O.R., her neck burning.

Maddox's voice brought her to a halt. "Dr. Kestrel, one more moment, please."

Hope forced herself to stop and turn back. "Of course."

Maddox dismissed the security personnel, emptying the hallway to the two of them. She leaned forward, steepling her fingers. "Do you think I don't know what happens in my hospital the moment it happens?"

The heat spread from Hope's neck to her cheeks. "Of course—"

Maddox abruptly pivoted. "Come, walk with me."

Hope cast a last fleeting glance back toward the O.R., then followed. They passed into one of the main hospital corridors, and Maddox's tone became soothing. "It's difficult to have had a non-responder. I know your empathy causes you to struggle with this. There's nothing more dangerous than a doctor who can't be objective."

Hope forced her feet to keep moving. "I'm not—"

"Your empathy causes you uncertainty. Uncertainty makes you lose focus." She halted in the middle of the hallway and laid a hand on Hope's shoulder. "I know what you want. The post-residency position. It should belong to you. I see it in you. The drive to be the best." Her hand squeezed. "I was once like you. So *zealous*. Before I learned—to see the bigger picture. But I wonder, are you strong enough? To truly succeed here?"

To the staff streaming around them, it had all the appearance of the Director giving a friendly gesture of encouragement to the High Resident. A faculty member passed them with a collegial dip of his head. Maddox's hand tightened further on her shoulder.

Hope clenched her jaw and stayed silent. Somehow, she knew it was a test of some sort, and she would pass it. She excelled at passing tests.

Maddox's eyes signaled her approval. A part of Hope responded to it— the resident's conditioned behavior to crave the validation of her higher-up—and suppressed any protest over Maddox's treatment of her. No one ever said residency was supposed to be fair. It was worth it—any moments of unhappiness or suffering were transient, knowing she was part of the team building a better system.

Maddox had no cause to doubt her. Hope *was* here at PRIMA to prove the algorithm's superiority in saving lives. She *was* strong enough. Because the entire reason—the only person who mattered, the person she'd vowed never to disappoint again—was her mom. After her death, she would never again break a promise to her mom—to her mom's memory.

Maddox released her. But before she drew away, she murmured one more thing. In such a low voice, Hope almost thought she imagined it. "I'd better not hear any more fucking rumors."

She pivoted on her heel and left Hope alone in the corridor. More staff hurried by, diverting around Hope like a boulder in the current. Everything had happened so fast. What rumors? She tried to read the expressions of the passers-by, as if they knew. But their faces held no answers.

Hope remembered her plan to find Cecilia and swallowed past a thickness in her throat. She'd been wrong in her thinking a moment ago—there was one other person she could still disappoint. How could she face her mentor now?

CHAPTER FIVE

Hope passed through the second security checkpoint to the research wing with Maddox's words still ringing in her ears. *I'd better not hear any more fucking rumors.*

She had no idea what Maddox had been talking about, but her mind had no problem conjuring up rumors, drawing on her deepest fears and insecurities. Among them, that she didn't deserve the top spot—or she only got it because of Cecilia. That she would not get the faculty position. She would be a failure.

Twisting her necklace in her fingers, she paused outside the door to the lab. These negative thoughts had to stop. She needed to focus and get back in control. She was the High Resident, damn it.

An appointed position.

She hadn't imagined the threat implied in those words.

I know what you want. The post-residency position. It should belong to you. I see it in you.

Was that why Maddox had pulled her from the O.R.? To judge her worthiness for the position?

Hope gave her badge a frustrated swipe over the door sensor.

Only to blink in confusion at the sight that greeted her beneath the fluorescent glare. Jacie, standing at Cecilia's side, her height dwarfing the petite Cecilia.

Cecilia spread her fingers out in a fan, gesturing upward. "Hope, meet Jacie Stone. Our new lab intern for the year. She has an impressive background in computer science."

Because of course she was, and of course she did. "We've met."

An awkward silence followed. Hope cleared her throat. "How'd Brayden's case go?"

"Good." Jacie slouched a little more. "At least from what I could tell. I mostly just tried to stay out of the way."

Hope grunted. "Finally, a smart decision."

Jacie opened her mouth as if to say something in reply, then closed it.

Hope's chest tightened. She shouldn't have said that. It was petty of her, but arriving to find Jacie with Cecilia had unsettled her. She only wanted to talk to her mentor—alone.

But why hadn't Jacie said anything about being Cecilia's new research intern? Her questions yesterday made more sense now. Jacie could have mentioned her computer science background, though. Hope had worked with Cecilia since her undergrad years, and surely Jacie would have known Hope's epigenetic DNA data had played a vital role in the machine learner training sets. She and Cecilia had published their research together.

"Can I talk to you?" Hope drew Cecilia aside and steered her through the communal work area to Cecilia's office in the back, shifting the mounds of paper to clear places to sit. The stale scent of dust floated up to tickle her nostrils. For a computer genius, Cecilia had obscene amounts of paper around.

Jacie followed, and Cecilia waved her to a chair.

The hum of the lab equipment filled the silence.

Fine. Hope was too tired to insist Jacie leave. She'd get back in control. Cecilia could always help Hope get back on track. "You heard about the non-responder, I take it?"

Cecilia peered over the wireframes of her glasses. She only needed them for reading, but if she took them off, she was forever losing them, so she'd adopted the habit of looking over them. Her straight, black hair framed her heart-shaped face, ending in a sharp line at her collarbone, with a few more gray strands than Hope had last noticed, reminding her Cecilia was nearing sixty.

Hope's gaze wandered to the framed photos on Cecilia's desk, landing on her favorite, an old one of her and Cecilia at the high school science fair. Where they'd first met.

"Yes, I heard about the non-responder," Cecilia said, her tone signaling she'd said it more than once.

Hope's jaw tightened. "So why weren't you there?"

Cecilia's brow furrowed. "Where?"

"Outside the O.R., with Maddox. She said she'd asked you to be there."

"I wasn't feeling well this morning—"

"I could have used you there. All Maddox wanted to talk about was some policy, rather than discussing how a non-responder ended up assigned as a responder. It makes no sense."

"I thought you said it happened one in ten thousand times," Jacie butted in.

"It does. It's just—I don't know. I want to know why it happened to a patient on *my* service—"

Cecilia's gentle voice broke in. "PRIMA's precision far exceeds the performance of human physicians, but even so, no algorithm can be one hundred percent. You are aware of this, Hope."

Hope's area of expertise was the DNA sequencing to generate the data sets. Cecilia was the expert on the neural network. Hope had to trust her mentor on this. "Yeah, I know. It's what I told the patient and his wife—"

"What does a machine learner do with a case that doesn't match its prior experience?" Jacie sat forward on the edge of her chair. "Where it has no prior data?"

Hope scrunched up her face and then released it, trying to remain calm. "Don't tell me you're one of *those*. Questioning whether algorithms can replace human intuition in medicine. Despite all the evidence—"

"It's the other way around." Jacie bounced in place, her words tumbling out. "Intuition can't replace *data*. No matter the algorithm, it's only as good as the data it gets."

Hope flashed a stiff smile. "I created vast tumor DNA data sets for the machine learner to compare the differences between the tumor genome and the normal genome—"

"Hear me out. The machine learner for PRIMA is a neural network essentially capable of learning on its own, right?" Jacie's voice sped up even more, something Hope didn't think was possible. "It's not programmed with the answers. Instead, it can come up with the answers *itself* after analyzing lots and lots of data. In a case where it has no prior experience—no data—it makes an educated guess."

Hope twisted her pendant and waited for Cecilia to interject, but her mentor appeared content to let the two trainees argue this out. "A *guess*—"

"Any machine learner will make assumptions." Jacie punctuated the air with a finger. "Learning from finite data *requires* making assumptions."

"So, you're saying it could, what? *Guess* and make a mistake?"

"Yes. Some events are simply unpredictable. Learning itself is uncertain. Remember the medical AI of a decade ago, and what happened when they first trained it to detect cancer in an x-ray? In the training data, sick people took the x-ray lying down, but the healthy control set took the x-ray standing up. So the AI didn't learn to detect cancer, but whether a person was lying or standing."

It was Hope's turn to snort. "PRIMA is far more advanced than those early neural networks."

Jacie jabbed another finger in the air toward her. "Is it, though? What if one person's cancer has new mutations never seen before? Mutations the algorithm couldn't have any prior data on, as none yet exists?" She made a sweeping arm gesture. "The machine learner would try to justify from what it's seen before to what it hasn't. This is one of the biggest problems in machine learning—*overfitting*. In essence, the computer hallucinates a pattern that isn't actually there."

Hope shook her head. Jacie was oversimplifying it. PRIMA's experts had disproven this theory already. She scoffed. "It can't *hallucinate*—"

"This problem with overfitting is the central problem in machine learning. The machine learner finds a pattern in the data that isn't true *in the real world.*" Jacie's eager gaze darted between Cecilia and Hope. "In a person, I think we'd call it hallucinating. Don't you see? Machine learning can extract knowledge from data, but it can't *create* knowledge—"

"Jacie's right." Cecilia broke in. "Overfitting can be a problem in any machine learner system. But we've been able to reduce any possibility to a negligible rate. I think that's all this non-responder was. The unfortunate one in ten thousand. Magnitudes of order less than the rate of human medical error. It wasn't so many years ago, 2016, that medical errors became the third leading cause of U.S. deaths. That's why we created PRIMA. Human beings can't do it alone."

Jacie muttered under her breath. *"The unfortunate one in ten thousand."*

But Cecilia either hadn't heard or ignored Jacie's comment and continued to address Hope. "This isn't worth your time. It's regrettable you had a non-responder. I know it's difficult for you, but it could have happened to anyone. This wasn't your fault. You need to move forward— do not let the past consume you." Cecilia's eyes widened in concern. "You'll only cause yourself needless distress if you choose to dwell on this."

Hope's attention wandered back to the photo of her and Cecilia from the science fair. Hard to believe, fifteen years ago now. She still remembered how Cecilia's eyes had widened upon taking in her project...

Hope had been fourteen and parentless at the fair.

Cecilia had been one of the judges. "You improved the yield on DNA extraction from organic materials substantially."

She'd grinned at Hope like someone who'd found a winning lottery ticket in her pocket. "Please, tell me more about your technique."

Hope had been so engrossed in their conversation that she hadn't noticed Cecilia steering her toward the stage until they were almost there. She stopped short, but Cecilia took her arm, guiding her up the ramp in a casual stroll.

"You deserve your award," Cecilia murmured in her ear. "Do not let fear rob you of respect. Especially respect so well earned."

She smoothed Hope's hair, and somehow Hope didn't mind. Her throat felt thick.

"Go on." Cecilia had smiled. "You won't be alone."

Hope had crossed the stage to where the principal had pointed. She'd tried not to shrink from the applause and glanced back at Cecilia, who gave her a decisive nod. The principal had cleared his throat...

The sound of Jacie clearing her throat brought her back to the present moment. Jacie was talking again. "How do you tell them they have no chance of benefit?"

"What?"

Jacie shoved her glasses up her nose. "For those not selected, when PRIMA gives its report, or whatever... and if it says the treatment won't work, how do you tell the patient?"

"We don't." Hope paused. "That's the nurse's job, of course."

Cecilia gave her a reproachful glance.

Hope backpedaled. "I mean, PRIMA has proven that training the nurses in the triage and delivery of test results allows the physicians to be more efficient. Physicians only meet the patients who've been properly identified as responders. Patrons, I guess we're calling them now. That allows us to focus all of our medical skills on the people we can truly help. PRIMA trains the nurses to inform those we can't help." She tilted her head at Jacie. "You should understand this."

"Oh, I understand." Jacie's voice was soft, but her jaw remained set. "So PRIMA doesn't have to pay for the cost of their care, you mean."

Hope couldn't believe her ears. "What? That's not the driving force. Not at all."

Jacie shrugged a shoulder. "Don't you worry even a little about their motivations? To make a profit?"

Hope's head went hot, and she spoke in a carefully controlled voice. "Doctors gave my mom chemo—before they had the tech to know she'd be a non-responder. Do you know what happened? All she did was suffer. *That's* the driving force. PRIMA helps us prevent unnecessary suffering."

Jacie didn't meet her eyes. "I guess—"

"No, there's no guessing about it. That's the entire point of what we're doing here."

Cecilia cleared her throat, and Hope dialed back down her voice. "Besides, if someone doesn't want treatment at PRIMA, they can go elsewhere."

Jacie raised her eyebrows. "Do you really think that? Do you know how hard it is for the uninsured?"

"They have the market exchanges."

Jacie mumbled something that sounded like, "Yeah, right."

Hope looked at Cecilia to interject, but her mentor was studying Jacie, a curious expression on her face. Hope shook her head in frustration.

"The reality is someone has to pay for healthcare. You don't know what it's like, outside of PRIMA." Hope thought back to her first year of residency before she'd transferred to PRIMA. "All those prior authorizations and denials. The insurance companies impede doctors at every step. But here, the algorithm guides our treatment decisions. PRIMA's going to improve the system for everyone."

"But..." Jacie trailed off.

Hope raised her hands in frustration. "But what?"

Then she recalled Jacie's words on the unit yesterday—*my sister*. Hope was truly sorry if Jacie had lost a sister, but Jacie didn't understand the suffering doctors caused by treating non-responders.

An unbidden image flashed through her mind of the first time she had seen her mom's bald head—the unexpected smallness. She'd wanted to cup her hands around it and feel the fascinating smooth beauty of it, but she'd been afraid, her mom's head so fragile, and her eyes so large without her hair to frame her face. So instead, she'd shoved her hands in her pockets and stared at the floor.

Hope forced those thoughts back into the compartment where they belonged. Jacie was making this unnecessarily difficult. All they had to do was perfect their medical skill-sets, and the algorithm would guide them. Yesterday had been an exception. That's all.

But another part of her mind whispered that she *had* administered treatments to a non-responder without knowing it. The algorithm had caused her to do what she most dreaded—the thing it was supposed to protect her from.

Maddox's voice echoed in Hope's head. *The AI doesn't make mistakes. People are a different story.*

Had it somehow been Hope's fault?

"I almost forgot." Cecilia interrupted her thoughts, holding out an envelope. "This came for you. I meant to give it to you at our last Saturday breakfast."

Hope took the letter, palms damp with sweat, her dad's handwriting visible on the outside. He'd long ago figured out mail had a better chance to get to her here, where Cecilia periodically rounded it up for her, than at her apartment.

It was the last thing she needed right now, and she shoved the letter into her bag without opening it. Cecilia was right. The best thing Hope could do was rededicate herself to her purpose.

An alert popped up on her tablet, drawing her attention, and she forgot all about the letter. She sucked in a sharp breath, not believing her eyes.

Her ranking.

It had dropped, and she no longer held the top position. It now belonged to Leach. But the only person who could dock points was...

Maddox.

It wasn't fair. The non-responder had been nothing under her control. She wanted to say something to Cecilia—to explain the unsettling interaction with Maddox.

The post-residency position. It should belong to you. I see it in you.

"Hope, if you could stick around, there's something else I need to talk to you about—"

Cecilia broke off as, behind Hope, a change in air pressure rustled the papers on the floor, signaling the door opening.

Hope rotated halfway in her chair and froze.

Silver hair. A sweater, red as arterial blood. Maddox strode through the doorway, her gaze sweeping the room as if she owned the place.

Jacie said something, but Hope didn't hear it over the rushing in her ears.

Maddox brushed past them both to get to Cecilia. A hint of her perfume assaulted Hope's nose. That sharp scent again.

Cecilia rose to her feet, her face pale. "Never mind, we'll have to talk later, Hope. I have another meeting."

CHAPTER SIX

TUESDAY 09 OCTOBER 2035
9:45 AM
Dr. Cecilia Li's Office, PRIMA

Marah's eyes lingered on the door after Hope Kestrel and her intern departed. These residents. It could be like herding goddamn lab rats some days.

But that flash of fear in her High Resident's eyes had been interesting. The intervention earlier today had been helpful, then.

Not that she wanted the residents to fear her. But they were like children—unaware of the dangers. That's why Marah protected them—even when they didn't understand enough to be grateful.

The irony was that if she did her job right, they never would.

She stretched out an arm and closed Cecilia's door with a lazy wrist flick, taking the chair Hope had vacated. Her hips and legs thanked her. Goddamn osteoarthritis, no time for that today. As much as she disguised it on the outside, her body reminded her daily she was getting older. Or just damn old. But retirement wasn't in her vocabulary.

The culmination of her decades-long journey, the thought of what she would finally accomplish, sustained her. Focusing on it helped her cordon off the physical aches to the back of her mind. She tapped open her tablet to check her messages and addressed Cecilia. "Where were you?"

Cecilia gave her a blank look. "Right here, of course."

Marah let the silence build between them.

Cecilia's expression faltered. "I may have lost track of time."

"Do I have to remind you of the critical position we're in right now?" Marah drummed her nails on her leg. Cecilia remembered nothing outside her precious lab. "The merger?"

Cecilia fiddled with her glasses.

"With Seattle Healthcare Associates." Marah pinched her brow. "Really, Cecilia, if you came to the goddamn meetings, you would know this stuff. It's only our crucial next step in solidifying PRIMA as the majority healthcare service provider in the greater Seattle area. You need to be there, the neural network's *creator*."

Cecilia remained silent.

"It won't be long before we have enough hospitals in our network to move forward with implementing the algorithm at all sites. This merger is critical, and it won't happen if I don't keep it on track."

Her tablet pinged. Noah Meier, her old colleague, *again,* emailing her about that young girl. Talk about irony. How many years had it been since their residencies? To think he'd reached out now. No matter, everything was coming into place. All that she'd promised herself, and he had no goddamn idea of what she'd been through, of how it had changed her. A stab of regret caught her off guard as it came and went. But she'd already told him nothing could be done about the girl. PRIMA couldn't work miracles. She deleted the email without responding.

Cecilia intruded on her thoughts in a shaky voice. "I have a new idea. On how to fix it."

Marah straightened her sleeves, smoothing the edge of her sweater over each cuff. Sometimes, she wished she didn't still need Cecilia. It would be easier to promote someone else in her position. But Cecilia was too well known, and Marah couldn't risk any negative press. She forced herself to use a calm voice. "There's nothing that needs fixing. Especially not when we're weeks away from acquiring our biggest new partner."

Cecilia replied in a subdued but even tone. "You and I both know that's not true."

Marah leaned back in her chair and crossed her arms. "Do I need to remind you how deep you are in this? You're equally responsible."

The color drained from Cecilia's face. "You made sure I had no choice."

"Typical Cecilia, always the victim."

"I'm making a different choice now. There's still a chance." Cecilia's last words were barely audible. "I have to believe it's not too late."

"You made the right choice when I presented the options to you. Remember? And it made your career. Get over it already." Every few months, Marah still had to deal with Cecilia's attacks of conscience. "What is it you're proposing now?"

Cecilia regarded her with a pained gaze. "I think we fail to account for the mutations that occur well after diagnosing cancer. Mutations that must occur in the last days, even hours, of cancer cell growth. If we can identify those mutations, we can account for them in the algorithm."

Marah studied her. She had to admit, it sounded a bit intriguing.

Cecilia's words quickened. "If I can obtain blood samples from patients at the end stages of cancer, I can use Hope's DNA sequencing techniques to identify the new mutations. At the end of life. We have those people in our system—at HEARTH. There would be no cost. Please—" Cecilia reached out her hand. "—I'll handle it all myself. There's no downside. If I can fix it, no one need ever know—"

"The visionary Cecilia." Marah scanned the cluttered room and curled her lip at the pathetic heaps of paper, careful not to show any sign of interest. "You're a scientist, my dear. Leave the strategy to people like me. It takes guts to take it to the next level. You scientist-types need so much coddling."

Not to mention this abominable timing with the HEARTH transfer. Of a *Patron*.

But Marah would handle that, too, and ensure Hope Kestrel understood who was at fault.

And it wasn't the goddamn algorithm.

That's why she'd had no choice but to knock down Hope's ranking. Hope needed to understand it wasn't all about her, and she shouldn't take her place for granted. Once she learned her lesson, Marah would restore her points. Most likely.

She didn't need any more hassles. All Marah wanted was Cecilia's cooperation with the merger campaign. But being an effective leader meant knowing when to toss out a carrot. She would indulge Cecilia. Besides, it had sparked an idea of Marah's own. Not one she would share with Cecilia, though.

"Alright, I'll take care of it." Marah pulled down her glasses and looked at Cecilia over the rims, brainstorming out loud. "We should be able to institute a protocol with HEARTH, so it becomes routine. I'll arrange for the samples to be delivered directly to your lab, and *you'll* respond to all media requests for the merger." She didn't make it a question.

Cecilia bowed her head.

Marah stood. "Oh, and one more thing. Make sure your residents aren't involved with this. Especially not Hope Kestrel."

Cecilia muttered an affirmative and then rushed out past her, leaving Marah alone, as if forgetting it was her own damn office.

* * *

Podcasts / Algorithm Anarchist Podcast / Why We Need to Keep Questioning PRIMA (and Why We Must Keep Talking About It, Part 2)

Rachael: Hi everyone, I'm Rachael, and this is *Algorithm Anarchist*. Where we remember, the most dangerous lies are the ones that use the truth to sell themselves.

[music]

Today on the podcast, more background on PRIMA. Did you all catch this article in the Daily? "PRIMA Promises to Save More Lives." Let me break this down, people.

Sure, PRIMA took off like a rocket five years ago. But without the market forces that uniquely aligned in the mid-2020s, it probably wouldn't have.

Think about it. Fifteen years ago, the COVID-19 pandemic. The catalyst which led to the end of the previous broken system—health insurance tied to employment. Once the Healthcare For All policy went into effect in 2028, and they issued the subsidies, the uninsured flooded the online insurance marketplace.

Here in Seattle, there was a hugely receptive market for PRIMA. Why? Because they promised no copays or deductibles—for those who test as responders. Is it any wonder the program rapidly filled?

This article says the plan is "thriving," and PRIMA will soon be the dominant force in the U.S. healthcare marketplace.

Listen to this quote from PRIMA's Director, Dr. Marah Maddox: "In the previous decade, the U.S. spent one-third of its health care dollars in the last month of life alone. Twenty-eight million Americans were uninsured. Implementing PRIMA has saved billions of dollars previously spent on ineffective treatments in the last months of life. Our algorithm ensures our healthcare resources are being used appropriately and effectively. To keep our hospitals from becoming overcrowded with those who don't belong there. Which allows us to save more lives."

Let me ask you, listeners. Think about what she means by "those who don't belong there..."

CHAPTER SEVEN

4:00 PM
HEARTH, Wallingford neighborhood, Seattle

Hope paced the empty lobby at HEARTH, regretting her uncharacteristically spontaneous decision. It had been a week since Sean Medrano had transferred to the hospice facility, and despite Cecilia's advice, she hadn't been able to put him out of her mind. On an impulse, she'd called her friend Poppy Hart, the hospice nurse, who'd invited her to visit and check on Sean herself. Before Hope thought it through, she'd said yes.

Worn sofas and squat chairs in various shades of browns and yellows filled the lobby, scattered in front of a sputtering fireplace, a dramatic contrast from the sleek whites and grays of PRIMA. The shabby coziness reminded her of her grandmother's living room and all the afternoons spent doodling in her sketchbook while her grandma crocheted.

But those days were long gone. She drew in a deep breath and released it. It didn't smell like a hospital here, either, although her nose detected a trace of a familiar scent she couldn't quite place—

Poppy entered from the hallway and waved, her brunette hair coiled in a long braid. The same style since she and Hope had first met five years ago—when Poppy had saved Hope as an intern from making a huge mistake in front of her attending. They'd been friends ever since. Poppy's brown eyes lit up with her equally bright smile, and with her typical efficiency, she showed Hope back to Sean's room after a brief greeting.

But before going in, she paused outside the door, using one hand to sweep her braid back over her shoulder, her eyes finding Hope's. "I'm afraid he's declined more quickly than expected. He's no longer interacting."

Hope acknowledged this with a slight nod, not allowing herself any emotion. "And the family?"

"They stepped out for a little while. Before I knew you were coming, I suggested they get a meal and some rest. I'll call them at the first sign of anything changing."

Poppy opened the door, and Hope followed her into the room. Sean lay in the bed, eyes closed, mouth agape, the sound of his raspy breaths filling the room. Hope didn't need to be a physician to sense the nearness of death.

She hung back, and Poppy dimmed the overhead lighting. The silvery light brushed his body with enough gleam to do her work, leaving the rest in shadow. Poppy adjusted the sheet folded over his chest, laid the back of her hand on his forehead, and then glanced self-consciously over her shoulder at Hope. "The skin sensors regulate the temperature to keep him comfortable, but I still value the human touch, however quirky the other nurses think me."

Somehow, it wasn't quirky at all to Hope.

Poppy held an outstretched arm to Hope, inviting her to come closer. "I've been in hospice for four years, but it always strikes me no matter how many patients. Everyone dies, yet death is never the same."

Hope hesitated, then crossed to the opposite side of the bed. She placed her hand on his arm, noting the papery texture and mottling of his skin, and spoke in a low voice. "Hi, Sean. It's me, Dr. K."

His eyes remained closed, and his body labored with each stuttering intake of air into the dying lungs.

Poppy smoothed his forehead. "The furrowing of his brow has relaxed since I gave him the last dose of morphine."

Hope swallowed. "I guess we should all be grateful the Opiate Ban doesn't apply to hospice—"

She broke off as the rattling breaths halted and held her own breath.

But his body shuddered, and the agonal breaths resumed—a reflex of the brainstem and no indicator of higher brain function. The irregular respiration pattern continued.

Poppy took his other hand and gave Hope a sad smile. "Some things the computers will never do."

The door clicked open behind them.

Startled, Hope let go of Sean's arm.

Another nurse entered, clad in the same lemon-yellow scrubs as Poppy, the HEARTH logo visible over the left breast pocket. *We are the heart in HEARTH.* The oddly cheerful slogan and bright color struck Hope as an inappropriate effort to gloss over the mortal nature of their work.

"It's time," the other nurse said.

Poppy's eyes darted to Hope before releasing Sean's hand and accepting the supplies from the other nurse, who then departed.

Hope watched in disbelief as Poppy applied a tourniquet to Sean's upper arm and prepared to draw blood. "Um, what are you doing?"

Poppy glanced to the corner where the ceiling met the wall and then back. "It's nothing. A new policy."

Hope tracked the trajectory of her gaze to a security camera. Her heart hammered in her chest. "What policy?"

Poppy's voice dropped to a near whisper. "The final draw. Two tubes to be drawn close to the end."

Final draw? The distaste in Poppy's expression made it clear she didn't want to be doing this. "But what's it for? We don't check labs on hospice. He's here for comfort."

Poppy's eyes shot toward the security camera again, and she shook her head quickly.

Hope bit her lip and waited for Poppy to finish the venipuncture. She wasn't the High Resident here, and she didn't understand what was happening yet.

Dark and sluggish blood filled the tubes as if his body knew it had no more to give. Poppy released the tourniquet and applied a bandage, not meeting Hope's eyes. "I need to turn these in."

She whisked out of the room, and Hope lingered, retaking Sean's hand. She squeezed it, but no response.

It still meant something to her to say goodbye—the chance she'd never had with her mom.

"Goodbye, Sean." She released his limp hand. "Your family will be back soon."

She waited a few more minutes, wanting to believe a part of him could still hear her. "Poppy's taking good care of you."

When she exited, she spotted Poppy at the end of the hall, handing the blood tubes to the other nurse.

Poppy gestured curtly for her to follow, heading back to the lobby.

Hope caught up with her. "What was—"

"Not here." Poppy cut her off. "Outside."

She didn't stop until they reached the parking lot.

Hope crossed her arms. "Okay, now will you tell me why you're drawing blood on a patient in his last hours of life?"

A miserable expression crossed Poppy's face. "I'm just doing my job. You don't know what it's like as a nurse sometimes. We have to follow policies, or we get written up. And it does no harm. It's only one blood draw at the end. It's part of the job. I don't have a choice."

Hope pressed her lips together. She knew more than Poppy might think about mysterious policies. "Part of the job or not, it serves no purpose for the dying. Hospice care is about comfort. Sticking people like a pincushion when the results won't change the plan of care—"

"I know—"

"The ethics committee signed off on this?"

Poppy rubbed her forehead. "I don't know—"

"You don't?"

"I didn't ask. You know how it goes. The orders are top down. And with Jake laid off and job-hunting, I need to keep this one." Poppy stared at the ground. "Especially since... we're going to try again. For a baby."

Her words caught Hope off guard. A few months back, Poppy had shared on her socials that she'd had a miscarriage. Hope hesitated, unsure what to say. "Hey, that's great you're ready to try again. Really."

Poppy's face brightened. "PRIMA has a new test. You must have heard about it."

Hope drew a blank for a second before recalling an internal email announcement about a new use for the algorithm—predicting the viability of pregnancies. She hadn't paid a lot of attention since she never worked obstetrics. "Oh, right, the early mis-pregnancy panel."

Poppy nodded.

"That's great," Hope repeated. "I think you should go for it."

Poppy rested a hand on her lower abdomen. "Thanks. We haven't told anyone else yet, but I think—I might be pregnant again already. It's too early to test, but I've got a good feeling. I have a PARC appointment later this week."

The *Prognosis and Results Center.*

Hope hugged her. "That's fantastic."

They both fell silent, and Hope shifted awkwardly on her feet. "Thanks for letting me come and see Sean. Knowing he's in such expert hands means a lot to me. Will you tell the family I came by? I'm sorry I missed them."

Poppy squeezed her hand. "Of course. I'm going to go call them now. I think it's time for them to return." She gave Hope another of her wholehearted smiles. It was no wonder she was such an incredible nurse. "I'm happy you came, too. Not many physicians bother to visit their patients here."

It wasn't until after Hope drove away that her thoughts returned to *the final draw*. Whose purpose did it serve?

CHAPTER EIGHT

TUESDAY 16 OCTOBER 2035
5:30 PM
PRIMA, Main Campus, Seattle

Hope passed through security, heading back to the lab, her thoughts as twisted as the passageways. The more time that passed since last week's encounter with Maddox, the more she considered she'd exaggerated it. No one had brought it up again, and she'd settled back into her familiar hospital routine. But witnessing this 'final draw' thing at HEARTH, and seeing how upset it had made Poppy, had her mind rehashing everything. Poppy's words replayed in her mind. *We have to follow policies, or we get written up... I don't have a choice.*

But they all had a choice, didn't they? Then she thought about how Maddox had swept into Cecilia's office last week and, before that, Maddox's fingers digging into her shoulder in the hallway. The feeling the Director was testing her.

That must be it. This must be some kind of test. If she could recover her top spot, she would regain her approval with Maddox, and the awarding of the faculty position would follow. She only needed to stay focused.

Resolved, she entered the lab to see Cecilia's back curved gracefully over the digital microscope, absorbed in her work. Hope tiptoed over to study the adjacent screen displaying the same view, a peripheral blood smear. But something wasn't right. Bizarre and fragmented cells crowded the high-powered field. She cocked her head. "What're you working on?"

Cecilia sprang up, placing a hand on her chest and letting out a short, high-pitched laugh. "I didn't hear you come in! It's only a small side project. Nothing too interesting for you."

She gathered the slides and swept them into an open drawer.

"I'd be happy to help—"

"No, no, I have another project I'm thinking of for you. This is nothing." Cecilia stepped over to the sink and washed her hands. "How's everything going with Jacie?"

Hope twisted her mouth. She hadn't told Cecilia yet. "I transferred her to work with a different resident last week."

Cecilia dried her hands. "I see."

"I have too much on my plate to mentor an intern."

Cecilia raised an eyebrow.

"She asked too many questions." Hope blew out a sigh. It wasn't so much the number, it was the nature of Jacie's questions. Questions that raised doubt—something Hope couldn't afford.

"Reminds me of someone else I know." Cecilia laughed again, but this time more naturally. Ten years disappeared from her face, but her worry lines returned as soon as the laugh faded.

Hope frowned. Cecilia definitely appeared more tired than usual—and like she'd lost weight. "Let me help. Whatever this new project is, you're working too hard. I can do both—"

"No."

Hope blinked at the unusual harshness of Cecilia's tone.

"I'm sorry, I'm not feeling well today." Cecilia pressed her hands over her stomach.

"What's wrong?"

Cecilia lowered herself onto the nearest stool.

Hope froze. "What aren't you telling me?"

Cecilia gave her a sad smile. "I was waiting until I had all the tests. I thought it was nothing and didn't want you to worry."

Hope's heart raced, and a visceral knowledge hit her. She didn't want to hear whatever Cecilia was about to say.

But Cecilia said it anyway. "I'm sorry, Hope. It's cancer... gastric cancer."

A trembling spread up Hope's hands to her arms, and she clasped her elbows to her body to get control. No, not again. *Not again.*

Her mind snapped into clinical mode. It would be okay—she could fix this. "What stage?"

Cecilia shook her head. "I don't know yet. I have my appointment at the PARC in a couple of days."

Just like Poppy.

Hope paced. "Okay, then. We'll just take it one step at a time. As soon as you receive your treatment plan at the PARC, we can move forward. Whatever you need, I'll—"

Cecilia reached out for Hope's arm, bringing her to a stop. "I know this will be hard for you, but it's not your job to fix me. I'm fine waiting a couple of days until we know more. Okay?"

"Of course. There's nothing to worry about. You're here, at PRIMA. Everything's going to be fine—"

Cecilia drew her in for a hug. "I promise to let you know as soon as I have the results."

Hope nodded, not trusting herself to speak, blinking back the tears that threatened to spill.

Cecilia released her and patted her back. "I think I'll head out early and work from home. We can talk more tomorrow, okay?"

Hope pressed her lips together and nodded some more. She helped Cecilia with her coat. "Do you want me to come over? Make you some tea?"

"Don't be silly. You're on duty this evening. I'll be fine."

Hope hugged her arms across her chest. "Okay, but call me if you need anything?"

After promising to do so, Cecilia departed, and Hope sank down onto the stool. She needed to go do her evening rounds, but the heaviness in her body glued her to the seat. She assured herself everything would be fine— this wouldn't be like what had happened with her mom. They had PRIMA now, the algorithm. Cecilia would get the best care. Hope wouldn't let herself think of any other possibilities. She would trust in the system, the reason she was here. That meant getting back to work.

She forced herself to pull out her tablet and catch up on her alerts before clicking on the ever-present box in the upper left-hand corner to view her ranking. No change. Still below Leach. But she had a complex case coming up later this week—a robotic Whipple procedure—sure to earn many points.

God, what was wrong with her? Worrying over her ranking when Cecilia had cancer. And she hadn't even gotten the chance to tell Cecilia about what she'd seen at HEARTH. But that had been for the best—Cecilia didn't need more worries.

Once they learned of her treatment plan, Hope would have to work out some way to lighten Cecilia's workload. Her eyes landed on the digital microscope. She'd peek at those slides, take some notes, and have some summaries ready for Cecilia tomorrow. No matter what Cecilia had said, now that she'd told Hope about her cancer, she would surely welcome some extra help.

With renewed energy, she rose from the stool and gave a tug on the drawer, but it didn't budge. Huh, Cecilia must have locked it. But they rarely bothered to lock anything inside the lab, the tight security leaving nil chance of anyone inappropriate being in there. She waved her badge over the wall sensor to unlock it, but it didn't work. She tried again—still nothing.

It was getting close to 6:00 PM, and she'd have to leave it for tomorrow. She grabbed her stethoscope. "*Osler*, light's off."

A few minutes later, she stepped onto the OASIS unit to the sight of the interns clustered around Leach in a semi-circle, Jacie included. Today's scarf was pink.

Even from the opposite end of the hallway, Hope could sense the interns' collective misery. She suppressed a slight grimace, telling herself it wasn't her business. They were Leach's team.

She took the closest workstation and asked Osler to bring up the day's lab results, trying to immerse her mind and not dwell on Cecilia. But Leach's voice kept drawing her attention. He fired questions, one after the other, down the line of interns, lording his senior resident status over them.

His voice grated in her ear while she finished reviewing her patients' labs, then closed the workstation and drifted closer to Leach and his team.

It had been the right decision to assign Jacie to another resident. But now, she almost felt bad about having stuck her with Leach. Cecilia's words floated to the top of her mind. *Reminds me of someone else I know.*

Hope shouldn't involve herself in how Leach treated his interns. She should be relieved. With Jacie out of her hair, Hope could focus on being there for Cecilia.

Leach barked a question at Jacie. "Dr. Stone, what are the branches of the celiac artery?"

Jacie answered with admirable confidence. "The common hepatic, the right gastric, and the splenic."

Leach's face broke out in his trademark charismatic smile, but Hope didn't miss the edge of derision to it this time. "Wrong. The *left* gastric."

Uh oh. This wouldn't be good.

"Are you sure?" Jacie tugged at a curl. "What about anatomic variation or anomaly? It could be the right gastric. Or, at least, it's theoretically possible...?"

Hope stifled a grin. Most interns wouldn't question their senior resident when told they'd gotten it wrong, nor try to point out a loophole. But Jacie wasn't most interns.

Leach's smile fell away, and he replied with an impatient snort. Hope advanced closer to the group, and Leach scowled at her.

An idea had popped into her head. She probably shouldn't do this—it would make things even worse between her and Leach. But somehow, she couldn't stop herself.

Someone needed to put Leach back in his place. Not because he was questioning his interns, but because of how he did it. Hope loathed this method of teaching the interns—hammering them with questions and embarrassing them in front of their peers if they couldn't regurgitate the correct answers. Seeing Leach treat his team like this was an uncomfortable reminder of the humiliation Hope had experienced in front of everyone outside the O.R. at Maddox's hands. It was a tactic that had existed for decades called "pimping," shorthand for Put In My Place. One acronym that didn't belong exclusively to PRIMA, it happened everywhere.

Residency programs somehow couldn't eradicate it, no matter how technology in medicine advanced. The innate competitive natures of those drawn toward medicine always emerged. At PRIMA, it had become a point of pride amongst the residents to demonstrate the most mastery of medical facts from memory without cheating and asking Osler. Hope had been the champion in her intern class.

But internship was brutal enough without being forced to compete against one's peers. Time to exercise her High Resident authority, to make a point of her own. For the sake of all the interns, not only Jacie. "You don't mind if I observe, Dr. Leach?"

"By all means." He flicked his hands at her. "After all, you're the High Resident."

He instilled the last two words with contempt. It was no secret he resented her for getting the High Resident position over him. She should be the better person, take the high road. But somehow, she couldn't.

"Keep going, please." Hope waved a hand. "Pretend I'm not even here."

Leach's jaw muscles tightened but then appeared to relax, and he beamed that smile at her. This time laced with guile. "Dr. Kestrel, why don't you take over?"

She twisted her mouth as if she hadn't expected this and was unprepared, scanning the row of interns, then holding up a finger as if inspiration had just struck. "I've got a good one. Who can tell me the signs and symptoms of an insecure sycophant?"

As soon as the words left her mouth, she knew she'd gone too far. Their longstanding rivalry notwithstanding, this crossed a line she hadn't meant to cross.

The interns' reactions varied. Some were slow to catch on and stood dumbfounded. A few sucked in sharp breaths. Some suppressed nervous smiles. Others darted uneasy glances between them. One frowned in worry.

Jacie stared at Hope with wide eyes, her mouth parted in an even wider grin.

Leach clenched his fists at his sides, and Hope couldn't mistake the flash of hatred his eyes directed at her. But she caught a flicker of something else, too. A blaze of hurt. He stalked off without another word.

Hope dismissed the stab of regret and told herself he'd deserved it. She hadn't forced him to act like a continual jerk. With a nod to the interns, she departed in the opposite direction.

From the nursing station, Abbie flashed her a discreet thumbs-up. The nurses weren't fans of Leach's methods either.

With the interns behind her, Hope allowed a satisfied grin to grow, trying to make herself feel something that wasn't there. The interns released their laughter after they must have imagined Leach and Hope were both safely out of range.

But after a few steps, her grin fell away. Despite putting Leach in his place, she found herself filled with emptiness, not satisfaction, and ashamed on some level she'd chosen to sink low herself to accomplish it.

It hadn't been worth it. He'd probably now try to undermine her further, and if the faculty found out, it could jeopardize her chance at the position. She should have thought it through beforehand. Hope needed to be at her best—to help Cecilia. Maybe that's why she'd done it, to distract herself. This wouldn't be like her mom. Hope wouldn't let it.

She passed through the elevator doors. Seconds before they closed behind her, a hand shot into the sliver of space between them. They parted to reveal an arm that belonged to Jacie, who darted in.

The doors closed, and they were alone in the elevator.

Jacie glanced at Hope out of the corner of her eye. "Thanks for that."

Hope somehow kept a straight face. "I'm afraid I don't know what you're talking about."

CHAPTER NINE

TUESDAY 16 OCTOBER 2035
6:15 PM
PRIMA CAFETERIA

"Come on, you might as well eat." Hope exited the elevator and waved for Jacie to follow.

They made their way through the food stations, and Hope noticed Jacie ignored the *Flourish* posters depicting the optimum meal balance and promptly loaded her plate with some pasta carb disaster. She glanced down at her own tray, where her meal could be featured on the poster. Funny, that had never bothered her before.

The auto-register scanned their trays and badges. Hope didn't have to check her display to know she'd nailed her protein goal and calorie count. Jacie's flashed yellow, but she didn't appear to notice, having added a burger to the pasta on her plate.

The melancholy strain of a Chopin nocturne on the piano wafted over the low hum of conversation. PRIMA treated its physicians to live music performances during peak meal hours, and tonight was a pianist. Hope recognized the piece as Opus 9, No 1, and tried to block it out—it had been one of her mom's favorites. If she thought about her mom right now, she would overthink Cecilia's situation, and she needed to keep them separate in her mind. Because they *were* separate.

She grabbed a seat at one of the window tables overlooking downtown Seattle, the sun near setting and the looming Columbia Tower dwarfing the lesser but stately old Smith Tower, her favorite architectural landmark.

Jacie approached and took the opposite seat.

Despite the dinner aromas, the ever-present citrus scent of the hospital sanitizer lingered in Hope's nose. Her stomach soured, and she moved her plate aside as Jacie took a large bite of her burger.

Should she tell Jacie about Cecilia? No, Jacie hadn't worked with her for long, and Cecilia was a very private person.

Hope distracted herself by tracing the symbol embossed on the cafeteria tray with her finger and remarked idly, "PRIMA sure likes to put the Caduceus everywhere around here."

Jacie jutted her chin toward the symbol. "That's not the Caduceus. It's the Rod of Asclepius. The single serpent."

Hope suppressed a sigh and pushed the lettuce around on her plate.

Jacie lowered her head and mumbled. "It's just the Rod of Asclepius is the true symbol of medicine. Not the Caduceus—"

"Does it matter?" Hope tried to concentrate on her salad. Cecilia would want her to eat. She forced a bite.

Jacie put down her burger and swallowed a gulp of water before speaking more forcefully. "The Caduceus has two snakes and isn't truly medical because it's the staff of Hermes."

Hope blinked. It wasn't Jacie's fault she was in such a foul mood, and if she couldn't tell Jacie about Cecilia, it wasn't fair of her to brood about it. She cleared her throat and tried to respond in a more friendly manner. "Hermes. The messenger, right?"

"And the trickster." Jacie's face lit up, and her voice sped up to match. "He had nothing to do with Asclepius, who was Apollo's son. His mom was killed when she was pregnant with him, but Apollo saved him from her womb, in possibly the first C-section in history."

Hope raised her eyebrows. "Fascinating. Somehow, they skipped that in my Ob/Gyn rotation."

Jacie grinned and talked around her next bite. "Of course, some versions of the myth conveniently leave out that Apollo was the one who ordered her death."

"Yes, the patriarchy tends to do that. Leave out their petty inconveniences in their myths, and somehow blame the woman." Hope folded her hands under her chin. "So, Asclepius. What else?"

"He learned medicine from Chiron—the wise centaur—"

"I know who Chiron was—"

"—and became so good, he could bring patients back from the dead. But that didn't go over so well with Zeus because it threatened his all-powerfulness—"

"One can imagine—"

"So he killed him with a thunderbolt. Now he's a constellation." Jacie pointed at the symbol on the tray. "The serpent-bearer."

Hope leaned forward and spoke in a conspiratorial whisper. "I've heard another theory about the rod and staff. More of a practical one. Do you know how physicians used to remove parasitic worms? By cutting a hole in the skin," — she reached her fork across the table to Jacie's plate and twirled a long noodle around it — "then, as the worm crawled out, wrapping it around a stick." She held up the fork. "Voila. A 'serpent' around a stick."

The noodle fell off her fork and onto her lap with a wet slop.

Jacie laughed.

Hope rolled her eyes. Interns. But soon, she joined in, and her laugh overtook Jacie's. It hadn't even been all that funny, but something inside of Hope loosened. She ignored the stares from the tables around them and scooped up the noodle with her napkin. It felt good—to let her control go. To let go her worry about Cecilia.

But at that thought, Hope's laughter trailed off. She recalled that one last word Jacie had said on OASIS. The one Jacie didn't know Hope had heard.

Sister.

Hope wasn't in the habit of prying into the personal lives of her interns and residents. Better to keep some distance, some separation. But something about the moment prompted her to ask, anyway. She cleared her throat. "Last week, on OASIS, I heard what you said... after I walked away...."

Jacie interjected in a soft voice. "It's okay. I don't mind talking about it. My baby sister. Osteosarcoma. *Refractory*. Sixteen years old."

Hope didn't know what to say. She lived with that aching void, and no words could ever be adequate. "I'm sorry for your loss—"

Her voice dropped off.

That scent. Faint but sharp. The barest trace reached her nose, and then it was gone.

Hope spun in her chair, and her eyes landed on Maddox. The din of the cafeteria receded. Maddox sat alone at a far table, her attention absorbed in her tablet. But Hope had the strangest sensation anyway she'd been watching her.

She whirled back around and busied herself placing her dishes on her tray, but then had an urge to glance again. The hairs on her arms prickled.

Maddox was no longer sitting alone. Someone had joined her.

Leach.

He appeared to be speaking to Maddox in some distress, his mouth moving too fast, and his hands punctuating the air. Was he telling her about how Hope had shown him up in front of the interns? Talk about snakes.

Hope snuck another glance in time to see Maddox hold up her hand. Leach fell silent, and Maddox rose from her chair.

And headed toward Hope.

The rest of the staff fell back from Maddox on either side like oppositely charged particles.

Leach trailed behind her.

Behind them, Hope glimpsed another resident approaching their table, only to spot Maddox and do a rapid 180-degree pirouette to flee in the opposite direction.

Jacie scooted aside, and Maddox took the vacated chair across from Hope without invitation.

"Dr. Kestrel, here's the thing." Maddox opened her tablet. "I've been getting reports, and I'm concerned. We're all concerned. About you."

Hope straightened in her chair, not sure she'd heard correctly. Plural, *reports*? She darted a glance at Leach. "Wait, what?"

Maddox caught her glance. "It's nothing to do with Dr. Leach. I'm afraid this was already coming. I tried to talk to you before to prevent this. You remember that, right?" Her lips pinched together, and she studied the tablet as if reading something. "You're under too much stress of late. It's affecting your performance. The Board has recommended you take a few days off. For your own benefit."

Hope's brain couldn't process the words.

Maddox didn't bother to lift her eyes from her tablet. "Effective immediately."

"I don't understand." The words formed thick in Hope's mouth. "Is this about that policy? But I told you, I didn't know—"

"Dr. Leach will cover your duties. It's all been arranged. He'll take care of your Patrons."

"Wait... you're asking me to leave?"

"No." Maddox finally raised her eyes and drummed her fingers on the table. "I'm telling you."

Hope's frantic gaze searched the cafeteria as if she would find someone who would step in and fix this. For the first time, she noticed a security guard and dog standing by the cafeteria entrance—Kyle and Bear. Next to them were the two suits that now appeared everywhere with Maddox. Watching Hope.

Wait, watching *her*?

Maddox held out her hand. "I'll need to hold on to your badge. For the time being."

Hope jerked back. This couldn't be happening. She was the High Resident and had worked her whole life to be here. "Wait, are you firing me? In the *cafeteria?*"

Maddox leaned forward and gripped Hope's knee. "No one said anything about firing. *Yet.* This could be temporary. That'll be up to how you choose to behave. I won't stand for insubordination."

Hope lurched up from her chair to escape. Her mind disconnected as if she were viewing this happening to someone else. In slow motion, she retrieved her bag from the floor.

"Hope..." Jacie murmured.

Maddox's attention seized on her. "Who's this?"

Hope spoke quickly. "Only an intern."

Come on, take the hint. Keep quiet.

Jacie's eyes darted between Hope, Maddox, and the male suit—who had crossed over to them while they'd been talking. To Hope's immense relief, she said nothing more for once.

The man grasped Hope's elbow.

Hope ripped her arm out of his grip. She enunciated each word. "Don't. Touch. Me."

He backed off, his hands up. "Sorry, miss. I've got orders to make sure you leave the building."

"It's *Doctor*." Hope ground out the words.

"Whatever you say, Miss Doctor," he said. "As long as you make your way out now."

The other residents and staff shifted their eyes elsewhere, colleagues she'd worked with for years. Not one of them made eye contact, let alone spoke up or rose to defend her.

Except one. The only one who had the guts to not look away—Leach. His eyes held a strange note of sorrow. But she didn't believe he'd be sorry.

Before she could stop herself, she leaned down and whispered in Maddox's ear. "Good luck if you think *Leach* can run this program better than me."

One corner of Maddox's mouth rose upward, slowly.

Hope flung her badge on the table and spun away to get control of her emotions. She'd heard of this happening to other residents, but never imagined it could happen to her.

Only Maddox had the power to place residents on leave—or reinstate them. There rarely had been unions for resident physicians, and PRIMA was no exception. After all, the term's origin dated back over a century, to when young physicians would "reside" in hospitals, where they essentially became a form of indentured labor as the price of learning their profession. Some things had improved since those days, but others had changed little, and a private program like PRIMA wasn't subject to national oversight.

But who had filed reports on her? Maddox had made it pretty clear by *reports* she meant *complaints,* but Hope didn't know why anyone at PRIMA would be upset with her performance. The only negative outcome she'd had was the non-responder—

The private security man grabbed her by the elbow again.

Then Kyle was there, stepping in between them. Hope slipped out of the other man's grasp, bending down to clutch onto Bear. But the private security woman interceded, shoving Bear away. A low growl emitted from the dog's throat, and the woman pulled out a taser.

"Stop!" Hope's breath hitched in her chest. "I'll go. Leave him alone."

Tears of rage threatened to erupt from behind her eyes. But she wouldn't cry—not in public. She forced them back.

Kyle had a hand on Bear's collar. "I'm sorry, Dr. K."

"It's okay. I'm going." Hope straightened her spine and stalked over to the stairs, flinging the door to the stairwell open. She'd be damned if she'd stand there waiting for the elevator with the entire staff watching. As soon as it banged shut behind her, she half-ran and half-stumbled her way to the ground floor.

The private security man dogged her heels. In the lobby, he stopped her by gripping her shoulder.

She slapped it off. Why did he think he had the right to keep grabbing her?

He extended his hand. "Your tablet."

Hope surrendered it, not seeing a choice. The tears threatened to spring forth again, and she struggled to understand what had changed. One minute she was High Resident—at the pinnacle of her career, achieving her promise—and the next, kicked to the curb by the Director. A horrible thought entered her mind. *Cecilia.* She needed to be at PRIMA to help Cecilia. Her lungs constricted, making it hard to breathe. She would lose her chance to fix things.

She needed time to think. There had to have been a mistake. What did she do that was so unforgivable? She stared at the automatic doors opening and closing, people coming in and going out in a steady stream, unable to bring herself to walk out. Not like this. But the guard wouldn't leave. His hand went to his hip and hovered over the taser there. It was all so surreal, she almost wanted to laugh. "What, you're going to taser me—like your partner almost did to Bear?"

The guard's eyes signaled the door. "Go on now, Miss."

"You really have a problem using the title Doctor, don't you?" But not seeing a choice, she held her chin high and stomped over the threshold.

The doors glided shut behind her with a quiet whoosh of air. In Hope's ears, it had a resounding and final note.

Rain poured down on her, but she didn't feel it. She didn't know how she got to her car, but somehow, she found herself standing in front of it. The sun had set, and the streetlights clicked on. She got in and hunched in the cold vehicle, using her fingertip to trace the patterns the streaming water made down the windshield.

Through the rivulets, the complex that formed PRIMA shimmered, and the pristine angles of the glass pyramids soared skyward. They'd always resonated in her as the physical manifestation of the perfection of the algorithm. Hope loved the complex of buildings and her role as the High Resident. She was nothing without this place. What had the loss of her mom meant if she couldn't keep her promise?

The towering structures had always imparted a sense of security and stability, but the looming glass surfaces now appeared threatening. Maddox had no right to treat her as disposable. Hope wouldn't let her. She would redeem herself in her colleagues' eyes. Her research, she couldn't lose that. No other residency programs could compare, and she didn't want to go anywhere else. Besides that, Cecilia needed her now more than ever.

PRIMA was where Hope belonged. By Cecilia's side.

But how? Hope's fists pounded the steering wheel. Without her title, without access to PRIMA, she was powerless.

PART TWO: *PROGNOSIS*

Do not allow thirst for profit, ambition for renown and admiration, to interfere with my profession, for these are the enemies of truth and of love for mankind and they can lead astray in the great task of attending to the welfare of Thy creatures.

—The prayer of Maimonides

CHAPTER TEN

TUESDAY 16 OCTOBER 2035
7:30 PM
Hope's apartment, University District, Seattle

Water pooled at Hope's feet, creating puddles on the floor from her sodden scrubs. She didn't know how long she'd been sitting in her darkened apartment, hovering on the edge of the bed. The rain lashing at the windows gradually brought her back to awareness of her surroundings, and she reached out to switch on the bedside light with numb fingers.

She stared at the blank, undecorated walls. Pre-furnished, the apartment could belong to anyone. It was PRIMA where she truly lived, where she belonged. She didn't have to check the refrigerator to know it was bare.

Time no longer had any meaning. How had it been only earlier today that she'd learned about Cecilia's illness and, before that, visited Sean at HEARTH? Had he drawn his final breath yet?

The hairs on her arms stood up like they had in the cafeteria. *Maybe that was why Maddox had docked her ranking*—intentionally distracting Hope from further investigating. But Cecilia had insisted it was nothing to worry about. *I think that's all this non-responder was. The very unlucky one in ten thousand.*

The same thing Hope had told Jacie.

For the first time in her life, she questioned Cecilia's advice. She might not have entirely concentrated on what Hope had told her, preoccupied with her diagnosis. And her distraction over her health issues might be why she'd locked up those specimens when she'd never done so.

Hope shivered, abruptly realizing she was freezing. She stripped off the wet scrubs and grabbed dry clothes from her dresser—running pants and a t-shirt. Her eyes involuntarily drifted to the bottom drawer where she kept the letters. An unwanted reminder of the other letter Cecilia had given to her last week, still buried at the bottom of her bag, best forgotten. A vague thought of retrieving it passed through her mind, but she dismissed it, the effort too vast.

She reached for her neck, fingers curling around the tiny bird on the silver chain. The splashing of tires through street puddles reached her ears from outside, and she fell into the memory...

She had just turned eight and resisted the pull of her mom's hand. The shininess of her green boots in the puddles had entranced her. Her new necklace peeked out from under her coat. The bird was called a swallow, and Mom said it was a special bird that stood for hope. She got it. All hope. Not her, Hope.

Hope wriggled out of her mom's grasp. She spotted a mama duck by the park with four baby ducks behind her. "I'm a duck, see?"

She flapped her arms, stomping and quacking in the puddle.

Mom reached for her again, but she dashed away toward the ducks.

The mama duck charged back and forth between her ducklings and a storm grate at the curb. By the time Mom caught up, Hope was sprawled on her stomach on the wet road, her eye to the grate. "I see them—they're down there! More baby ducks!"

Mom crouched beside her, fingers groping around the edges of the storm grate. "Aha!" She flipped up a latch, and the grate came free. "Now, if I can reach...."

Mom stretched out on the dirty ground, ignoring the grime that coated her jeans and red trench coat. Her blonde head and then her shoulders disappeared into the storm drain. Hope held her breath until Mom emerged with three soft yellow-gray bundles in her hands. The mother duck weaved around her ankles, quacking up a storm. Mom bent down and released the ducklings with gentle hands.

They joined their brothers and sisters, cheeping in circles around the mama duck. Hope was so thrilled at their reunion that she didn't notice one small bundle of feathers remained still and not moving. Not until she saw Mom crouching down.

Her stomach felt funny. "Why isn't that one with them?"

Mom's eyes met hers. "I don't think this one made it, little goose."

Her lip trembled. "Is it dead?"

"I'm afraid so."

Hope wiped her runny nose with the sleeve of her jacket.

The mama duck fluttered back and forth between her live ducklings and the unmoving bundle. After a few minutes, she stopped her agitated quacking and rounded up the live ducklings to head into the park. Six ducklings followed her, all in a row. The seventh duckling remained still at their feet.

"Why's she leaving it here?" The tears dripped down Hope's face and mixed with the rain. "How could she?"

Mom held her gaze. "She needs to take care of her other six babies. There was nothing more she could do. It's nature's way."

Hope pushed her hood back, the cold raindrops a relief on her feverish head. "But... isn't she sad?"

Mom straightened. "I think she's very sad. But I think she knows she needs to be strong for her other ducklings. That's what mama ducks do everywhere."

After that, every puddle they'd passed had received a fierce stomp from Hope. She hadn't cared what her mom had said. She never forgave that mama duck for leaving...

When she was older, she'd realized her mom had already been sick by then.

More splashes on wet pavement, and a car horn from outside brought her back to the present. She shivered again despite her dry clothes. Now Cecilia was sick, too.

No. She swiped at the wetness on her cheeks. That was the past. She wouldn't get sucked back into those memories. They would not define the future. She was stronger than this.

But part of her was an eleven-year-old girl again, thrust into a vacuum of space where her mother's sudden absence ripped away her ability to breathe. She couldn't go through that again. She yanked open the nearest window and sucked in great gulps of air. Then dashed to each window in the apartment and flung it open in turn, not caring about the additional puddles forming on the floor. She needed the air, she craved it, she would die if she didn't get fresh air into her lungs.

She stood in the center of the room, panting, needing more. More air, more space.

Pulling on her running shoes, she didn't bother with a jacket, and her feet were at a run before they even hit the Burke-Gilman trail access at the end of her block. The rain lightened. She passed the familiar trees lining the path, steady giants, a mix of Douglas fir and birch. The nighttime air, the wet-grass scent, and the rhythmic pounding of her stride steadied her thoughts.

She forced the memory of the ducks out of her head. No more memories of her mom, either, and no more thoughts about Cecilia. Instead, she focused on replaying more details from the conversation with Maddox. Something she could act on.

Reports. Maddox had mentioned reports. But from who?

Footsteps behind her, heavy breathing. Hope often ran this trail in the evenings and hadn't ever had cause to worry. But her heart raced beyond the demands of the run. She swept a hand across her forehead to get rid of the sweat and made an abrupt 180-degree turn, fists in a defensive position in front of her face.

"Aaaaack!" Jacie veered off the trail to avoid running into her and narrowly avoided colliding with a Sitka spruce. Still dressed in her scrubs, she bent at the waist, hands on knees, panting. "I've been... trying to catch up with you... for half a mile..."

Hope stared at her, incredulous. "You followed me?"

"Well, yeah... you didn't answer your texts." Jacie clambered back onto the paved trail.

"You almost gave me an arrhythmia." Hope scrubbed at her face. The wetness on her cheeks was only rain. Damn it, she wasn't weak. She wasn't vulnerable. She was not a scared little girl missing her mom anymore.

Jacie scuffed her toe in a pile of wet leaves. "What was that all about tonight, anyway? With Maddox?"

"I don't know." Hope swiveled away and bent forward into a hamstring stretch. She didn't want the events of tonight to be real. She needed time to figure something out.

"Maybe it won't be that big a deal." Jacie's voice lacked conviction. "You'll be back at the end of the week."

Hope resumed a slow jog to keep her muscles from seizing up.

Jacie trailed behind her for a hundred yards before she spoke up again. "Can't Cecilia help?"

Hope's head throbbed. She couldn't explain to Jacie why she wouldn't add this to Cecilia's worries, and she didn't have Cecilia's permission to tell Jacie about her cancer. She changed the subject. "It must have been Leach. He must have told Maddox lies about me."

Jacie slowed to a stop. "That's something else...."

Hope drew up short. "What?"

"After you left. I'm sorry." Jacie rubbed her arms, a miserable expression on her face. "Maddox made the announcement. They're going to give Leach the faculty position at the end of the year."

Hope's lungs constricted, and it became hard to breathe, like back in the apartment. In one night, her entire world had fallen apart.

She'd underestimated how much power Maddox could wield over her career. Her muscles quivered. But Maddox shouldn't underestimate how vital Hope's mission was to her, especially now that Cecilia would need treatment at PRIMA. She wouldn't just give up. She clenched her fists.

Jacie started to say something, then stopped, then started again. "It seems like it might not be a coincidence that Maddox put you on some sort of leave soon after you had a non-responder..."

She was right. Hope couldn't ignore the timing, either, or simply wait to be allowed to return and then pretend it all hadn't happened. To do so would violate her ethical code. As Sean's physician, she had a moral duty to determine if something more had factored into his non-responder status and why Maddox had paid so much attention to Hope for it.

Jacie ran her hand over her head, pushing the water off her curls. "Isn't there anyone else who could help?"

Hope shoved her hands in her pockets. "I have to do this on my own."

Jacie twisted her lips. "There must be someone."

Hope did know someone else who might help. Someone from her past. Someone Maddox herself had triggered Hope to think about when her question had reminded Hope there'd been another non-responder the previous year.

Cecilia's words from last week came back to Hope. *Do not let the past consume you.* But another voice inside her whispered that only by examining the past could she decipher the present. She would have to choose—to let her past in.

But there was only one problem. He was the last person Hope wanted to see. Her former High Resident.

"I'm going to find Dalton Fall."

CHAPTER ELEVEN

THURSDAY 18 OCTOBER 2035
9:05 AM
Green Lake Park, Seattle

Dalton appeared as if out of thin air, two paper cups in hand, offering one to her without a word. His brown hair was longer, and he hadn't shaved, his nose and cheeks above his short beard tanned, as if he'd been spending a lot of time outside. Dressed in jeans and a form-fitting long-sleeved t-shirt, he didn't resemble the type-A, perfectionist High Resident she'd known. He looked... good. Better than he had a right to.

Hope accepted the coffee, sipping at it to hide her disorientation. It was the perfect temperature. Of course it was. He never got anything wrong. She mumbled a thank you.

He took a seat at the other end of the bench, the one he'd specified on the park's west side near the boat dock. Two days ago, when she'd tracked him down by phone at the nonprofit Jacie had traced him to, he'd practically hung up on her. He'd refused to communicate further except in person, and today had been the soonest he could meet, the two days an eternity to wait and do nothing.

Cecilia had called to update her. She planned to work from home until her PARC appointment, giving Hope the perfect opportunity not to tell her about Maddox kicking her out of PRIMA. It wasn't a lie, she rationalized. Not if she got reinstated by the end of the week. Then she'd never have to burden Cecilia with it.

Dalton raised his cup toward hers. "I don't know how you drink those. Mochas were always too sweet for me."

Her cheeks warmed and not from the coffee.

"You look tired," he continued. "But PRIMA will do that to you."

She gripped the cup. No 'hello' or 'nice to see you again, Hope' or 'great to hear from you' or, maybe, even 'I missed you.' She didn't know why she'd expected anything different. It wasn't like he'd made any effort to reach out to her after leaving the program. After he'd left *her* without a word. She flexed her fingers to stop herself from crushing the cup. She'd ask the questions she needed to ask and move on. No need to tell him about Maddox placing her on leave—too humiliating. She cleared her throat and managed a civil response. "Thanks for meeting me. I won't take up too much of your time."

When he'd vanished from PRIMA last year, mere weeks before finishing his residency, it had been as if he'd dropped off the face of the earth. He'd deleted all his socials. Total ghosting. She hadn't heard his name mentioned at PRIMA until she'd spoken it last week outside the O.R.

His non-responder case—the one Maddox's question had made her recall—had been switched to attending-only. Hope had to admit she'd never tried to find out what happened after. She'd been too upset about Dalton leaving without a word and then caught up in her subsequent promotion to High Resident. It had been a relief when the attending assumed the case.

Now, something convinced her on a gut level that his prior case could shed light on her current situation. Something only Dalton would know—about Maddox and her putting Hope on unjustified leave. Something connected to *his* disappearance last year.

But how to start? She squinted into the sunlight. Lumbering slate clouds approached and threatened the sun break wouldn't last long. A steady stream of bikers and walkers mobbed the path—a mix of determined exercisers in spandex, more casual senior citizens, and young parents out for air. The latter pushed their offspring in various types of strollers, some of which had more the appearance of bizarre high-tech grocery carts than conveyances designed to carry human children.

She took a deep breath. "I need to ask you about that patient. The one from before you left."

He didn't appear to be listening, his gaze on a distant point out on the lake.

Snatches of conversations reached Hope's ears, and the breeze carried the scent of impending rain. A red balloon hovered above the trees, no doubt escaped from a child's hand. It floated higher and higher, a speck in the looming sky.

Just when she thought he hadn't heard her and she needed to repeat herself, Dalton spoke. "Ah, PRIMA. To optimize and flourish..."

Hope had forgotten his habit of philosophizing. In the past, it had made her dismiss why she'd been upset, but this time, she couldn't afford to forget. She wouldn't *let* herself forget. They'd been a team, or at least she had thought so. He might pretend that meant nothing now, but Hope couldn't. She took another careful sip of coffee. She needed to focus on why she was here. Focus on what she could control. "I'm sorry to have dragged you away from your job. But I think you might help shed light on a... situation... at PRIMA—"

"To optimize." He went on as if she hadn't spoken. "From the Latin root *ops*, referring to power. To make as perfect as possible."

The air, for a moment, carried the scent of Maddox's perfume. *Power with a capital P.* Hope shuffled her feet under her. It was only her imagination.

Dalton chuckled to himself before taking a long drink. "A *situation* at PRIMA. Surprise, surprise..."

She studied his profile, the addition of the facial hair camouflaging the firm lines of his jaw, and considered whether his recollection of what coffee she preferred was simply a function of his perfect memory, or if it meant anything more. She cleared her throat again. "I had a non-responder, and I realized it was the first time since—"

"PRIMA is supposed to weed out the non-responders, isn't it, Hope?" His voice flat, almost patronizing.

Hope pressed her lips together. The wind picked up, creating waves of ripples that spread outward to the banks. She blurted out the question she really wanted to ask. "Why the hell did you leave?"

His eyes met hers—the same stare he'd used to pin down the junior residents and interns on rounds. But now, she detected something more—a sense of yearning mixed with it. Was it for her? Or something else? She felt herself flushing again, not wanting to admit a part of herself still hoped it might be the former.

"Don't you think it's a little late to ask that?" His voice contained the barest hint of a tremor that disappeared so fast, Hope almost wasn't sure she'd heard it.

But it's not like she could have asked him sooner. "*You* were the one—"

"Why did you think I left?"

"I didn't—I mean, none of us knew—there was a rumor..." Flustered, she glanced at the ground. There'd been a lot of rumors. "Some people said you couldn't handle the stress."

Stress. An alarm sounded in her mind, reminding her of something. *Maddox's voice, telling her she was under too much stress—*

Dalton laughed, a sudden harsh sound. "Because I had such a weak personality?"

"No, of course not." Heat flared behind Hope's eyes. "But what was I supposed to think?"

What were any of them supposed to have thought? He'd abandoned them—abandoned *her*. Without a word. With no explanation. Hope struggled to understand how that day had led to her current situation. But her gut instinct told her somehow they were connected.

He leaned back and draped his arms over the bench. "Who made the announcement back then, anyway? Maddox?"

Hope hesitated. "I don't recall."

Dalton's lips formed a wry smile, as if he didn't want her to see he might care about her response.

The wind picked up some more, and she pulled her jacket closer around her.

He raked his hands through his hair. "Fine. Tell me about your non-responder."

She was no longer certain telling him was the right thing, but she had nowhere else to turn.

He listened to her story of Sean Medrano in silence, waiting until a cluster of speed-walkers on the trail had passed, then gave her that intense stare again. "How much do you want to know?"

Hope resisted an urge to reach out and trace her fingers over the stubble of his jaw, busying her hands by twisting her pendant instead. "Everything. That's why I'm here."

"I'm not sure you know what you're asking, Hope."

A flash of anger rose in her chest. How dare he treat her like she wasn't deserving of the information? "That's kind of dramatic, don't you think?"

Dalton leaned farther back on the bench and tilted his head toward the clouds. "When you figure out the answer to that question, let me know."

"You—egotistical—" she sputtered and cut herself off.

She'd been a fool to think he would help her. As if he'd have some explanation for his disappearance that would erase the past year. As if he'd be willing to help her after he'd abandoned her then, and they'd somehow return to PRIMA and resume where they'd left off. She gave a slow, disbelieving shake of her head, then got to her feet.

Instead of getting up after her, he continued to sit with infuriating calm. "Where would you go if you could go anywhere in the world?"

More philosophizing. Her anger crumbled, leaving a hollowness in her chest. Maybe they'd never been a team at all, and she was better off without him. She downed the last of the mocha. "What kind of question is that?"

"Humor me. Where would you go?"

Hope released a heavy sigh. "Like on a trip?"

"Sure, a trip. If PRIMA ever allowed you a vacation, where would you go?"

She turned her face to the blast of cold air from the lake. A memory of the beach cottage surfaced in her mind. Her mom's laughter trailing on the wind...

Dalton was studying her. "It's still the ocean, right?"

He didn't have the right to ask her that.

"Good to see you haven't changed." Dalton rose from the bench abruptly and lifted his cup, almost as if toasting her. "Don't forget to recycle."

He stepped onto the path, melding into the crowd in a way he never would have before. And like that, he was gone again.

Hope's muscles quivered, and she hurled the now-empty cup at the grass. A pigeon fluttered indignantly, and a pair of older women strolling by cast disapproving glances at her. She swiveled back to catch one more sight of Dalton, but the crowd had assimilated him.

A blonde figure caught her attention, something familiar about the woman's profile. Her mouth went dry. It was *her*—Maddox's private security guard. But the next moment, the woman swung a toddler in her arms, laughing. Hope shook her head at herself. She'd become paranoid now.

The breeze picked up, shaking the trees. The sky had darkened, and the relaxed nature of these people taking their recreation no longer struck her as enviable. Didn't they have jobs?

She shook her head a second time. When did she become so bitter? She didn't have a job to go to, either. A strange, untethered sensation floated in her chest. She scanned for the balloon on the horizon, but it was gone. Vanished, just like Dalton.

She'd made no progress and was right back where she'd started.

Don't forget to recycle. What a jerk. She glared at the discarded coffee cup in the grass. A spiteful part of her wanted to leave it, but having grown up in Seattle, littering was against her genetic code. She shooed away the pigeons and retrieved the empty cup, angling toward the nearest solar recycler.

It wouldn't fit through the opening. Hope tried to force it with no luck, then realized the cup had an unusual shape—wider on the bottom than the top. The new trend from the popular chain where Dalton had purchased the coffee. She inverted it and started to shove it in the slot top first, but something on its bottom caught her eye. Her arm froze in place. She slowly withdrew the cup.

A series of numbers and letters in precise block print snaked around the bottom of the cup. She rotated it in her hand.

2.20.29 CL

5.15.34 DF

Precise block print she would recognize anywhere. The meticulous handwriting of Dalton Fall.

It would appear he'd decided to help her after all.

But what did it mean?

CHAPTER TWELVE

FRIDAY 19 OCTOBER 2035
5:00 AM
Puget Sound Pastries, Seattle

"Damn, this is early." Jacie sank into the chair across from Hope with a groan. Her scarf today was orange, fitting the season. She'd agreed to meet Hope before her rounds, and, thankfully, Seattle's coffee shop hours accommodated them.

"Yeah, welcome to intern life."

Jacie rolled her eyes, and Hope smiled to herself. How touching—her sarcasm was rubbing off on Jacie.

The sharp aroma of the freshly ground coffee beans saturated the air, and Hope pulled out her phone to place their order. The app suggested the latest drink special, but she stuck with her usual mocha. Take that, Dalton Fall.

She quirked an eyebrow at Jacie. "My treat. What do you want?"

"Anything venti sized."

Hope added a venti mocha to the order, and a few minutes later, the barista brought the drinks to their table.

A Pearl Jam classic played in the background, and the song triggered a memory from the days before her mom got sick, singing the lyrics to old 1990s songs with her parents in the car. Her mom had the most beautiful voice, and her dad would add harmony. Before he changed—before the cancer changed them all. It was hard now to believe those days had ever existed.

Hope blinked the memory away, trying to shed the uneasiness created by this public place. Like it had been in the park... like she didn't belong anywhere outside of PRIMA.

Double-checking no one was within earshot, she retrieved from her pocket the piece she'd torn off the cup and placed the fragment before Jacie. "Okay, Ms. Alpha Geek, what do you make of this?"

Jacie nudged her glasses up her nose and scrutinized the paper. "It looks like dates and initials." She sat up straighter. "DF... Dalton Fall? You met with him? What did he say?"

Hope snorted. "Nothing useful. But after he took off, I spotted this on the mocha he brought me."

Jacie scrunched her eyebrows. "What do you think the dates mean?"

Hope had an idea, but she'd need help to chase it down. Hence, asking Jacie to meet her this morning. "5.15.34 would've been right around the time he left the program."

Jacie squinted at it. "What about the other initials?"

"CL? I hadn't thought about it yet." Hope lied.

Jacie's eyebrows shot up. "Cecilia Li."

Hope snatched back the fragment. The last thing she needed was Jacie digging into Cecilia's status. "CL could be lots of different people. We don't even know for sure it's someone at PRIMA."

Jacie gave her a pensive stare. "How do you know he even wrote it? It's a weird way to give you a message."

"He brought the coffee, and I recognize his handwriting. Besides, he made a point of telling me to recycle the cup. It was one of those funky-shaped ones that wouldn't fit in those new city recyclers without flipping it upside down. He would've been sure I'd see his writing once I did."

Jacie took another slug of her latte before reaching into her bag and retrieving her tablet.

Hope's fingers itched to grab it, tired of being so helpless without her PRIMA access. Having to rely on someone else went against everything she'd been and reminded her of what she had to lose.

"There's something I need to say first." Jacie folded her hands. "I need to continue to work with Dr. Li. You can't mess that up for me."

That might not be up to either Jacie's or Hope's control. Until Cecilia received more info on her treatment plan, it wasn't possible to know how much she'd be working these next few months. "Okay—"

"I'm serious. This is another level beyond me tracking down your boy's new workplace a few days ago."

"What? He's not my *boy*—"

"I can't have you later having second thoughts and throwing me under the bus if I do this."

"I would never—"

"Just so we're on the same page, then."

"You have my word." Hope met Jacie's stare, then leaned back and crossed her arms. "Besides, it's yet to be proven you're as good a hacker as you claim to be."

Jacie's mouth opened, then widened into a grin. "Watch and learn."

She connected to the Wi-Fi, then angled the screen toward Hope. Next, she unrolled a portable keyboard and attached it. "Commencing Project Coffee Cup Code."

Hope rolled her eyes. "We hardly know if it's a *code*—"

But she broke off as she realized Jacie was no longer listening, her fingers flying across the keys. Hope forced herself to wait and sip her coffee, no longer tasting it, her muscles tense.

After a moment, Jacie's voice startled her out of her reverie. "That's strange."

Hope leaned forward. "What?"

"Nothing." Jacie shook her head. "I mean, there's nothing here."

Hope tried not to show her disappointment. She should have known her first instinct had been right, and this would lead nowhere. Or worse, Dalton's idea of some practical joke. She should call him and demand he give her a straight answer.

But then she remembered his words from the park. *When you figure out the answer to that question, let me know.*

Jacie popped a piece of gum in her mouth. "I've got another idea."

A few minutes later, Hope sucked in a sharp breath at the view on the screen. "If I didn't know better, I'd say that's Dalton's personnel file."

"I gave myself administrator privileges." Jacie winked. "Don't worry—it's untraceable. It'll erase the access record as soon as I log out. Brilliant, right? Let's see what comes up under 5/15/34..."

This was getting riskier. Hope glanced over her shoulder to ensure the surrounding tables remained empty, then leaned in closer. Jacie could still get caught, despite what she said. Personnel files were highly protected.

But she forgot all else as the last entries leaped off the screen:

CONFIDENTIAL SUMMARY—INCIDENT REPORT—DALTON FALL MD, HIGH RESIDENT

- 5/15/34 PATIENT [REDACTED] EXPIRED ON THE OASIS UNIT.
- RN [REDACTED] REPORTED MEDICATION ORDER ERROR BY DR. FALL.
- PEER REVIEW COMMITTEE CONCLUSION: DR. FALL OVERRODE THE PHARMACY SYSTEM TO ORDER [REDACTED], CONTRIBUTING TO THE PATIENT'S EXPIRATION.
- DR. FALL CONTESTED HE DID NOT WRITE THE ORDER.
- PEER REVIEW COMMITTEE VERIFIED HIS ELECTRONIC SIGNATURE ON ORDER.
- RN [REDACTED] TESTIFIED DR. FALL GAVE THE ORDER.
- PEER REVIEW COMMITTEE RECOMMENDATION: SUSPENSION OF PRIVILEGES AND INSTITUTION OF A PERFORMANCE IMPROVEMENT PLAN.

Hope chewed on her lip. This had to be the same patient she remembered, the one she'd gone to ask Dalton about. This report must be why he couldn't talk about it, but had to give her a cryptic clue instead.

She recalled the details of the case. There had been no medication error, she was sure. Despite the PRIMA analysis, the patient hadn't responded as expected to treatment. Like her patient—Sean Medrano.

Hope continued to read:

- 5/22/34 DR. FALL DECLINED TO SIGN PIP TO REINSTATE PRIVILEGES AT PRIMA.
- 6/6/34 DR. FALL SIGNED SEPARATION AGREEMENT, INCLUDING NDA.

END FILE.

Dalton had wanted her to find this. But what did it mean?

Jacie blew out a long breath. "Performance improvement plan and separation agreement, and... what's an NDA?"

"Non-disclosure agreement."

Jacie's fingers flew on the keyboard again. Before Hope could stop her, she accessed Cecilia's personnel file and searched the date on the cup next to the 'CL' initials, 2.20.29. Nothing.

Hope covered her mouth with a hand to hide her relief. Maybe the initials 'CL' *didn't* belong to Cecilia Li, and this was all a colossal waste of time. She crossed her arms. "I don't think we're on the right track with this."

Jacie took her hands off the keyboard. "Do you think he really did what this file says?"

"It doesn't matter, and it's none of our business." Maybe the stress *had* gotten to Hope more than she cared to admit. She was leading herself on a wild goose chase, which wouldn't help her. "That's why it's confidential and in his sealed file."

Her non-responder had only been bad luck—like Cecilia had said. Hope was chasing down a dead end. There was no point in revisiting the past.

All she needed to do was convince Maddox to let her finish out the year as High Resident. Then, she could ask to stay on with PRIMA in an interim capacity despite Leach getting the secured faculty position. She could still apply for her own lab, even if it meant a few years later than she'd hoped. That would be okay if it gave her more time to help Cecilia through her treatment.

But even as she tried to convince herself, her mind refused to comply, flashing back to the locked lab drawer. She shifted in her chair. "Do you know anything about a new project Cecilia's working on? Something to do with peripheral blood smears?"

Jacie shrugged one shoulder, her attention focused back on the tablet. "I saw her working on the slides, but she told me it was some boring side project I wouldn't be interested in."

The same thing Cecilia had told Hope.

Jacie's fingers clacked at the keys. "I figured it had something to do with the biohazard box from HEARTH."

Hope frowned. "HEARTH? That can't be right."

Jacie's eyes flicked to meet her gaze and then back to the screen. "I know what I saw."

Nothing was making any sense, and Hope needed to make it all fit together, to get control over it. An urge to go to Cecilia for help, despite the health issues she was dealing with, seized her. Ever since their first meeting at the high school science fair, Cecilia had been there for her. To mentor her research, to remind her to eat when she got too caught up in her experiments, and even as a shoulder to cry on when her college boyfriend had dumped her. She wanted Cecilia to tell her the reason behind the sequence of events. There had to be a logical explanation for Maddox's actions.

But something held her back. Not just Cecilia's cancer diagnosis. Another unwanted thought arose in her mind. What else had Cecilia kept from her? Things about the lab? About PRIMA?

A news alert on the café's wall screen caught her attention. Hope read the taglines to distract herself from her disturbing thoughts while Jacie resumed her search.

... Powerful windstorm to hit Pacific Northwest over the upcoming week. Typhoon will pass over Japan and continue as extratropical circulation moving east across the Pacific. By next week, expected to merge with hurricane-like storm moving north from Hawaii. Global warming or the perfect storm? ...

... Seattle Healthcare Associates expected to join PRIMA, Prognostic Intelligent Medical Algorithms...

The merger—how could Hope have forgotten? Everyone had been talking about it. The vote was coming up, and everyone expected it would go through. She swallowed. The step PRIMA needed to expand, the healthcare mission she was supposed to be a part of.

Her phone buzzed on the table, and Poppy's photo appeared on the screen. Hope could think of only one reason she'd be calling this early. She hesitated, then picked up the call.

"Oh, Hope, thank you for answering—" Poppy broke off. She sounded like she'd been crying.

"He's gone, then?" Hope rotated away from Jacie, speaking in a low voice.

"What? Oh, Hope, yes, I'm so sorry. Sean passed away yesterday evening. Peacefully, with his family at his bedside. I should have called you sooner, but that's not—" Poppy broke off with a shaky breath. She definitely was crying. "I'm so sorry to even ask this, but could you meet me at the PARC later this morning? 9:00 AM? I have my appointment, and Jake— well... we got in a fight—"

Hope twisted back to find Jacie closing her tablet and pushing back from the table. She held out her hand to signal Jacie to wait and spoke rapidly to Poppy before ending the call. "Of course, I'll meet you there. Whatever you need."

She stood. "Wait, you're leaving already? What'd you find?"

Jacie slipped on her coat. "Nothing else yet. I've got to get going so I'm not late to rounds. I'll spend more time on this tonight."

It wouldn't be fair of Hope to ask her to stay longer and risk being late, especially not on Leach's service. She'd have to let Jacie leave and simply wait until evening. She nodded and fidgeted with her cup. "Hey, thank you."

Jacie popped a fresh piece of gum in her mouth and shrugged. "You're welcome."

"Be careful."

Jacie cocked her head, then smiled. "Always."

Hope lowered herself back into her chair and remained at the table after Jacie departed, thinking of Sean and his family, unable to escape the feelings of guilt that overwhelmed her. What could she have done differently?

The café was getting busier, the before-work crowd picking up. She gathered up her trash, and a movement out of the corner of her eye caught her attention. A tall, broad-shouldered man slipped out the door, and the hairs on her arms prickled in warning. It took her brain a second to make the connection—Maddox's *other* private security guard.

She pushed past the line of customers to get to the door, her heart hammering. "Excuse me, excuse me—"

"Hey, watch it!"

"I'm sorry—"

She burst out onto the sidewalk.

He was gone.

CHAPTER·THIRTEEN

Podcasts / Algorithm Anarchist Podcast / What is Machine Learning (And Why You Should Care)

Rachael: Hi everyone, I'm Rachael, and this is *Algorithm Anarchist*. Where we remember, the most dangerous lies are the ones that use the truth to sell themselves.

[music]

This week I'm continuing my exploration of PRIMA. So, here's something you need to understand about their algorithm. At its most basic, machine learning AI is a system that learns from data sets to perform and improve upon a specific task. In PRIMA's case, healthcare. Or so they claim.

But to be useful in the real world, a machine learner healthcare algorithm needs to not only diagnose but prognosticate. To predict if treatments could be expected to change disease outcomes on the individual level.

PRIMA claims to have the first neural network to succeed at both levels. The first level—diagnosis. And the second level—treatments and responses.

But what about those who buy into PRIMA's plan but are never allowed through their doors? Who are never given a choice? What about them? Don't they deserve doctors too?

CHAPTER THIRTEEN

FRIDAY 19 OCTOBER 2035
6:30 AM
PRIMA, Main Campus, office of Dr. Marah Maddox

Marah scrolled through the files on her tablet, not yet sure what she searched for but equally confident she'd find it. She opened the transcript of Hope Kestrel's initial interview with PRIMA:

DR. GLASS: WELCOME, MS. KESTREL. I'M EMMA GLASS. I'LL BE ONE OF YOUR INTERVIEWERS TODAY.

HOPE KESTREL: PLEASED TO MEET YOU.

DR. GLASS: YOU'VE GOT A STRONG CV, BUT I'M SURE I DON'T HAVE TO TELL YOU THAT. WE'D BE LUCKY TO HAVE YOU TRANSFER INTO OUR PROGRAM. WHY DON'T YOU TELL ME A BIT MORE ABOUT YOUR RESEARCH? EPIGENETICS, ISN'T IT? YOU'LL HAVE TO FORGIVE ME. I'M A PSYCHIATRIST TURNED ADMINISTRATOR. I'M AFRAID BIOCHEM WASN'T MY FORTE.

HOPE KESTREL: THINK OF THE GENOME—THE ENTIRE DNA CONTENT OF THE CELL—AS THE COMPUTER HARDWARE. EPIGENETICS IS LIKE THE MODS. IT CAN CHANGE WHAT DNA EXONS ARE EXPRESSED.

DR. GLASS: SO, HOW DOES THAT HELP EXACTLY?

HOPE KESTREL: BECAUSE IN CANCER, SOMETIMES IT'S NOT A FLAW IN THE DNA ITSELF, BUT IN THE INTERPRETATION—IN THE DNA CODE-READING ALGORITHMS OF OUR CELLS.

DR. GLASS: AH, LIKE DNA IS THE CODE, BUT THE TRANSLATION COULD GIVE YOU TWO DIFFERENT MESSAGES DEPENDING ON YOUR CODE-BREAKER.

HOPE KESTREL: EXACTLY. FACTORS *OUTSIDE* OF THE DNA SEQUENCE CAN AFFECT WHAT PROTEINS ARE MADE. EVEN WHEN THE GENE SEQUENCE ITSELF IS UNCHANGED. EPIGENETIC CHANGES CAN TRICK DNA INTO CHOOSING TO BEHAVE IN A WAY IT SHOULDN'T.

DR. GLASS: AND YOUR UNDERGRAD WORK WITH DR. LI? WHERE DOES THAT FIT IN?

HOPE KESTREL: SHE'S INCORPORATING THE EPIGENETIC DATA INTO THE MACHINE LEARNING ALGORITHM. IF WE CAN UNMASK THOSE CHANGES IN TUMOR CELLS, WE CAN UNCOVER NEW GENE MUTATIONS TO DISCOVER NEW THERAPIES.

DR. GLASS: SOUNDS PROMISING. I THINK YOU'LL BE HEARING FROM US SOON.

A security alert popped up in the middle of the screen. Ah, the intern had arrived, exactly on time. Marah would pick this up later—finding more clues to what made Hope Kestrel tick.

She reached the security checkpoint in time to see the intern pass through and stepped in front of her, blocking her path. "Dr. Stone, isn't it?"

"Dr. Maddox! I mean, yes, I'm Jacie Stone," the young woman stammered. "I'm not really used to the whole doctor title yet."

Marah aimed a reassuring smile up at her. The girl was indeed *tall* and, curiously, wore an orange scarf around her neck. Marah ignored the nonstandard attire for now. "Why not? You're here, aren't you?"

Jacie gave a slow nod.

Marah pivoted, gesturing for Jacie to follow her. "Come, I'll walk with you. Where are you headed?"

The girl glanced at her tablet, hesitating a second before closing it and following. "OASIS. Morning rounds."

"Who's your senior resident?" Marah knew the answer, of course, but wanted to get Jacie talking.

"Dr. Leach."

"Ah, yes. You're lucky then. He's one of our best."

Jacie's lips flattened into a straight line. "Yes, that's what I tell myself every morning. How fortunate I am to work with Dr. Leach."

Marah fought to keep a straight face. She liked this young woman. The algorithm had done an excellent job selecting her for the program, but she needed a boost in confidence. "You shouldn't sell yourself short. We only take the best of the best, and I hear Dr. Li selected you for her lab. Congratulations."

"Thank you." Jacie's lips twitched into a nervous smile, and she stopped walking as they reached the end of the hallway. "Dr. Maddox, it's an honor to talk to you, but I'm sure you have more important things to do—"

"—and that means you're working with Dr. Kestrel, of course." Marah continued as if Jacie hadn't spoken. "Yes, I remember you were with her in Cecilia's office, and that was you with her in the cafeteria a few evenings ago, too, wasn't it? I'm sorry you had to witness that. Dr. Kestrel's a good resident. She needs a bit of help from us right now, that's all."

Jacie offered another timid smile that faded quickly. "I didn't think you would have noticed me."

Marah needed to gain Jacie's confidence. She gave her arm a brief squeeze—a slight touch to show her support. "You'll find I take my role in overseeing the residency program seriously. I make it a point to get to know all my interns and residents." Marah made a tsking noise. "Such an ugly business that night. Poor Dr. Kestrel, I'm afraid she let her performance slip of late. It can happen even to the best of us. That's why I had to put her on leave. It hurt me as much as it hurt her, but the program will do everything we can to help her."

Jacie rubbed her arm where Marah had touched her. "Oh. That's good, then."

Marah studied her face. "You haven't had any contact with her, have you—since that night?"

Jacie's expression remained blank. "With Dr. Kestrel? Why would I?"

Interesting. The girl would lie for Hope Kestrel. Marah pasted a smile on her face. "No particular reason. I only thought it a possibility she may have reached out to you." She pinched the bridge of her nose and then brought her hand down as if it pained her to say the next words. "I didn't want to have to say anything, but I think it's important you're aware—in case she does contact you. Please understand this is confidential between us. Hope Kestrel has had some, shall we say, personal difficulties. I've tried to give her every opportunity. Still, despite the program's best efforts, I'm afraid she let those personal difficulties affect her performance."

A look of confusion passed over Jacie's face. "I'm sorry to hear that."

Marah affected a sigh. "Not as sorry as I am. But I sincerely believe we can still help her turn her performance around. I hope you understand the gravity of the situation now. Can I count on you to report to me if she contacts you?"

Jacie pressed her lips together. "Sure thing."

"Good." Marah raised her wrist and tapped the commands on her smartwatch. "Now, you might find a little bonus added to your ranking this morning."

"Oh, but that's not necessary, really—"

Marah brought up a hand. "Nonsense. You'll find excellent performance around here is rewarded. Now, keep up the good work."

The ranking system had been Marah's best idea. It never failed to amaze her how the trainees would fall in line with being able to track their rank continuously in direct comparison to their peers. A Pavlovian response, really.

Jacie had brought out her tablet. Her eyes widened. "Thank you, Dr. Maddox."

Marah smiled and then winked at her. "It's my pleasure. I can't tell you how happy I am you're a part of PRIMA—"

Both of their devices chimed. An email alert. It appeared to be nonsense, and Marah deleted it with a swipe of irritation. "Damn phishing emails. I've asked I.T. to improve our filters." She glanced over at Jacie's screen. "You should delete that, too."

Jacie closed her tablet. "Yeah, be careful of those. Sometimes they're malicious."

Marah scrutinized her. "Yes. Aren't they, though?"

Jacie shifted her weight from one foot to the other. "I really better get to rounds. I mean, this has been an honor to talk with you, and thank you for my points—"

"Excellent performance is rewarded," Marah repeated, holding her gaze for a few seconds more before waving an arm up the hallway toward OASIS. "Give my regards to Dr. Leach."

CHAPTER FOURTEEN

FRIDAY 19 OCTOBER 2035
8:45 AM
The PARC (Prognosis and Results Center), Seattle

The PARC building had a more industrial appearance than PRIMA's main campus, all steel and dark glass. Poppy waited outside, appearing to have come straight off a night shift at HEARTH, her yellow scrubs rumpled and eyes puffy. If only *Cecilia* had been the one to ask Hope along to her PARC appointment. But right now, Poppy was the one who needed her.

Hope jogged up to her. "You okay?"

"Thanks for coming." Poppy gave her a quick hug, then flashed a nervous smile.

Hope tried not to show her surprise. Jake and Poppy were the most stable couple she knew. "The two of you doing okay?"

Poppy shrugged. "We disagree on the testing. He doesn't trust the science."

"What's not to trust?" Hope took Poppy's hand and gave it a squeeze. "Come on, let's get you inside."

She led Poppy through the check-in procedure, grateful to feel useful for the first time in days. They settled themselves on a vinyl sofa in the crowded waiting area. Hope scanned the room just in case, but no Cecilia in sight.

Poppy shrank away from the others. "God, they all look so impossibly happy. Like they're in some secret clique of parents-to-be, only no one gave me the password."

Hope had to admit, the room contained a buzz of excitement. Many of the partners holding hands or arm-in-arm. The two women cuddling across from them appeared particularly ecstatic. "Hey, don't worry about them."

Poppy suddenly fanned herself with her hands. "Ugh, I think I might throw up."

Hope nudged her with a shoulder. "That might be a good sign, no?"

Poppy gave a half-hearted laugh.

A middle-aged blonde nurse in caterpillar-green scrubs appeared in the doorway leading back to the clinic area. "Poppy Hart?"

Poppy clutched Hope's arm. "I don't want to go. If I don't find out, nothing will change. All the possibilities can still be open. But once they reveal it, there won't *be* any more possibilities, only the one probability."

The nurse called her name again, this time with an edge of annoyance.

Hope waved her hand and called out, "She's right here." She turned to Poppy and squeezed her hand again. "Come on. I'll be right by your side."

They trailed the nurse down the hallway into an empty exam room. Poppy remained silent while the nurse took her vital signs.

"Excellent," the nurse said. "Let me double-check something, and I'll be right back."

Poppy turned to Hope, a harried, wild appearance to her eyes. "It's going to be bad news. The smile on that nurse's face wasn't congratulatory—I know that kind of smile."

"Hey, you can't be sure—"

The nurse returned wearing a somber expression and took Poppy's hands in hers. "I'm sorry, it's not good news."

Hope remained silent while the nurse explained to Poppy that the mis-pregnancy panel results predicted this pregnancy, too, would not go to term. Poppy would have another miscarriage. Hope's heart broke for her, and she couldn't help feeling angry. Jake should be here. She focused on that anger rather than allowing another thought to enter her mind—what if Cecilia's test results today didn't reveal good news, either?

Poppy leaned into her. "All I want is to give Jake his dream. A baby, a family. He's been through so much."

Hope put an arm around her. "This isn't your fault."

"It's neither your fault nor your partner's." The nurse chimed in with artificial brightness. "At least you found out in the earliest stage. We can spare you progressing through a pregnancy destined to end in miscarriage. Only a mis-pregnancy."

Hope restrained the impulse to slap the false smile off the nurse's face.

"What if it's a mistake?" she said over Poppy's head. "How can you be sure?"

The nurse went on to explain about the clinical trials that validated the mis-pregnancy algorithm. How women with a history of miscarriage diagnosed with mis-pregnancy by the new PRIMA testing all subsequently miscarried. How the medical community, and even the Catholic church, accepted the mis-pregnancy results as indicative of not an actual pregnancy. Ending the mis-pregnancy thus wasn't considered an abortion. The religious types argued it was best to clear the womb so the woman could try sooner for another healthy pregnancy. The healthcare administrators made the financial argument that treating a clump of nonviable cells was a lot less expensive than treating a miscarriage, especially a later-term one. Hope noted grimly that neither of these arguments bothered to center the woman's point of view, the *actual person* it was affecting.

But it seemed too perfect a result, even for PRIMA. Although Hope assumed the one in 10,000 error rate also applied here. "All of them?"

The nurse affirmed, turning back to Poppy and continuing in her artificially bright voice. "But this doesn't mean Poppy won't have a healthy pregnancy and baby, eventually. Ending the mis-pregnancy now increases your chance of the next pregnancy being healthy. You'll avoid the risks and complications of miscarriage, including hemorrhage, sepsis, and the potential need for emergency surgery, including a hysterectomy. How awful would that be? Why would you risk that?"

Poppy was nodding, but her eyes were vacant, like someone who'd just walked away from a car accident.

Hope spoke for her. "What happens next, exactly?"

"We'll give Poppy a prescription, and she can take it in the privacy of her own home. The mis-pregnancy can be ended. It will prevent the emotional and physical toll of waiting for the inevitable miscarriage."

Back at Poppy's house, Hope hovered in a chair in the living room. Poppy lay curled up on the couch, holding two pill bottles.

She held one bottle up toward Hope. "I guess I take this one first. Ironic, isn't it?"

Hope twisted her mouth. "I don't see—"

"The pain pill. There are few exceptions to the opiate prescribing ban. One is for mis-pregnancies. Another is for hospice patients." Poppy choked out a laugh that sounded more like a sob. "Beginnings and endings, I guess."

Hope searched for the right thing to say. She wanted Jake to get home already. With Poppy's permission, she'd called him from her car to fill him in on what was happening.

She recalled what she'd learned about miscarriages in med school, searching for something to say. "It's very common. Twenty-five percent of women in the U.S. will experience a miscarriage—"

Poppy cut her off. "Yeah, one in four women, I know. When I had the first miscarriage, I tried consoling myself with that statistic. It didn't work." She let her arm drop by her side, still holding the pill bottle. "Then I looked up second miscarriages. Any guesses on chances of that?"

"I don't—"

"One in seven at best. One in five at worst. But this testing—it says it's one hundred percent for me, for this pregnancy, right? So what do those other statistics matter?" Poppy pressed her hands to her face. "What if I can't ever carry a pregnancy to term? Jake told me it doesn't matter to him, that he loves me no matter what. But he had such a lonely childhood. I want to give him his dream of a big family. If only my body would stop betraying me."

Hope hesitated. "Poppy, why'd you decide to do the mis-pregnancy testing? Help me understand what's going on here."

Poppy reached for a tissue and blew her nose. "You wouldn't understand."

"Maybe not. But I'd like to."

Poppy wiped her eyes. "I couldn't live through a miscarriage again. I—I can't. Jake doesn't understand what it was like for me. The first one, we were at thirteen weeks. Everything was supposed to be safe past the first trimester. Then, with no warning, waking up to the bleeding, the cramps, the hospital, the procedure... I can't go through that again. I can't. It would break me."

Hope moved over to sit next to her. "I'm so sorry that happened to you."

"I mean, working at HEARTH, as part of PRIMA, we get access to the most advanced healthcare in the world. An opportunity most of the world doesn't even have yet. So when I learned of the new mis-pregnancy testing, I told Jake I wanted to do it. I tried to explain... if the inevitable was destined to happen, at least I could choose how and when. To have some control. It would be physically safer for me, too."

Hope's phone alerted her to a text message, and she quickly silenced it without looking at the screen.

Poppy continued in a shaky voice. "Once I learned of the option for the mis-pregnancy testing, I had to do it. It's like... the burden of devastation would somehow be less if I at least had this small measure of control over my body. Does that make any sense?"

Hope put her arm around Poppy and drew her close. "Yeah. I got you. It makes perfect sense."

CHAPTER FIFTEEN

Hope shut off the auto-drive and parked on the street near the address Jacie had texted her in North Seattle. She scrutinized the message one more time. *Can you meet me? Something to show you. My house, tonight, 8:00 PM.*

It had been a day. After Jake had finally returned home, Hope had left to give Poppy privacy to speak with him. The rest of the day had passed at a glacial pace while she waited for evening, eager to meet Jacie. She'd hoped Cecilia might call with her own update, but she hadn't yet. And after Poppy's experience at the PARC, Hope couldn't bring herself to call Cecilia, telling herself no news was good news.

Hope didn't want to allow herself to think of Cecilia potentially being in the same situation, receiving bad news alone. Why hadn't Cecilia let Hope go with her? Why hadn't she called yet?

She winced as she recalled the conversation between her, Jacie, and Cecilia last week.

"*... when PRIMA gives its report, or whatever... and if it says the treatment won't work, how do you tell the patient?*"

"*We don't... That's the nurse's job, of course.*"

She hoped Jacie had better news for her tonight. Anything would be better than what they'd found in Dalton's personnel file. She couldn't help but think Maddox was retaliating against her the way she apparently had against Dalton—for having a patient become a non-responder, something neither resident could have been responsible for—but she needed more evidence. She couldn't go to the authorities with only a copy of a confidential NDA—especially when she couldn't explain how she'd gotten it. They needed something more.

Hope stepped out of the car and walked up the gravel driveway. The house was older, circa 1980s, but cozy-appearing, newly repainted, light green with gray trim. She climbed up the three front steps and pressed the bell.

The door swung open to reveal Jacie, still in her white scrubs. "Hey, thanks for coming."

She beckoned Hope inside and showed her to a living room, where Hope took a seat on a checkered blue sofa. Plants filled the room, and family photos lined the walls. Two parents and two girls spanning a sequence from babies to teen years. In each one, the smiling face of the younger girl drew her focus. The sister who had died.

Jacie crossed to a door on the opposite side and closed it, but not before Hope glimpsed a desk covered with computer equipment—multiple monitors and a microphone. She then took the chair opposite Hope.

"My parents' house. I'm saving money and all that, you know." Jacie shrugged. "They're at work—we own a restaurant."

The house had a warmth that Hope hadn't experienced in a long time— one that had disappeared from her childhood home soon after her mom died. She cleared her throat. "It's a beautiful home."

"Thanks." Jacie glanced around as if seeing it for the first time. An uncomfortable silence followed. "Anyway, there's someone I want you to meet. Wait here."

Hope tapped her foot. Didn't Jacie have some news for her? Or was the 'something' a person? Her eyes drifted back to the photos while she waited. She wondered if her grief would have been easier if she'd had a sibling to share it.

"This is my sister, Izabella."

Hope jumped to her feet, unable to cover her surprise.

Jacie pushed a wheelchair ahead of her. In it sat the girl from the photos, dressed in shorts and a t-shirt. A younger, frailer version of Jacie, painfully thin, with limp curls plastered to her forehead and an oxygen cannula hooked under her nose.

"But—" Hope's eyes darted from Izabella to Jacie. "But I thought…"

Jacie mouthed the word "later."

Why hadn't Jacie told her that her sister was alive? Hope focused back on Izabella, who gave Hope a smile that brightened her entire face. "Nice to meet you."

Hope found it impossible not to return the smile. She crossed the room and shook her hand. "Nice to meet you, Izabella. I'm Hope."

With her other hand, Izabella waved downward, and Hope noticed a below-the-knee amputation of the left leg. "Sorry, I don't have my prosthesis on. But Jacie said you wouldn't mind, since you're a doctor and all."

Hope kneeled to bring herself to Izabella's eye level. "I don't mind, and not because I'm a doctor. If you ever meet anyone who does mind, you let me know." Her clinical eye noted the scar. Well-healed. She would estimate the surgery had been some time ago, probably years. The wheelchair likely had more to do with whatever additional condition necessitated the oxygen tank. Hope shifted her weight back on her heels. "You had an excellent surgeon, and you are, if I may say, a superb healer. Your skin looks fantastic."

Izabella's cheeks pinked a little. "Thanks. Jacie helps me a lot."

Hope rose to her feet. "I can see that."

"Is she helping you, too? Did she tell you about the time she hacked into the school website—?"

"*Izzie*," Jacie cut her off. "Hope's kind of like my boss, so please, let's not tell her that one."

Hope grinned. "No, I want to hear this. Please, tell."

Izabella giggled. "There was this girl, in the grade above me, and she was bullying me, and Jacie found out, and—"

"Okay." Jacie wheeled Izabella around. "We don't want to tire you out. Let's get you back to your movie. Then I'm going to chat with Hope a little, okay?"

Hope winked at Izabella. "Next time."

Izabella winked back. A chirp sounded from her pocket, and she pulled out her phone. She swiped the screen and giggled again. "Oops, Jacie, this is yours."

Jacie snatched it and brought out the phone she had in her pocket. She compared the two and made a noise of exacerbation. "You've got to quit mixing up our phones."

The two continued to bicker as Jacie wheeled her down the hall, but Hope sensed the love beneath the words. She had nothing to compare it to. The family photos drew her gaze back. Now that she knew, she could see where Izabella began to appear ill, around age twelve.

A few minutes later, Jacie returned, waving Hope back to the sofa and sinking into the chair across from her again. She let out a long sigh. "We've been trying to get her one of the new robotic prostheses, but it's too expensive without insurance coverage."

Hope frowned, wanting to know why Jacie had allowed her to believe her sister was dead, but first asking about the prosthesis. "Why won't insurance cover it?"

Jacie slid a piece of paper across the coffee table to her. "Because of this."

Hope picked it up and read:

PATIENT: IZABELLA STONE
DOB: 3/01/19
PREDICTION OF RESPONSE BY PROGNOSTIC INTELLIGENT MEDICAL ALGORITHMS

YOUR PRIMA ANALYSIS CUSTOMIZED REPORT AND RECOMMENDATIONS:
MUTATIONS DETECTED: 37
RESPONSE RATE PREDICTION: 0%
RECOMMENDED TREATMENT: HOSPICE

THANK YOU FOR TRUSTING PRIMA WITH THE PRIVILEGE OF YOUR HEALTHCARE.
WE OPTIMIZE, SO YOU CAN FLOURISH.

Jacie's voice broke the silence. "Osteosarcoma of her leg. Resected four years ago—the amputation. We thought she was cured. But last year, it came back, metastatic to her lungs. This is the PRIMA report for the metastases."

Hope remained silent, unable to find any words to respond.

"Yeah, funny thing, insurance won't cover a high-end prosthesis for a *non-responder*." Jacie picked at the cushion on the chair, then pressed her hands together as if keeping herself from coming apart. "My parents were uninsured. Small business owners who couldn't afford it, even with the subsidies. Until PRIMA came along, offering their fixed, affordable premium for everyone. My parents thought their prayers had been answered. An insurance plan the subsidies could actually cover, with no deductibles or copays, sounded like a miracle."

Hope spoke in a slow voice. "Because the algorithm individualizes treatment and keeps costs down."

Jacie let out a bitter laugh. "Yep. And my parents were so grateful. Weren't we lucky to live in Seattle, the birthplace of this newest medical technology? And we were. We really were. Izzie had the surgery, and we thought the worst was behind us."

Hope wasn't sure she wanted to hear the rest of the story. She glanced up the hallway toward Izabella's room. "What happened?"

"Last year, we realized something was wrong. She was listless, pale, losing weight. But it took forever for someone to listen to us and run the tests. We were right. Something *was* wrong with Izzie. Lung metastases. Three of them. But she wouldn't be offered treatment. Because of what's on that slip of paper. *That's* how PRIMA keeps costs down. Denying surgery to the refractory cases. Even a kid."

Hope's mouth had gone dry. She couldn't have spoken, even if she somehow could formulate the right words.

Jacie let out a rueful laugh. "I looked into everything. Because to not even try? I couldn't accept that. I called experts, universities. There was a chemo pill, but they explained it would cost over twenty thousand dollars per month without insurance to pay for it. *Twenty thousand* dollars. A *month*. My parents would do anything—*anything*—in the world for her, but there was no way. Even if they sold the house, it would only cover a few months. So I kept asking, why not operate? Why not resect the damn metastases?" She jabbed a finger toward the paper on the table. "Because of that. That piece of paper—that said even if they operated, the cancer would come back. It's a piece of paper, but they might as well have set it in stone. Even if we found a surgeon who would operate despite PRIMA's prediction, the total cost, without insurance coverage, would exceed half a million dollars. She'd never even get admitted without insurance prior authorization. I called everywhere, but that damn PRIMA report attached itself to Izabella's record, no matter how hard I tried to separate it. Even the non-PRIMA facilities embrace the algorithm's clinical predictions—for insurance coverage purposes. Since there was no guarantee of prolonging her life, they all said 'don't bother,' especially not on their dime."

It did not surprise Hope to hear it, as sorry as she was for Izabella's incurable situation. It's what the algorithm was for.

Jacie continued. "I called the pharmaceutical companies and applied for assistance programs. But when the companies got that report—and they always did—they denied our applications. They weren't willing to give away their expensive drugs for free to someone they believed *wouldn't respond*. Thanks to PRIMA."

"I'm so sorry—"

"I got desperate and discovered that purchasing medications from other countries is a legal gray area. The U.S. rarely prosecutes if you have a valid prescription and resort to foreign pharmacies only because of financial barriers. So, we needed a valid prescription from a physician. I only knew one, our old family practitioner—Dr. Noah Meier. I collapsed in relief when he returned my call and agreed to write the prescription."

Hope sat up straighter. "Wait, you're saying she's been getting the oral chemotherapy, anyway?"

Jacie nodded. "My parents took on a second mortgage for the house and the restaurant. Used up all their savings. It's *only* costing us five thousand a month instead of twenty."

Hope tilted her head. "But that's—for how long now?"

Jacie's mouth flattened into a straight line. "That was over a year ago. With Dr. Meier's help, Izzie's still alive. But time's running out. My parents are going to go bankrupt, and the targeted therapy won't work forever. I have to get her into PRIMA for more definitive treatment. If the lung metastases can be resected, she has a chance. She would've had the surgery a year ago if it wasn't for that piece of paper."

Hope stared at her. "That's why you applied to PRIMA. What you meant in the café. Why you want to work in Cecilia's lab."

Jacie met her eyes. "I'm not like you. I didn't join PRIMA for some imaginary greater good. There's only one reason I'm here. To help my sister."

Hope rubbed her forehead. "But what exactly do you think you'll be able to do for her?"

"I don't know. I only know I have to try."

Hope tried to process it all. If she hadn't met Izabella, she might not have believed it. But as much as she sympathized, there was nothing she could do. "Why did you ask me here tonight?"

Jacie hesitated. "I found something else. After this morning, I kept searching. I started thinking, maybe we were looking in the wrong place for 'CL.' What if it was a lab file, not a personnel file? So I dug around some more and found a sub-folder in Cecilia's lab archives with the date from the coffee cup: 2.20.29." She pulled out her tablet and slid it toward Hope. "I think you better see this."

Hope lowered her eyes to the screen. It was an email.

From: Cecilia Li <li.cecilia@seattle.edu>
Sent: Monday, February 20, 2029, 3:56 PM
To: Marah Maddox <mmaddox@seattle.edu>
Subject: Re: error rates
Marah, please see the attached files for your review. Unfortunately, we're still getting about a five percent error rate. However, I did an exploratory analysis. If I exclude certain data sets (attached), the algorithm will align with the goal error rate of one in ten thousand. I wanted to send this over to you to

analyze and give me your thoughts on how we can use this to hypothesize to adjust the algorithm further.

Thank you,

Cecilia

Hope lifted her finger in slow motion and clicked on the icon to open the attachment.

It couldn't be.

She examined it again. And yet again. She broke out in a cold sweat. If this meant what she thought...

No, it *can't* be.

"The attachment. The excluded data sets..." Nausea rose in Hope's throat. "They're mine. My data. The epigenetic data. The unmasked tumor DNA sequences. They were supposed to be part of the training sets for the machine learner."

The date of the email sank in. The implications of this—but no. Hope had to double-check. She opened a new browser window.

Jacie reached toward the screen but let her hands fall. "Is that...?"

"The press release. From 2029." Hope had to force the words past the tightness in her chest. "The press release that announced PRIMA's launch into clinical practice...."

"That's the day after this email—"

"Let me think for a minute." Hope snapped at her.

She pressed her fingers to her temples. According to the email, Cecilia had excluded some data sets to see how the machine learner would respond. But only as an exploratory analysis.

Cecilia excluded my data sets.

Because with including her data sets, the accuracy rate plateaued at 95 percent. Which would mean a five percent error rate. Way too high for precision clinical practice—and too high for PRIMA's bottom line.

"Does this mean what I think it means?" Jacie spoke in a carefully controlled voice. "Because the timing of this email makes it look like they launched a machine learning system into clinical practice—despite a decision to *leave out entire sets of data*. If that data wasn't in the learning sets for the machine learner, it would skew the algorithm."

Jacie was right. Hope didn't need to be a programmer to understand that. "If they didn't provide the machine learner with the data to account for epigenetic changes in DNA—"

Jacie finished the sentence for her. "Its accuracy rate is only 95 percent. And they knew it. *She* knew it. She lied to us."

"No." Hope's stomach clenched. "Cecilia wouldn't have done this."

Jacie jabbed her finger at the screen. "This kinda sorta makes it look like she did."

"The email said it was exploratory only."

Because if it were true, it meant the chance of the algorithm making an error was, in actuality, five times in a hundred.

One time in twenty. Not one time in ten thousand.

And they implemented it anyway.

Maddox—and Cecilia.

The ground fell away beneath Hope. She grabbed her coat and headed for her car. She needed to get out of there.

Jacie chased her outside and grabbed her arm. "You can't run away because you don't like what we found." She let go of Hope and clenched her fists at her sides. "I knew there *had* to be a fundamental error in the PRIMA algorithm to explain Izabella's response. Why she's responding to the oral chemo even though the algorithm predicted she wouldn't—"

Hope paced, unable to stand in one place. "What do you want me to do?"

Jacie gave her a pained stare. "Don't you see? Izzie's cancer must contain a mutation that the machine learner algorithm had never seen before and thus failed to identify, even though it *is* responsive. The algorithm couldn't account for a random event it couldn't predict."

"Overfitting." Hope shivered and recalled Jacie's words from that first day in the lab. *The computer hallucinates a pattern that isn't actually there.* "But if Izabella isn't a non-responder—"

Jacie finished her sentence in a choked voice. "She's an exception."

The wind picked up, and dead leaves whirled around them.

Jacie was right. Hope couldn't run away from this. She had a duty, a responsibility, to further investigate. The algorithm—the system she believed in—couldn't be flawed to this degree.

Hope folded her arms across herself, bracing against the wind. Her mind refused to believe it. The email couldn't mean what it appeared to imply. The file might not even be real. How had Jacie even found it? She must have done something wrong.

Jacie moved closer. "A machine learner will only be as accurate as the amount and quality of data you give it. Aside from the omitted data, have you examined the subjects' demographics in your datasets?"

"Of course, that's all on record—"

Jacie crossed her arms. "Less than five percent of the DNA data is from Black patients. Maybe that's part of the problem."

Hope blinked into the wind. "But it's not like that's intentional—"

Jacie's expression tightened. "Tuskegee. James Marion Sims. Henrietta Lacks. Holmesburg Prison. COVID-19. I could go on. Our healthcare system is built on the backbone of structural racism."

Hope fumbled to pull her collar higher. She knew about structural racism in medicine, of course. The Tuskegee syphilis "study," where doctors intentionally withheld penicillin treatment from Black people. James Marion Sims, the so-called "father of gynecology," had become so by experimenting on Black, enslaved women without consent, including surgeries with no anesthesia. Henrietta Lacks, a Black woman and mother of five who died of cervical cancer in the 1950s, but researchers continued to grow the cells from her cancer in a lab—without her family's consent—and then commercialized the cell lines, leading to millions of dollars in profit for the medical researchers who patented her tissue. Holmesburg Prison, where they used inmates for medical experiments, injecting them with chemicals to test products for anything from the cosmetic industry to industrial warfare agents. And COVID-19, the recent pandemic of their lifetime, with widely disproportionate mortality rates that had exposed the country's fault lines of racial injustice and revealed just who was considered "essential."

As the country had moved on from the pandemic, Hope believed things had improved. But what evidence did she have for that? She was ashamed to realize she had no answer. She'd been too busy focusing on PRIMA, her research, and trying to leave her past behind her. But PRIMA was guilty of the same thing. Her cheeks went hot. What would her mom think of her having been blind to this?

Jacie was still talking. "Big Data increasingly controls every facet of our lives. There's no dataset on this earth free of bias, but we're letting these faulty algorithms control home loans, college admissions, credit scores, employment, court rulings. Who gets parole and who doesn't. Who gets bail, even. Do you think PRIMA is any different?"

Hope met Jacie's eyes. "I did. I thought our objective, DNA-based data was the solution."

Jacie snorted. "It's not objective if the data's being manipulated or deliberately left out."

Hope shook her head in denial. "But it's not possible Cecilia's been intentionally omitting my data. Not for all these years."

They were a team. Cecilia understood how much PRIMA meant to Hope. What it represented. How she'd invested every part of herself in building a better system. How every cell in her body was driven by the memory of her mom. Cecilia would have an explanation. It wasn't what it appeared. Someone else had to be at fault.

"The data." She grabbed Jacie's arm. "Whoever controls the data controls PRIMA. What if—"

"—it wasn't Cecilia who kept your data sets from reaching the machine learner." Jacie finished her sentence.

Hope gave voice to the name they were both thinking. "Maddox."

Then another implication of their discovery knocked the breath out of Hope. *Five percent chance of error.*

She whispered another name.

"*Poppy.*"

CHAPTER SIXTEEN

Hope cursed the traffic and pounded the horn as a silver BMW cut in front of her. On her left, the auto-truck lane penned her in, and her right was bumper to bumper.

She tried calling Poppy again, but still no answer. When she'd left their condo earlier, Poppy and Jake were going to have a long discussion ahead of them. Hope might not be too late. If Poppy knew the truth, it might make a difference in her decision. The choice was hers, but it should be a fully informed choice. A vast difference existed between a one in ten thousand error rate and a one in twenty.

Poppy had trusted in a flawed system. PRIMA had lied to her and all its employees—and patients. Was Cecilia a part of this lie? It couldn't be true. It had to have been Maddox. Hope only wanted Cecilia to be okay and to know her PARC testing result.

But first, she needed to reach Poppy. She curled her shoulders forward over the steering wheel. The sky unleashed a downpour of rain, and the wipers automatically responded, increasing to high speed. Spotting an opportunity to squeeze in front of an SUV, she switched to manual drive and pressed the gas pedal toward the floor, fighting her way into the express commuter lane and ignoring the angry horns that blared behind her.

Her brain continued to wrestle with the question of how Cecilia could have allowed PRIMA to go forward with such a significant error rate. Had she not cared how many lives would be affected? Hope couldn't come to any understanding of it, nor reconcile such a cold, unfeeling decision with the intelligent, caring mentor and friend she knew. It must have been Maddox who unilaterally decided the cutoff on the accuracy rate. What had given her the right?

The line of traffic in front of her came to a dead stop, and Hope's car took over, activating the brakes and throwing Hope forward against the shoulder belt. She smashed the horn again out of frustration. If only everyone engaged their auto-drive, these jams wouldn't happen. But some people still loved to drive manually, causing chaos for everyone else. Her eyes darted between the side mirrors, trying to spot an escape from the gridlock. All six lanes were at a standstill. She used the moment to call Poppy again. Still no answer. Hope punched in a repeat text. *Call me. Urgent!* She didn't want to text *'don't take the pills,'*—in case Poppy already had.

The rain grew heavier, and she swore again. She had to get off I-5. A motorcycle passed her on the left. Without stopping to worry about whether it was a good idea, she disengaged the auto-drive one more time, choosing chaos. She swung out behind the motorcycle into the shoulder lane, avoiding eye contact with the red-faced drivers she passed who hit their horns and raised shaking fists at her.

Forty-five minutes later, she swerved into the parking lot for Poppy's building in the Queen Anne neighborhood, taking the first spot she saw and disregarding the 'reserved' signs. A group of young women had just exited the lobby, and Hope grabbed the door before it closed. She ran up the four flights of stairs and pounded on Poppy and Jake's door.

It took forever before the door opened.

"Hope?" Poppy blinked at her, clad in pajamas and slippers. "What are you doing here?"

"Hey," Hope shifted her feet. "I know it's late. Sorry."

Her eyes traveled up and down Poppy's body. Was she too late? But she couldn't blurt out a demand about the pills. What would Hope say if she'd already taken them? She stalled. "Um, can I come in? There's something I need to talk to you about."

Poppy shuffled back, and Hope followed her into the living room where they'd been earlier.

Hope cast a glance around. "Where's Jake?"

Poppy's face twisted. "He went out again."

"What? I mean—"

"Do you think I'm a terrible person?"

"What kind of question is that? No—"

"Jake left because I asked him to. I couldn't bear having him hovering over me, like another layer of sadness to smother me. I'm so selfish, but I can't comfort him on top of everything—"

"You're not selfish—"

"I couldn't imagine going on with the pregnancy, knowing it wouldn't go to term—the *waiting* for the inevitable miscarriage. I wouldn't know when. It could happen next week, next month, or even further along. If it couldn't be stopped, and the only thing I could control was when and where it happened, does that make me a monster?"

"Of course not. You, and all women, deserve to be in control of your body—"

"I feel like I'm losing my mind." Poppy released a short laugh that morphed into a sob, sinking to the floor. "I keep having this thought. I know it's crazy, but you know how some cultures believe a pregnant woman shouldn't attend a funeral? What does it mean that I attend to the dying? Is it all my fault? I feel like an angel of death—that my body can't carry a baby—"

"No, Poppy, it's not your fault—"

Poppy let out another sob-laugh. "I'm a midwife of death—"

"What?" Hope crouched and put her arm around her.

"That's what people used to call early hospice workers decades ago."

"You do important work, and you do it well, and it has nothing to do with the miscarriages. That's just superstitious nonsense from people trying to blame women for something that's not their fault." Hope gently helped her stand. "Let's get you to the couch."

Poppy allowed herself to be pulled up, leaning heavily on Hope, her gait unsteady. She mumbled as Hope steered her to the sofa. "I feel like I'm a failure... or I must not deserve to be a mother because my body betrayed me again...."

Hope settled her on the couch and assessed her with a clinical eye. "Um, sorry to ask this, but have you been drinking?"

Poppy flapped a hand. "Not booze. It's the damn opiate pill."

Hope's stomach dropped. She was too late, then.

Poppy turned her head up at Hope. "You know what's great about you? I can tell you all this shit, and you don't pity me. I don't think I could stand to be pitied." Her words became more slurred. "But sometimes, I think I hate you. I hate all the doctors. It's their fault, this test result, and that nurse, too..."

Hope ignored her words, doubting Poppy would remember much of what she said after the drug wore off. Her eyes flicked toward Poppy's lower abdomen. "Do you need anything? Are you in pain? Cramping?"

"I don't want to think about that..." Poppy drifted off, but then startled awake and pushed herself up. "Why are you here again?"

Hope needed to ask her own questions. "What time did you take the pills?"

"A while ago. The first ones." Poppy held up her hand and rotated it in slow motion, a fresh-appearing Band-Aid wrapped around her index finger. "I was going to take the second ones, but I dropped the glass of water and cut my finger. I had just finished cleaning everything up when you knocked on the door."

Wait, what was Poppy saying? Hope crouched down and gripped Poppy by the shoulders. "You didn't take the second pills? Are you sure?"

"Is that why you're here? To check up on me?" Poppy lurched backward out of Hope's grasp. "No, I didn't take them yet. But I will. I'm going to—"

"No!"

Poppy jerked her head back.

"Don't take them. At least not until you've heard what I have to say." Hope hugged her arms across her body and gazed down at her knees.

"I don't know how to tell you this..." She forced herself to look Poppy in the eyes. "It's possible there's been a mistake."

"I'm sorry—what?" Poppy blinked.

Hope repeated herself and explained about the five percent chance of error.

Poppy raised her arm.

And punched Hope in the face.

CHAPTER SEVENTEEN

SATURDAY 18 OCTOBER, 2035
7:00 AM
Hope's apartment, University District, Seattle

Hope sprinted through PRIMA, the passages twisting and dead-ending, becoming more and more lost. She searched for her mom's room, even though she was her adult self, not a child—the way time can become fluid in dreams. The glass walls morphed into mirrors, and no matter what direction she faced, her reflection stared back at her in endless multiples. She came to a door. Locked. She pummeled it with her fists, kicking and flinging herself at it, screaming her mom's name, until a hand on her shoulder startled her into silence. Cecilia whispered, *"What have you done, Hope?"*

She woke with a strangled gasp. If only yesterday's events could be a dream, too. Shuffling out of bed, she checked the bruise on her cheek, opening and closing her jaw a few times in front of the bathroom mirror. Only a mild ache, no need to ice it again. It had been a glancing blow. Poppy didn't have it in her to harm anyone.

It had been worth it to have reached Poppy in time. Last night, she'd called Jake and explained it to him too, and once he'd returned home, Hope had left them to process the possibility their pregnancy had a five percent chance of going to term. Small, yes, but not insignificant.

Yet to accept it—and the evidence in the files—meant acknowledging everything was out of Hope's control, and she couldn't afford that. She was always in control.

But no new solution had presented itself. Cecilia had allowed the use of her flawed algorithm to affect the lives of thousands of people. Her actions had allowed people to die. Now she'd fallen sick, too. How would it affect her treatment? What had the PARC told her? Hope still hadn't heard from her.

Her mind veered away from the implications. The many others it could have falsely affected. Poppy, Izabella...

Sean Medrano. A wave of dizziness made her sway on her feet. Did this mean he would have had a five percent chance of being a responder if they'd given him another chance? If so, would that have justified more treatment instead of sending him to HEARTH? They would never know.

One thing she did know. If Maddox had her way and PRIMA won the merger vote, they'd gobble up one healthcare center after another until millions more would be at risk.

Too many pieces still didn't fit together, and Hope ran through them in her mind. The information in Dalton's personnel file that didn't match what she remembered about his prior non-responder patient, the mystery slides in the lab Cecilia had wanted to hide from her, the 'final draw' procedure, and a biohazard box from HEARTH in Cecilia's lab. They had to be connected.

The beginning of a plan formed in her mind.

She texted Jacie. *My apt tonight. Come as soon as you're off duty.*

• • •

At 9:00 PM, Jacie paced the short length of Hope's apartment. "Let me get this straight. You want me to hack into PRIMA, but this time, into Maddox's files?"

Hope gave her a curt nod. "I know it's risky, but it's the only way."

Jacie stopped her pacing and squinted at her. "What happened to your face?"

Hope rubbed a self-conscious hand over her cheek. She'd forgotten about the bruise. "I walked into a door."

Jacie gave her a flat stare. "I don't get it. Yesterday you weren't very convinced, and now you want me to hack into the Director's files?"

Hope hesitated, then filled Jacie in on Poppy—omitting anything about Cecilia being sick.

Jacie met her story with silence.

Hope crossed her arms. "So... what do you say?"

"I don't know." Jacie shook her head. "But your career is pretty much over. It's not hard to piece it together—Maddox is going to do to you what she did to Dalton Fall. So I'm the only one risking mine here. Why should I stick my neck out for you?"

Hope turned her palms outward. "To help people—"

Jacie snorted. "Rich, white people, you mean."

"To help Izabella, too. Once we have more evidence—"

"No. It'll take too long." Jacie resumed her pacing, her manner again reminding Hope of the coiled-up spring, waiting to unfurl her pent-up energy. "Let's say we find something. How long would it take for the authorities to investigate? Months? Years? Izzie doesn't have that long."

"I've been thinking about that too," Hope admitted. "Who would we even go to? The state medical board? The FDA?"

Jacie gave off a short laugh. "Like they'd even believe us."

Hope had to agree with her. "I'd only look like a disgruntled employee going after her employer. Now that I'm on this forced administrative leave, my credibility's shot."

Jacie's finger punctuated the air in front of her. "Dr. Li just sat there, refusing to admit the flaw in the algorithm, not to mention omitting data. Meanwhile, all this time, PRIMA denied my sister care."

Hope resisted the impulse to jump to Cecilia's defense. A few days ago, she would have declared it impossible. Now, she didn't know what she believed anymore. Even if Maddox had been the main bad actor, Cecilia's silence made her complicit. Had it been because of her illness? Had it compromised her job performance? Hope didn't want to believe the falsified error rate could be true. But then there'd be no hope for Poppy's pregnancy—or Izabella.

Jacie halted in front of her, a gleam in her eyes. "I'll make you a deal. I'll hack the system if you figure out a way to get Izzie the surgery. To resect the metastases from her lungs."

Hope hesitated. A gust of wind rattled the building.

Jacie's face twisted. "I see."

She grabbed her coat and made for the door.

"Wait." Hope caught her sleeve. "It's not that. It's... I don't want you to go through what I did."

Jacie faced the door. "Explain."

Hope drew in a deep breath. "I was just a kid when my mom got sick. Before, in Cecilia's office, I told you a little about her suffering..." She gathered her strength to keep going. "Ovarian cancer. She did all the treatments and everything they told her to, but it returned. Metastatic. She tried chemo after chemo..."

She'd never tried to explain this to anyone other than Cecilia. "The false hope was worse than the cancer. In the end, chemo had only a ten percent chance of helping. But I didn't understand that until later, when I was older. I wished the doctors would have told me the truth as a kid. Doctors shouldn't give people false hope."

Jacie spun around. "At least your mom got to choose to *try*."

"Some choice. Doctors shouldn't offer the illusion of choice when no actual choice exists. To not go through all that... *poison*. When the cancer was terminal, no matter what."

Jacie threw her hands up in the air. "But PRIMA is terribly flawed. We just discovered that. How can you defend it?"

Hope's voice rose to match hers. "I didn't know. Until yesterday, I thought it was infallible."

"PRIMA is *not* infallible." Jacie crossed her arms. "My sister is living proof."

"You think that now." Hope lowered her voice. "But there's no guarantee, even with the surgery—"

"Life doesn't come with guarantees. All my family wants is for Izzie to have a *chance*."

They faced off in silence until a slow laugh emerged from Jacie's throat.

Heat crept up the back of Hope's neck to her ears. "What?"

Jacie snorted as the laugh grew. "It's funny—for someone named Hope, you sure don't know much about the concept." She popped a piece of gum into her mouth, then broke into a furious grin. "What other choice is there for any of us but to keep hoping?"

Hopefulness promised everything and got you nothing. Hope had reminded herself of that every day since her mom had died. Because *hope* was too risky. It's not that she didn't understand the concept. She rejected it. She'd embraced PRIMA instead and clung to the algorithm—to protect herself.

But this wasn't about her anymore. A girl's life was at stake. Still, part of herself urged sticking to the original path, with PRIMA—the secure path, the stable path. No, the path built on deception. Hope closed her eyes and let her arms fall to her side. "I'll do it."

"You? You're going to hack into Maddox's files? I'd like to see this—"

"No." Hope opened her eyes. Once she said it, there'd be no going back. But she realized she'd already made her decision. Yesterday, when she'd met Izabella. She spoke in a quiet voice. "I'll do the surgery."

Jacie said nothing for a moment. Then her eyes lit up. "You would do that?"

Hope crossed her arms. This wasn't about her anymore. "Absolutely."

•   •   •

Twenty minutes later, they sat at the kitchen table, drinking the tea Hope had scrounged from the back of a cupboard.

Jacie's face lit up, then her eyebrows squished together. "But, how?"

A million details sped through Hope's mind. "We'll need a surgical team. Leave that to me. But the harder part is you'll have to get us into the system, get Izabella assigned a Patron number—and on the O.R. schedule."

Jacie's eyes lit up to match her face. "I can do that."

"Not to mention you'll have to get me back inside, despite my suspended privileges."

"No problem."

But there was a problem, a rather large one. Even if they accomplished the first step—getting access to the O.R.—they wouldn't be able to access the augmented reality. Not without an authorized retina. Something Jacie couldn't hack, and they weren't going to resort to violence. Which meant Hope would have to operate old-school, without the AR. She'd done a handful of open thoracotomies but never on her own. She needed another surgeon to assist—one with more experience than her, one who could operate without the AR.

Hope knew who she had to call. Admitting it to herself was more difficult. She made the call before she could talk herself out of it.

· · · ·

Dalton accepted her call voice-only.

"You found the files," he said. A statement, not a question.

"Yeah."

Silence on the other end.

"It's why you left," Hope said.

She'd finally pieced it together. How the information in Dalton's personnel file connected to the old email — to the omitted data, and the error rate of PRIMA. She couldn't believe she hadn't seen it before.

"Maddox framed you. She made it appear like you'd made a mistake when that patient didn't respond as expected. So it wouldn't appear the algorithm was in error, and no one would be tempted to investigate further. A human error, nothing more."

Dalton didn't speak.

Would he confirm the truth? Or would he disappear again? Hope's pulse hammered in her ears. "But you refused to play by her rules. You left instead."

Dalton's breath sounded in her ear. "What would you have done?"

The rest of the pieces clicked together. "Maddox trumps up a 'human error' for any non-responder. To avoid bringing attention to the algorithm's actual error rate." Her mouth went dry. "I had a non-responder, so now I'm the one in her crosshairs..."

Dalton's silence was her confirmation.

Hope's next words came out too fast. "Why didn't you tell me?"

"I couldn't. The document I had to sign barred me from contact with anyone affiliated with PRIMA."

That's why he'd never called. The NDA. She twisted her necklace.

He spoke again before she could. "You know, nothing was preventing you from calling me."

Maybe he was right. But she'd been hurt and couldn't let herself call him. She'd been so sure if he'd wanted to contact her, he would have called. How was she to know it was so much more complicated? She wished she could go back and fix it. She should have tracked him down a long time ago. But there was no undoing the past.

Something still didn't quite fit. "How did they get the original publication past peer review? And the data monitoring committee?"

Dalton snorted. "Look up the committee members. They're all part of the Corporation now."

Another way Cecilia had betrayed her. Hope had been so naïve. It had all been a lie. She was that eleven-year-old child again, alone and motherless. *Cecilia, why haven't you called?*

But she had to focus. Compartmentalize. "I need your help."

Hope explained everything—the email, the falsified error rate, Izabella, and her plan.

"It's been over a year since I picked up a scalpel." The reluctance in Dalton's words didn't hide the note of yearning in his voice.

Her palms grew sweaty. He had to say yes. "We need you. You were the best."

"I don't know if that's me anymore."

"It is. Maddox can't take that away from you."

Dalton let out a long breath. "That's not who I am now."

No, he couldn't do this. Not again. "Dalton, please—"

He ended the call.

Hope couldn't meet Jacie's eyes.

Jacie sank onto the couch. "What do we do now?"

"Not to worry. I can do it without him." She'd have to.

· · ·

Rachael: Hi everyone, I'm Rachael, and this is *Algorithm Anarchist*. Where we remember, the most dangerous lies are the ones that use the truth to sell themselves.

[music]

Today, I want to talk about what I like to call The Watson problem. Yeah, that Watson. The AI that won the TV game show 'Jeopardy' in the early 2010s.

The funny thing was, it didn't work out so great when applied to healthcare.

It comes down to this—you have to look at the data sets. They used the medical literature and chart data. Watson couldn't mine the info as expected, so it couldn't extract the insights they wanted.

Let me tell you, people, it was useless. It mostly suggested standard treatments that the treating doctors were already well aware of.

But PRIMA's telling us its AI is genomic-driven. It's not trying to extrapolate from chart records. It's ingested and learned from DNA mutations.

If that's all true and good, why won't they make their data sets public? That's the question you should ask, people.

CHAPTER EIGHTEEN

MONDAY 22 OCTOBER 2035
6:30 AM
Hope's apartment, U-district, Seattle

It was a bad sign to awaken Monday morning, surgery day, to discover the storm had snowed in the city overnight. Of all times for the weather report to be accurate—blizzard in October. The climate disaster brought it earlier every year.

Hope had made two more phone calls after Jacie left on Saturday night. Both Abbie and Poppy had agreed to help with Izabella's surgery. Abbie would function as the O.R. nurse, assisting Hope, and Poppy would run the AAU, the Automated Anesthesia Unit, but only after Hope repeatedly assured her she'd forgiven her for the slug in the face.

She'd then spent the rest of the weekend reviewing open thoracotomy technique and trying not to think about Cecilia, who still hadn't called. No news was good news, she kept telling herself. But another part of her acknowledged she hadn't called Cecilia herself due to fear. She'd rather be in the dark than find out it was another situation like her mom's—not to mention confronting Cecilia about the falsified accuracy rate. She didn't know if she could handle facing her mentor. Not when she had to focus on Izabella's surgery and everything required to pull it off.

After Dalton had refused her, she didn't have anyone else at PRIMA she could trust. She'd have to manage with Abbie assisting her and Poppy running the AAU. It was risky, but she didn't see another alternative.

One thing she knew for certain when she awoke—there was no chance her electric car could drive through the snow. Good thing she knew someone who still owned a gas-powered four-wheel-drive—Poppy's husband. She called Poppy to ask if she might borrow Jake's truck to pick her up.

Poppy arrived promptly at 6:30 AM. They made their way onto I-5. The wind whipped snow drifts across the near-empty highway, and the tire chains' rumble vibrated through Hope's body.

"How's this going to work again?" Poppy's gaze didn't stray from the road.

Hope clutched the door handle as the truck skid on a patch of ice, then recovered. "Jacie's going to let us into the lab, and Abbie—she's the charge nurse I told you about—will meet us there."

Poppy downshifted. "What about Cecilia? Won't she want to know what's going on?"

"Um, she called out sick this week."

At this, Poppy risked a quick glance at her. "For the whole week?"

The temptation to tell Poppy everything almost won out, but Hope instead forced a lightness to her voice she didn't feel. "Yeah, GI virus or something."

Poppy swerved around a tree branch in the road. "What happens after Jacie hacks the system?"

"Her parents will bring Izabella to PRIMA this evening, and providing Jacie is successful, Izabella's name will be in the system for a direct admission for surgery. If all goes as planned, we'll take her to the O.R. at seven PM."

"But why so late?"

"Fewer cases, fewer people around."

Poppy fell silent as she concentrated on the road. Seattle had become a ghost city overnight. The change in state from liquid to solid of a simple molecule had rendered the city nonfunctional—plain old H-2-O. Seattle could cope with wet. Rain of all forms—from a gentle drizzle to a torrential downpour. But Seattle didn't do frozen.

Poppy took the James Street exit, and they ascended Pill Hill. A sedan without chains skidded the other direction and plowed into a snowdrift. Poppy didn't dare stop. Hope cast a backward glance to see the driver emerge to kick at the snowbank. Their truck crossed 9th Avenue and broke out of the fog. The PRIMA complex dazzled ahead, the streetlights reflecting off the whiteness of the snow.

Hope twisted her pendant, second-guessing her decision to ask Poppy to help after what she'd been through only two days ago. "You don't have to—"

"Shut up." The corners of Poppy's mouth twitched upward. "Or I'll slug you again. And then profusely apologize again."

Hope rubbed her cheek but smiled.

They turned into PRIMA's visitor parking lot a few minutes later, unusually empty because of the storm. Poppy took a ticket, and the gate swung up. She gaped at the sign. "Fifty dollars a day? You've got to be kidding me. How can family members afford to visit anyone?"

Hope pressed her lips together. She'd never been to the visitor's parking lot before and hadn't known the rates. But she should have.

Poppy parked, and they made their way to the main hospital entrance. Someone had shoveled a partial path down the sidewalk, although it had done nothing to help with the ice. Hope took Poppy's elbow to steady her. Poppy patted it away. "I'm pregnant. Not incapacitated."

They picked their way over the icy concrete to the side of the building, where Jacie awaited them at the employee entrance, stamping her feet to keep warm. She'd been on call overnight in the hospital, so she hadn't needed to worry about transportation through the storm. Poppy thrust a hand out to introduce herself, but Hope shooed her along. "Introductions later. Shelter from Siberia first."

Jacie swiped her badge, and they hurried inside, stomping the snow and ice off their shoes. Hope and Jacie started up the hall, but Poppy remained behind, contemplating the door.

Hope swiveled back. "What is it?"

Poppy shook her head. "Nothing. It's just, it's almost too easy. I mean, why don't they go to fingerprints or retinal scanners or face recognition? With all the other technology."

Hope had never thought about it before. "True. They use the retinal scanner to secure the AR."

"Simple." Jacie popped a piece of gum into her mouth. "Cost."

Poppy grimaced and placed a hand over her lower abdomen. "Of course. Cost."

They rounded the corner and approached the security checkpoint to the research wing. It was less busy than usual because of the weather, but Hope kept her head down. Jacie would sign in both her and Poppy as guests and hope no one was reviewing the live security camera feed too closely. They'd counted on the usual lobby crowds, but the storm had reduced the typical flood of patients and visitors to a trickle.

Then, to make matters worse, a familiar voice caused Hope to freeze in her tracks. She risked a cautious glance upward and swore under her breath—Leach, on the other side of the checkpoint, speaking with those private security guards. The three of them scanned the line.

Hope hissed a warning and performed an abrupt pirouette. She backtracked to the door and waved Jacie and Poppy back outside.

Jacie glared at her. "What?"

"Those guards standing with Leach. They're some sort of private security detail for Maddox. They know who I am. Even if they somehow don't recognize me, I don't have a chance of getting past Leach."

Poppy cast a worried glance at Hope. "What are we going to do—"

"Dr. K!" a booming voice interrupted them. "It's so good to see you back!"

The next thing Hope knew, a cold nose snuffled in her hand.

"Bear!" She crouched to sink her fingers into the dog's warm fur and wrapped her arms around his neck. He nuzzled her jacket. "Sorry, boy. I don't have any treats for you today."

Hope straightened to face Kyle before remembering the last time he'd seen her had been when Maddox kicked her out. And here she was, dressed in street clothes, not scrubs.

"What are you ladies doing out here? It's freezing!" The big man reached over them to open the door, gesturing them back inside.

None of them moved. Jacie and Poppy looked to Hope to take the lead. "Um, just waiting for someone, you know."

Kyle motioned with his arm again to usher them through the door. "Wait inside before you make yourselves sick."

Still, none of them budged.

He tilted his head. "What's going on here?"

Hope stalled, rubbing her hands on her arms. "We can't go inside right this minute."

Kyle released the door. "I think you'd better explain."

She shuffled her feet. Could she trust Kyle? She remembered the way he'd reacted to Maddox's guards. How he'd tried to help her in the cafeteria. He and Bear both. She'd have to take a chance. "All I can tell you is we need to avoid those private guards. And they're at the security checkpoint."

Kyle's mouth turned downward. "Those penguins? I can't believe the way they treated you that day."

Jacie blew on her hands to warm them and stomped her feet. "Maybe we can just wait them out and try again later."

Kyle shook his head. "They've been there all day the past few days. Like they're watching for someone."

Hope exchanged a look of dismay with Jacie and Poppy. She couldn't explain it, but somehow, Maddox must have the guards watching out for her.

Jacie swore. "I can't believe this. Not when we're this close."

Kyle's eyes narrowed. "I don't know what you've got going on, Dr. K., but I know Bear here has never let me down, and you're number one in his book. Come on, follow me."

The three women exchanged glances of cautious encouragement. Kyle led them around to the back of the building—a loading dock—where his badge unlocked the security gate.

"But what about the inner checkpoints?" Poppy asked.

Hope chewed at her lip, trying to think of a new plan.

"There!" Jacie pointed to a row of stretchers, a gleam in her eye. "Staff all need to sign in at security checkpoints, but *inpatients* don't."

Hope surveyed the stretchers. Yes, this could work.

But one intern couldn't push two stretchers. Hope eyed Kyle again. If they got caught, it could cost him his job. But she didn't see an alternative. If she could tell him about Izabella, she knew he'd want to assist. "If I promise you it's a matter of life and death, will you help us one more time?"

Kyle tied Bear's leash to one of the stretcher's guardrails and made a grand gesture with his arms. "Your chariot awaits."

A few moments later, she and Poppy were each lying on a stretcher. Surgical caps covering their hair, masks over their faces, safety glasses over their eyes, and white sheets pulled up to their chins.

"Just keep your eyes closed," Jacie said. "Here we go."

• • •

Whatever you do, don't open your eyes. It was harder than Hope thought it would be. Her ears picked up voices, a sign they must be nearing the security checkpoint, and she forced herself to take steady breaths through her nose. *In, out. In, out.* She hoped Poppy was doing okay on her stretcher.

They came to a halt, and Leach's voice rang out. "Dr. Stone, what are you doing with these patients?"

Hope's heart pounded as she waited for Jacie's response. It followed a beat later. "I got pulled for transport. The storm's caused short-staffing everywhere. All the interns are getting tasked with other duties. Hadn't you heard?"

Hope was grateful for the mask as a smile played about her lips. Jacie had struck the perfect tone between the frustration and resentment of an overworked intern and then closed with the perfect ending—the oh-so-slight challenge to Leach's authority.

Kyle's voice chimed in. "Excuse me, doc. I don't have all day. They've got us security guards stretched thin, too."

Hope's stretcher moved again. Was it going to work? Or would Leach recognize her and rip the mask off her face? She counted her breaths. When she got to twenty, she started to believe they might be safe. But it was forever until they came to another stop. Hope's heart pounded.

"All clear." Jacie's voice contained equal parts relief and excitement.

Hope opened her eyes and sat up, blinking to orient herself. They were in the hallway outside the lab. Jacie had stopped them at a point in-between the security cameras.

"Jesus, Mary, and Joseph!" A woman's voice exclaimed.

Hope hopped off the stretcher, pulling off her mask and safety glasses. "Hi, Abbie. Thanks for coming."

Abbie placed her hands on her hips. "This better be good."

Hope grinned, reaching over to give Poppy a hand off her stretcher. "It's kind of a long story. We should get out of the hallway."

Kyle saluted them. "It's been my pleasure, Dr. K. I didn't see anything." He and Bear headed off down the corridor.

Jacie used her badge to let them all into the lab.

This time, it was Hope's turn to be startled. Someone was already there. The last person she would have expected—Dalton.

But different. Clean-shaven, and he'd cut his hair. Like the High Resident she remembered. As if no time had passed. Hope's eyes took in his face, the firm angle of his jaw. The curve of his lips—her gaze remained stuck there a second too long.

One corner of his mouth quirked upward. "Hello, Hope."

She opened and closed her mouth. "How—?"

Dalton's eyes flicked to Jacie. "That's quite an intern you've got there. Reminds me of someone."

Jacie shrugged at Hope. "You said he'd be the best person to help you accomplish Izzie's surgery. So... here he is."

An expectant silence filled the room.

Hope scanned the group. "Alright, then. Introductions." She raised an arm toward Dalton for Poppy's benefit. "This is Dalton Fall, surgeon and former High Resident. My predecessor. I've asked him to assist me in Izabella's case."

"You forgot *the best*." Dalton settled back on a stool with exaggerated casualness. "*The best surgeon.* Isn't that what you said when you called me?"

Jacie gave him a skeptical once-over with her eyes. "Gosh, how'd you fit your ego through the door? I hope you didn't hurt it."

Hope rolled her eyes. "I guess you all now know Jacie Stone, my intern. She knows her way around computer systems. She's going to get us into the O.R."

Jacie cleared her throat. "You forgot, *genius hacker*."

Dalton cupped a hand over his mouth in an exaggerated whisper. "And she's worried about my ego?"

Abbie crossed her arms. "Do you both need a minute to get your heads on straight?"

Dalton straightened. "No, ma'am."

Hope suppressed a grin. "Poppy, I think you're the only one who doesn't yet know Abbie Fuentes, charge nurse extraordinaire. She's going to be our prep nurse."

Abbie regarded them all with a steady gaze. "That's right, I'll be keeping you all in line."

Hope put a hand on Poppy's shoulder. "This is Poppy Hart, RN. She'll be running anesthesia, monitoring the AAU."

Poppy's cheeks pinked. "I'll do my best."

Dalton brought his hands together in a single clap. "So, where do we start?"

Jacie tapped him on the shoulder. "I believe this is my part."

Hope gestured to Jacie, "Please, go ahead."

Jacie launched into the first part of the plan. "I'll need to hack into the central system to reinstate Hope's privileges. I'll assign Poppy and Abbie duty transfers to the O.R. here at PRIMA Central. That's the fairly straightforward part. The harder part will be to set up Izabella's Patron code to show she's assigned to surgery."

Jacie omitted that the other half of their plan entailed finding more evidence about the falsified error rate in Maddox's files. For now, she and Hope had agreed that part would be only between them.

"You can't do it from here," Dalton was saying. "The spyware would detect you immediately. At least, I strongly suspect Maddox has spyware on all the computers."

"That's the tricky part. I'll need to get behind the firewall." Jacie delivered a measured look to each of them. "I need to get into Maddox's office."

Dalton's laugh boomed and then fell away as he realized Jacie was serious.

Jacie dangled out a badge. "This identifies me as a housekeeper who cleans her office twice a week. We know tonight she'll be downtown at the merger meeting with Seattle Healthcare Associates at six PM."

Hope chimed in. "She won't miss one more chance to persuade the members to vote in favor of the merger. The voting closes at midnight. After that, there'll be too much attention on the algorithm to slip Izabella's surgery under Maddox's radar. It has to be tonight."

Dalton gave Jacie a grudging nod. "The badge might work, but what about the security cameras?"

Jacie held up a small device the size of a portable charger. "Scrambler. It'll interrupt the cameras and give me five minutes of static."

Dalton didn't laugh this time. He frowned down as his tablet pinged, muttering a brief excuse.

Poppy spoke up for the first time, her voice timid. "Is five minutes going to be enough?"

A determined gleam flashed in Jacie's eyes. "I'll make it be."

CHAPTER NINETEEN

MONDAY 22 OCTOBER 2035
4:55 PM
Conference Room, Seattle Healthcare Associates

Across the city, at Seattle Healthcare Associates, Marah tapped her foot under the auditorium's side table and checked the time, awaiting her turn to address their staff physicians about the merger with PRIMA. They'd bumped the meeting up an hour because of the storm, but the previous agenda items dragged on. Despite the weather, the physician turnout was large, and the auditorium packed. Her knees ached, and she uncrossed and crossed her legs.

"Let me get this straight." A tired-appearing physician was on her feet. "You want us to increase our patient clinic load from twenty patients to twenty-five in a day while simultaneously cutting down waiting room times?"

"Our patient survey scores tell us patients want more access to their doctors and shorter wait times." To illustrate her point, the woman administrator at the podium raised one hand high and the other low, like a balancing scale. "We must make changes if we're going to stay competitive in the market."

Another physician in the audience called out. "If I have to add five more patients per day, I'll have less time to spend with *all* my patients. It's not calculus."

"If you each see five more patients per day, that increases the number of appointment times by 2500 per week." The administrator spoke as if she were addressing a room full of kindergarten students. She put a pie chart up on the screen. "With one hundred physicians, times five additional patients per day, times—"

Marah closed her eyelids to suppress a roll of her eyes. If it were her turn to speak, she could show them how PRIMA's algorithm would solve all of this. Her eyes then snapped open at the next speaker's voice. A voice she'd recognize anywhere—Noah Meier.

"We see your mathematical point." Noah had an earnest expression on his face. Still handsome, even with the lines the years had added. He still had his hair, too, although gray had replaced the black, and he still wore that damn bow tie. Polka-dot, no less. "For those in the room who don't know me, I'm Dr. Meier, Family Practice. My good colleague here is saying we cannot provide superb care if we have to shorten the time we spend with each patient. Surely what the patients are most interested in is the quality of their care—"

"Access." The administrator interjected in a flat voice. "Access is the only patient-reported outcome the Board of Directors will track. You get more money from the budget if your department access score is good. If your access is bad, well, we don't want to go there—you won't have the budget to keep your current staff."

Noah's eyebrows shot up into his forehead. "Do you even hear yourself? Essentially, you're saying if we don't see more patients in less time, you'll punish us by taking away our staff, resulting in even *fewer* resources to take care of the patients."

The administrator continued in a practiced monotone that told Marah it wasn't the first time she'd given this speech. "The Board of Directors has determined access is the number one measure to prioritize for every department. But," — she shifted her gaze to Marah — "if we go forward with the merger with PRIMA, perhaps their famous algorithm will make all these problems obsolete. Which is the perfect opportunity to introduce our next speaker..."

Finally. Marah tapped her stylus on her tablet to open her notes. The lights dimmed, and she strode to the lectern, not letting her knees affect her stride. She had no question which way the merger vote would go. Not after listening to that discussion—their clinics were a disaster.

She breezed through her presentation. There were no interruptions, and it concluded with loud applause. She opened the floor for questions and spotted Noah leaning back in his chair. She'd avoided making eye contact with him during her presentation, but had been acutely aware of his presence the entire time.

Some physicians rose and voiced support, which Marah acknowledged. A few voiced minor concerns about their group merging with PRIMA, for which she had an answer ready for each.

Then Noah took his turn. "Thank you, Dr. Maddox, for an excellent presentation. My first question is this. Can you please tell us what prospective data validation you have or plan to do?"

Marah forced a warm smile. "Noah, so nice to see you here. I'm so glad you asked that. Before we opened our PRIMA treatment centers, we used the algorithm to run hundreds of independent simulations—"

"I'm not asking about simulations." Noah broke in with a polite raise of his finger. "I'm asking about real data with actual patients—"

"Whoa, whoa, whoa. Excuse me." One of her private guards, Vincent, appeared and motioned for Noah to give him the microphone. The other guard, Sydney, would be stationed outside the door. Marah had learned she couldn't be too careful in these public forums.

Marah gave Vincent a pointed stare. It had taken him long enough.

Vincent's voice was friendly, as if this all only a misunderstanding. "Dr. Meier, let's remember to keep this professional, okay? There's no need to yell."

Noah squished his eyebrows together. "I'm not yelling."

"It's okay, Vincent," Marah said from the podium. She and Vincent had their routine down pat, even if he'd been a little slow tonight. She addressed Noah. "Of course, we have data from prospective clinical trials and track all our data at PRIMA. I condensed and summarized a lot of that tonight, given the shortened time we had for the presentation because of the weather, but we'd be happy to provide it to your group after the meeting."

Noah tilted his head to the side, raising his voice to be heard without the microphone. "This AI of yours. It's got a perfect track record?"

Marah chuckled in a way that got several in the audience to join her. She had to be careful to finesse the audience, as if letting them in on an inside joke at Noah's expense.

"Extremely close to it. We estimate the error rate at one in ten thousand."

Noah crossed his arms. "I'm afraid that's not good enough for me."

"Not good enough for... *you*?" Marah raised her eyebrows, again inviting the audience in on the joke. She gestured to Vincent to give Noah the microphone back.

Noah took it. "Not good enough for me, my loved ones, or my patients."

Marah kept the pleasant smile plastered on her face. Goddamn same old Noah Meier. This was the last thing she needed tonight. His emails about that girl had been irritating enough.

Noah continued. "I know you've already taken over a good share of the healthcare market in the greater Seattle region. But I don't think you've shown us enough solid evidence to convince us our group should merge with you."

Marah took off her reading glasses and folded them in a slow and deliberate manner. "And tell us, Dr. Meier, what is *your* accuracy rate in practice?"

Several in the audience shifted uncomfortably. Noah took a few seconds to appear to compose his thoughts, his eyebrows furrowing and releasing. "Einstein said, 'The most beautiful thing we can experience is the mysterious. It is the source of all true art and science.' Do you genuinely believe you can encompass the entire human condition in your algorithm? Furthermore, why would you want to?"

Marah tapped her fingers on the podium. She needed to shut him down fast. "Are you avoiding my question, Dr. Meier? Do you have something to hide?"

Murmurs spread throughout the audience.

With a wistful shake of his head, Noah turned to his colleagues. "I know most of you are worried about job security and your families. I am, too. But many of you, I hardly see anymore. Why is that? We've all tried to please the administration by seeing more and more patients, and working harder and longer. Pushing through exhaustion and burnout. We've lost touch with each other and the camaraderie of medicine. But is this, really, the answer? Am I so outdated to believe machine algorithms cannot—*should not*—replace the practice of medicine? Do people no longer want a human doctor who can hold their hand at the bedside? History has shown over and over, those who look away and stay silent allow evil to triumph. There's a famous speech about that—"

"History lesson aside, I hate to think you're avoiding answering the question."

"'Medicine is a science of uncertainty and an art of probability.' Osler said that." He met her stare with a brightness in his eyes. "Perhaps you've heard of him. Sir William Osler, that is."

From Einstein to Osler, please. Marah would lose the audience if she didn't put an end to his rambling. They were done here. She signaled to Vincent with a subtle whirl of her finger at the podium's edge, then clasped the other hand to her chest as if grievously affronted.

Vincent retrieved the microphone and covered it with his hand. "I think that's enough, Dr. Meier."

Noah gave him a blank look. "But I didn't do anything."

Other than coming close to ruining everything. Marah wasn't about to let the seeds of doubt he'd already sowed in this group grow. The merger would succeed, no matter what it took. She took a step back and manufactured an expression of alarm.

Vincent positioned himself between Noah and Marah as if Noah posed a threat, his stance resembling a bouncer at the door to a club. There was a reason she'd hired him. "Again, Dr. Meier, there's no need to be confrontational. My job is to facilitate and make sure this meeting is conducted professionally. Now, if you can't do that, I suggest you leave."

Noah's gaze darted around the auditorium and took in Sydney, who'd stepped inside the doorway. He twisted his mouth in a wry smile and glanced back at Marah.

Marah shook her head in silent warning. He had to realize he couldn't win. Not this time.

He picked up his jacket and headed for the door.

Marah's stomach twisted. It was his own damn fault, the same as forty years ago. She wouldn't regret it, then or now.

Noah paused, eyes sweeping over the portraits lining the walls. "I always liked these. Our medical group's past presidents watching over us with their auras of wisdom and caring. Their presence has reassured me through countless meetings and presentations in this room. The legacy of medicine, standing on the shoulders of giants. But tonight, this decision fills me with a sense of doom—a vision of the giants of medicine falling all around us."

He exited to silence.

Marah took a deep breath. She could salvage this. *Wisdom and caring, my ass. More like constipated and senile, and hardly a woman among them.* She conjured back the warm smile for her audience and gestured to the portraits. "Dr. Meier made a valid point. When they were in practice, they were giants of medicine. But now, *you* all should be the giants. But why aren't you? It's because the untenable demands of the current healthcare environment have dragged you all down."

She was glad she'd arrived early to hear the initial gripe session. "You trained hard, devoted your lives to your profession. For what? To be treated like numbers on a pie chart?"

Marah could feel the energy in the room surging back to her. "With PRIMA, we envision an era where physicians won't need to waste time on tasks the algorithm can do, such as interpreting images and reading biopsies, with higher efficiency and accuracy. Some are pushing back, worried it's going to take away jobs. But it's the opposite—it's going to empower physicians to provide the best possible patient care. PRIMA has the potential to unify medical care to eliminate disparities between different

regions. *We* are the healthcare revolution. *We* will prove it to the world."
And, she didn't add, *we'll be the government's top choice when they're ready to privatize Medicare.*

She swept her arm toward the first woman who'd spoken out. "PRIMA is here to help *you*. To restore you all to your rightful place. With PRIMA, *you will be giants of medicine once again.* With PRIMA, we will build a new legacy of Medicine. With PRIMA, with your vote tonight, *you* will choose your future."

The wave of applause washed over her and filled any holes of regret Noah Meier might have left in his wake.

CHAPTER TWENTY

"Should we wake her?" Dalton's voice intruded on Hope's thoughts.

Hope contemplated Poppy's sleeping form and checked the time. Still not 6:00 PM. "We can give her a little longer. Jacie should be almost to Maddox's office. We can wake her when Jacie returns."

Poppy had dozed off a few hours ago, her head on Cecilia's desk, while Hope and Dalton had spent the day visualizing the surgery. After the group had met this morning to review the plan, Jacie had needed to head to rounds and Abbie to her OASIS shift. Jacie had left them with Izabella's records, including, most importantly, her imaging.

Dalton, Poppy, and Hope dared not leave the lab until they were ready to implement the plan since they couldn't risk being spotted where they didn't belong. Fortunately, Cecilia kept a refrigerator in the lab stocked with food and water.

Hope draped her jacket over Poppy's shoulders.

Dalton shook his head and smiled. "You haven't changed, have you? Always looking out for everyone else."

Hope fidgeted with the equipment, trying not to think about the possibility of Jacie getting caught. Her nerves were more on edge than she cared to admit. She cleared her throat. "Thanks for changing your mind. To be here, I mean."

She hadn't been sure what to think when he'd initially refused to assist with Izabella's surgery. But somehow, Jacie had convinced him, and they were a team again.

Dalton glanced away and then back. "That's what friends are for."

"Are we still? Friends?" Hope attempted to make her words casual, but her voice came out strained.

"We worked together for years." He closed the distance between them. His eyes seemed to darken. "Didn't you consider us friends?"

Hope straightened the equipment more and tried to ignore the sensation of her heart rate speeding up. "Did you? I mean, since..."

She trailed off.

Dalton gave her a pained stare. "I didn't have a choice. I was the High Resident, and I had to keep things professional. But I'm not, now."

Hope forced a lightness into her voice. "Not keeping things professional?"

"Not your High Resident anymore." He took her hand. "Do you want me to keep things professional?"

Dalton's thumb traced small circles into her palm, and her mind headed toward places she didn't want it to. She couldn't afford to be distracted right now, but she was tired. So tired of being strong, of being alone. He was here now. He'd come back for her, hadn't he? She must be at least part of why he'd allowed Jacie to convince him, even if he hadn't said so aloud. They could be a team again, not just in the operating room. He understood her for who she really was. And he smelled so damn good...

No—there wasn't time for this. What was he implying? That he'd wanted more all along? Did she want that, too? She didn't know. Or did she?

His other hand found its way to the back of her neck, his thumb and fingers digging into her tense muscles.

Hope cast a guilty glance toward Poppy, but her friend remained asleep, emitting quiet snores from the desk. Her body leaned into Dalton's, even while she told herself to move away. She yearned to rest, just for a moment.

Dalton's arms moved around her.

She closed her eyes and relaxed into his warmth. They *were* friends. Dalton understood her in a way only someone with intense shared experiences could. The stresses of being a physician, being the High Resident—and targeted by Maddox. Working so hard, devoting one's entire self to the greater system, only to have it all taken away. To have the belief you were in control of your life dissolve into illusion.

Hope was hurting more than she would admit, consumed with worry over Cecilia. She wanted to let herself feel safe, if only for the briefest of moments. To set down her burden and let go of the grief.

Dalton gave a slight lean back, a question in his eyes.

She tilted up her chin.

And then... her phone chimed.

Poppy startled awake.

Hope tore away from Dalton, lunging for her phone, heat flushing through her. Their lips had been only a micron apart. What had she almost let happen here?

She ran her hands over her clothes, smoothing them.

Dalton regarded her through half-lidded eyes that made her heart forget to beat, and he leaned casually against the opposite lab bench.

Hope's pulse recovered and pounded in her ears. She forced herself to focus on her phone, but it took her brain a second to process the message on her screen.

Dalton must have seen something in her expression. He straightened and crossed over to her, his demeanor back to his businesslike baseline. "What is it?"

Poppy blinked at them both. "What's going on?"

Hope's mouth opened, but nothing came out. She swallowed and tried again.

"Maddox," she said. "It's Maddox."

Jacie had programmed an alert to notify them when Maddox arrived back in the building. Something about hacking the primary security protocol that tracked the badges of everyone in the complex.

Dalton blanched, running his hands over his newly short hair, and paced the room in quick steps. "What's she doing back so early?"

Hope's stomach sank. "The storm—they must have changed the meeting time."

They all looked at the clock. 5:59 PM.

Jacie.

Hope raced for the stairs, leaving Dalton and Poppy behind.

Hope burst out of the stairwell, pressing her hands to her stomach to catch her breath. A wave of relief washed over her to find the hallway deserted and Maddox's office door closed. Was Jacie inside? Only one way to find out.

She rapped on the door. "Jacie, it's me!"

Nothing.

Hope pulled out her phone and texted. *"In hall, let me in. Code Blue."*

The doorway opened a crack, and Jacie peered out, the green scrubs from housekeeping too big on her thin torso and too short on her long legs, her hair hidden under a cap. "What are you doing here? You gave me a heart attack."

Hope pushed past her. "You're out of time. Maddox is back."

Jacie shut the door behind her. "But it's too early."

"So don't just stand there!" Hope waved Jacie to the desk and computer. "Did you have any trouble getting in?"

Jacie took up her position at the keyboard. "No one gave me a second glance. People see what they expect to see."

"Lucky for us, they don't know you're a brilliant and extremely determined hacker-doctor-sister-genius." Hope eyed the door, wishing it had a window to give them a view into the hallway. "What about the cameras?"

Jacie's brow furrowed as she typed furiously. "We've got two minutes left."

"You're almost done, right?"

A bead of sweat trailed down Jacie's temple. "It's possible my decryption program hasn't given me the password yet."

"*What?*"

Jacie bared her teeth. "It'll get it eventually, but I may have been a tiny bit overly optimistic in estimating the timeframe."

Hope stared at her in disbelief. "What do we do?"

Jacie wiped the sweat off her brow. "Got any guesses as to her password?"

"Are you serious? You are." Hope cast wild glances around the office as if she might spot some clue. But the office was empty of clutter. "I don't know. Does she have a pet? I don't think she has kids. Birthdate?"

Jacie shook her head without taking her eyes off the monitor. "Already tried it."

Hope's mind flailed. What did Maddox care the most about? "PRIMA?"

Jacie lifted her eyes only long enough to give her a flat stare. "Really? Besides, tried it. Nada."

Hope spun in a slow circle. Her eyes landed on the desk, the surface bare except for a small statue, a bust with an inscribed plaque, appearing out of place amid the office's minimalist style. She seized the figure, bringing it close to read the inscription. *The Virchow Award. Dr. Marah Maddox. 1995.*

Virchow... a synapse in her brain connected to a memory from outside the O.R., when Maddox had quoted Virchow.

Rudolf Virchow, the so-called father of modern pathology. What was this to Maddox? Unless...

It was worth a shot. "Try 'Virchow.'"

She scooted behind Jacie to see the screen and bounced on her toes as Jacie typed it in. *virchow*

Hope's posture deflated as Jacie shook her head. "Nothing."

Damn it. Any second, the cameras would come back on—and worse, Maddox would arrive. They needed to get out, but Hope wasn't ready to give up yet. "Maybe it's caps sensitive—try again."

Jacie typed.

VIRCHOW

Nothing happened.

"No, not all caps. Just capitalize the first letter."

Jacie shot her a glance over her shoulder but typed again.

Virchow

Hope held her breath.

The screen changed.

Jacie let out a short laugh. "I can't believe that worked—I'm in."

"Hurry." Hope watched her pull up the employee tracking board. Under status for Hope Kestrel, it listed "Suspended / Under Review." Jacie changed it to "Physician / Active Status." She then pulled up her own name and changed it from "Intern / OASIS" to "Intern / Central O.R."

Jacie next switched to the master patient database, locating Izabella's name and deleting the "0 percent chance of response," then changing the treatment recommendation line from "HEARTH" to "OASIS." Then she pulled up the OASIS census, confirming Jacie's name now appeared. For the disposition plan, she typed in "O.R. / Kestrel."

Hope scanned the list of patients while Jacie worked, and her heart skipped a beat at something that appeared on the screen. She leaned in closer. "What the hell?"

"What?" Jacie squinted at the monitor.

Hope went cold all over. "What's Cecilia's name doing on the inpatient census?"

But before she could read more, Jacie logged out, and the census disappeared. "No time. We can figure it out later."

"But what about changing Abbie's and Poppy's assignments? And searching Maddox's files?"

"No time," Jace repeated. "We have to get out of—"

She fell abruptly silent.

Hope heard it too. The staccato click-click of heels coming up the hallway.

No time to come up with a plan. She'd have to improvise.

"Stay here." Hope didn't wait for Jacie's answer and slipped out the door into the hallway, closing it firmly behind her.

Maddox came to a halt in front of Hope and crossed her arms, giving Hope a withering look from head to toe. At least her guards weren't with her for once. "Dr. Kestrel. I'd ask what you're doing here, but I truly don't care. It won't be for long."

She reached into her bag.

Hope held out her hands. "Wait, please—"

She had to keep Maddox from calling security and distract her until Jacie could escape—whatever it took for the plan to succeed, to give Izabella a chance. Even if she had to debase herself, grovel before Maddox, she'd do it. Her words rushed out. "I'm sorry, and I came to say you were right. I screwed up. Let me fix it. Tell me what I can do to get my job back. Anything."

Maddox studied her. "How did you get in here?"

Hope's thoughts raced. She didn't want to get Kyle in trouble. "Cecilia let me in."

Maddox's eyes narrowed. Hope was gambling she didn't know Cecilia was sick and, apparently, on OASIS as a patient. A pang of worry stabbed her chest, but thoughts of Cecilia would have to wait. Maddox gave an impatient snort. "I wouldn't put it past Cecilia, misguided as she can be, but that doesn't explain what you were doing in my office."

Hope shrugged a shoulder. "Housekeeping let me in."

"Really." Maddox drummed her fingers on her hip.

Hope cocked her head. "I thought you'd appreciate a bold action. Showing up in your office to show you my commitment."

It was a risk, and Hope held her breath.

Maddox withdrew her hand from her bag. Empty.

Hope braced an arm on the wall to keep from collapsing in relief.

Maddox pursed her lips. "And how committed *are* you?"

Hope didn't want to give Maddox this power over her, but she'd do it for Izabella. She dropped her eyes. "I'll do whatever it takes."

Maddox tapped her finger on her chin. "I'm pleased with your reaction. You clearly feel bad about your prior behavior, as you should."

Hope kept her eyes on the ground to hide the flash of rage, even as the two private guards appeared at the end of the hallway and strode toward them. Of course they wouldn't be far behind.

Maddox raised her eyebrows at them in an expression of mild surprise. "I didn't call for you."

"No, ma'am," Guard #1, the man, said. "Something triggered the silent alarm."

Guard #2, the woman, took in Hope's presence and stepped closer. Hope scowled at her and then forced herself to make her face go blank.

"It's merely our wayward High Resident." Maddox waved her hand in dismissal. "Not to worry, I've got the situation under control." Her voice turned icy. "If you're needed, I'll call for you."

Hope exhaled. She couldn't believe their good fortune. They might still pull this off. If she distracted Maddox for a little longer, Jacie could get out undetected.

The guards retreated, and Maddox flicked her hand at Hope. "Now, where were we? Oh yes. Whether to reinstate you. I'm willing to consider it, but it's going to take your total cooperation."

Hope's skin crawled under Maddox's dissecting glance. "Like I said, anything. Name it."

Maddox leaned in. "Tell me what happened. With your mom."

"What?" Hope's head whipped up. "What do you mean?"

Maddox lowered her voice. "You know."

"She died." Hope forced the words out through gritted teeth. "The end."

One side of Maddox's mouth curved upward. "I guess you don't want your job back after all—"

"No—wait." Hope closed her eyes. She understood now, on a visceral level, what she hadn't been able to see before—Maddox was nothing but a bully who thrived off the pain of others. No wonder Leach treated the interns like he did, with Maddox as his mentor. Hope had respected Maddox's accomplishments, wanting to be like her, but she now saw the truth.

She lowered her chin to her chest. Maddox must have used her position to gain access to her personal records. Hope knew what would satisfy her. What she'd told no one—not even Cecilia.

Hope opened her eyes. "It was my fault."

Maddox waited.

Hope whispered. "I broke my promise."

"I can't hear you."

Hope's muscles strained against her skin. "Does that make you happy? Is that what you want to know?"

"Go on."

"I promised her—I promised her I'd go see her in the hospital every night. And then, one night, I didn't. I was tired of her being sick. I wanted to... I don't know, punish her. So I refused to get in the car. My grandma had a bad back and couldn't lift me. Couldn't make me go. She called my dad, who said it was fine, to let me stay home."

"Then what happened?"

A dull heaviness spread from Hope's chest to her limbs. But she made herself angle around so that Maddox circled with her. The door opened a crack behind her, and Hope talked louder. "The next day, I regretted it. I wanted to go see her—I missed her. I asked my grandma to take me. We got there, and—"

She hated Maddox for making her say it. Her fingers curled into claws at her side. "They were coding her body, and she was already dead. Okay? Is that what you wanted to know?"

"Oh, but I knew that part already, my *dear* Dr. Kestrel. I want you to tell me about the next part."

Hope's breaths were too loud. "There is no next part. I told you, she was already dead."

"And what did you decide at that moment?"

A roaring filled her ears. For Jacie, she reminded herself. For Izabella, she could say it. Because nobody else could save the girl if Hope didn't give Maddox what she wanted.

"I decided she must have died from—because I..." Hope's voice shook, betraying her. "Because I broke my promise."

Maddox brought her hands together in a single clap. "Excellent! There it is. Poor little Hope made the wrong choice and regretted it ever since."

Hope bit back the bile in her throat. As an adult, she had, of course, realized the fallacy in her childhood logic. But a part of her still blamed herself. Even though the underlying events had been outside of her control, some part of her believed she should have been able to stop it if she'd only been stronger.

But now, she stood exposed in front of Maddox, reliving her mom's death all over again.

Maddox steepled her fingers together in front of her. "Perhaps you do have what it takes. But you won't work for Cecilia anymore. You'll work for me. Directly."

"But my research projects—"

"Forget those." Maddox flicked her fingers in the air. "I've got bigger plans for you."

Behind Maddox, the office door cracked open a little wider. Maddox started to turn toward it, and Hope's pulse soared. She infused her voice with contempt and said the words she knew would keep Maddox's attention. "Good, it's about time. I'm tired of working for Cecilia. For someone with no ambition."

But as soon as she'd said it, she wished she could take it back. Not because it was a lie, but because she recognized the truth in her words. Heat rushed into her head. It was what she'd always wanted, wasn't it? A powerful position at PRIMA.

She tried to hide the hitching in her breath as Maddox circled back and appraised her. "I knew you were a smart girl."

The crack in the door widened further. Hope had to keep talking. "But what's in it for me? How do I know *you'll* deliver?"

Maddox stepped away from the door and jabbed her finger into Hope's sternum. Her voice rose. "I'll tell you what. The next step in the algorithm. The next goddamn breakthrough for humankind."

Behind her back, Jacie finally squeezed through the office doorway, emerging into the hallway before Maddox finished her diatribe.

Hope forced herself to keep her eyes only on Maddox's face.

Jacie dashed away around the corner.

All Hope wanted now was to extricate herself and go after Jacie. But the hairs on her neck had lifted at Maddox's words. "What breakthrough?"

"While Cecilia's been working on her useless experiments, I've been working on my own. Tell me, Dr. Kestrel, what's the next step in the evolution of machine learning?" Maddox didn't allow Hope to answer. "The first breakthrough happened when machine learning became accurate enough for PRIMA to make reliable diagnoses. The second breakthrough occurred when PRIMA could predict the right treatments." She counted off her points on her fingers. "The third breakthrough was the logical corollary—predicting when disease would not respond to *any* treatments. Once we had those three steps, we launched PRIMA. But that's still only the beginning."

Hope wanted to scream that she knew about the lie, how Maddox and Cecilia had omitted her DNA data sets to falsify the accuracy rate. But she couldn't—not yet. She had to wait until after Izabella's surgery.

"It's true the system isn't one hundred percent perfect." Maddox waved her hands as if brushing away a mosquito. "But no algorithm can ever be. You have to allow the system some margin for error as it learns, or else it overfits the data."

"So you decided," Hope murmured. "What margin was acceptable."

"Somebody had to, for God's sake." Maddox had reached her office door. She paused, considering the housekeeping cart inside the room, her eyebrows pulling together. "You and I both know it's still *much* better than the average track record of human physicians. You and I, we're realists, Hope."

Hope willed her face to remain blank and not show the horror inside.

Maddox went on. "If we asked the machine learner to reduce its margin of error below that, it *over*-diagnosed, instead of the small margin of under-diagnoses. Over-diagnosis means over-treatment, which means higher costs."

"But doesn't everyone deserve a chance at healthcare? Isn't healthcare a basic human right?"

Maddox's mouth smiled, but it didn't reach her eyes. "That's the age-old problem with healthcare in this country, isn't it, Dr. Kestrel? How can healthcare costs be contained if each individual physician can choose the most aggressive treatments no matter the prognosis?"

She pivoted in the doorway. "The next step in the evolution of PRIMA will be to diagnose disease *before* it manifests. Say you're a fifty-five-year-old man. A tiny number of your cells are harboring a mutation. A time bomb. In ten years, those cells will grow a tumor."

Hope didn't want to admit it made some actual sense. "Diagnosing pre-cancer before it becomes cancer."

Maddox broke out in a self-satisfied smile. "Cecilia's research made me think of it. The DNA analysis done from the blood drawn right before death."

At first, Hope had no idea what she was talking about. Then it hit her. *The samples from HEARTH.*

The 'final draw.'

She put forward a vague probing statement, hoping her voice sounded neutral. "I didn't know Cecilia had shared the HEARTH data with you yet."

Maddox scoffed. "She's been looking for the late-stage mutations immediately *before* death, but why not simply analyze the tissue right *after* death? We can feed all that data into the algorithm, enabling it to become even better at identifying cancerous mutations. Then, working backward from those mutations, analyze the DNA to diagnose their precursors."

Hope spoke in a low, slow voice. "So we could treat those people before they manifest full-blown cancer?"

"In some cases, yes. For those who have a responsive mutation."

Hope twisted her necklace, not wanting to ask the question. "And for the others?"

"We can weed them out from the healthcare system, saving resources all around. An enormous advantage for us, don't you think, for when our government is finally ready to privatize Medicare? We'll be a shoo-in for the contract."

Hope couldn't breathe. This was never what she or Cecilia had wanted.

This... what Maddox was talking about... went far beyond what Hope had ever envisioned. It was wrong. She could see that now. All she'd wanted was to prevent suffering at the hands of false hope. The AI should make doctors deliver better, more accurate care. But Marah Maddox wanted to play God.

Worse, if the past few weeks had never happened—Sean Medrano, Maddox targeting her, and meeting Izabella—Hope would have gone along as before, following the path Maddox had laid out. But she could see clearly now who she'd become if she stayed—a person just like Maddox.

No, she would never let that happen. She would never be like Marah Maddox. As soon as Izabella was safe, Hope would find a way to stop her. For now, she would play along.

She forced herself to respond, cracking a grin. "That's genius."

That's insane.

"Exactly," Maddox said. "It's the future. And the future is now."

CHAPTER TWENTY-ONE

MONDAY 22 OCTOBER 2035
6:35 PM
Main Campus, PRIMA

Sweat soaked the back of Hope's shirt. This was a nightmare, but it hadn't been a dream this time. She slowly came to her senses, uncertain how long she'd been standing alone in the hallway. Maddox had retreated into her office after telling Hope to go home and that she'd be in touch soon about her decision.

Why was she still standing here? The lab. She needed to get back to the others.

She slipped inside with no one noticing and breathed easier to spot Jacie safely there ahead of her, seated between Abbie and Poppy.

For a moment, warmth surged in Hope's chest. A relief to share the burden of worry and responsibility with others. Everything back in control, safe, among friends. But the illusion dissolved as she watched them. Nothing was as she'd believed.

And Dalton... she didn't know what to think now. He stood apart from the others. Hope's eyes traced his face, his shoulders, and her body again felt the warmth of his embrace, wondering what might have happened if her phone hadn't interrupted them—

But wait. He hadn't come after her when she'd rushed out to help Jacie. True, she wouldn't have let him even if he'd tried, but that wasn't the point. Now, she didn't know whether to be grateful he hadn't overheard the exchange between her and Maddox or angry with him for not having attempted to come along. Even if Maddox spotting him would have ruined everything.

The rapid shift in emotions unsettled her. Maybe he'd changed in ways she didn't understand yet. After all, she hadn't seen him for an entire year. A chill in her veins displaced the warmth.

Dalton was interrogating Jacie. "Did it work?"

Jacie bit her lower lip. "I think so."

A muscle flickered at the edge of his jaw. "You think so, or you know so?"

"It's done." Jacie crossed her arms. "My part, at least. But—"

Hope stepped forward and cleared her throat to announce her presence. Had Jacie overheard everything? "Maddox knows I'm here. I had to stall her so Jacie could get out."

She avoided eye contact with Jacie.

"Damn it." Dalton punched the air. "What does that mean for the plan?"

"No changes to the plan," Jacie bristled. "If they caught me on the security footage, they'll only see a housekeeper with a cap pulled low over her face. They shouldn't be able to connect it to the rest of us."

"I don't think they're going to have any reason to review the security footage." Hope tried to imbue the confidence she didn't feel. "Maddox thought *my* presence triggered the alarm. She sent her security guards away."

"Are you sure?" Poppy spoke up. "I've got a bad feeling about this."

Hope drew herself up. "I told Maddox what she wanted to hear, so she thinks I'm on her side and will do everything she asks to earn my way back. We'll proceed on schedule to get Izabella to the O.R."

It wasn't the right time to reveal everything Maddox had said. She couldn't risk distracting them from what had to happen next, needing them to focus wholly on Izabella's surgery.

Jacie hadn't mentioned the other thing they'd discovered in Maddox's office—Cecilia's name on the OASIS patient census. Hope shot her a glance, but she was busy peeling off the green housekeeping scrubs to reveal her white scrubs underneath while continuing to argue with Dalton.

Despite Hope's anger at Cecilia's actions, she wanted to run to OASIS to find out the truth. If Cecilia was on OASIS, did that mean her treatment had started tonight? Or did it mean something else? What if she'd been given bad news at the PARC, like Poppy?

Hope's gaze landed on Abbie, and a jolt of awareness coursed through her. Of course—Abbie had just come from her OASIS shift. She would know—

Dalton made an impatient sound. "I'll do the surgery without Hope."

Hope's eyes shot to meet his. "What?"

Dalton crossed his arms. "It's too dangerous, now that Maddox saw you—"

Hope glared at him. "It will take both of us. There's no other way."

But a moment of doubt threatened to overwhelm her. How could she go forward with the operation for Izabella without the absolute confidence of success PRIMA used to give her? They were about to embark on the case not because the algorithm predicted they would succeed but because they hoped the algorithm was *wrong*, and Izabella in the five percent error bar where she might survive her cancer despite the PRIMA prediction.

She had an unwelcome flash of insight into her mom's doctors' decisions so many years ago, then rejected it. She didn't want to experience any understanding toward them. If she let the anger go, it would be too painful. Unacceptable.

But to believe in the algorithm meant choosing to let Izabella die. Something she would never do. What PRIMA had asked Jacie and her family to do.

Hope's hands clenched into fists. She drew in a deep breath, forced herself to unclench them, and then discreetly pulled Abbie aside from the others.

Abbie looked her up and down. "You feeling alright?"

Hope hesitated, knowing Abbie wouldn't take it lightly to give out private patient information. "I need to ask you something. Is Cecilia Li a patient on OASIS?"

Abbie let out a heavy sigh. "Yes, she's there."

Hope swallowed hard. "Which room? Please, I'm practically family."

Abbie narrowed her eyes, and Hope waited, counting her heartbeats. After several seconds, Abbie's face softened. "Room Seventeen."

Hope exhaled. "I need to see her."

Abbie glanced at her watch. "The parents are bringing the girl at 7:00 PM, right? That gives you twenty minutes."

Hope shook her head. "I won't be able to get in. No badge."

Abbie rolled her eyes. "I'll get you in."

Hope glanced around at the others before giving Abbie a nod. They headed for the door, and she caught Jacie's eye. "Be right back."

• • •

The corridors were eerily quiet, the effect of the ongoing storm. Abbie gave Hope an appraising glance. "You'd better change first."

She used her badge to acquire a pair of scrubs for Hope from one of the vending machines and then access the call room, where Hope made a quick change.

Abbie smiled when she emerged. "Better."

Hope had to agree. She felt the most like herself since that night in the cafeteria.

Abbie gave Hope an encouraging nod as they entered OASIS. "I'll be in the break room and come get you in fifteen minutes."

Hope paused outside Room Seventeen to gather her thoughts, unsure what she'd even say to Cecilia. She glanced around, only to spot Leach at one of the far workstations, shoveling his dinner into his mouth. Of all the bad luck. Their plan would be ruined if he reported her presence on OASIS to Maddox.

But wait, he couldn't know she wasn't supposed to be back. He'd assume they had reinstated her if she acted like she belonged, but even so, it might be best if he didn't see her here.

Leach paused in his bite to scowl at the screen in front of him. The odor of jalapenos and melted cheese from his burrito wafted over and turned her stomach.

Before risking him looking up and spotting her, she slipped into Cecilia's room. The familiar hospital scents of bleach and citrus sanitizer filled her nostrils, and at the sight of Cecilia, all worries about Leach faded away.

Cecilia had dozed off, reading glasses still perched on her nose, her petite frame so fragile in the large hospital bed.

Hope cleared her throat.

Cecilia startled awake, blinking up at her. "Hope? What are you doing here?"

Hope wanted to rush and embrace her, but she held herself back. Cecilia had lied to her, destroyed her research data, her life's work. For what? To help Maddox with her deluded scheme? But now Cecilia was on OASIS, a patient. Hope couldn't focus. She didn't know where to start.

Her voice came out a croak. "Why—why didn't you tell me?"

Hope didn't know if she meant about her destroyed research or Cecilia being admitted to OASIS—or possibly both.

Cecilia responded in a gentle voice. "I'd already done my PARC testing before I told you about the cancer. I'm sorry—I got my results a while ago, and I should have told you."

Hope's heart lifted. PRIMA must have admitted her to start treatment, and everything would be okay. "You got your staging then. What is it?"

"They said... stage two."

Hope drew in a steadying breath, her mind racing ahead. "That's good, stage two. It'll be an extensive surgery, but you can handle it. You're otherwise fit. You'll need chemotherapy and radiation after surgery, but—"

"No." Cecilia cut her off. "You're not understanding me. They admitted me as a professional courtesy, only for pain control, not treatment."

Cecilia's eyes held Hope's. "I'm sorry. It's a refractory subtype, and you know what that means. Even if they cut it out, it'll inevitably relapse, come back, metastasize. Incurable. There won't be a surgery. It won't be offered... you know this. I'm a non-responder."

Hope braced one hand on the wall. *Non-responder.* But that didn't mean the same thing now, not with a five percent error rate. And Cecilia knew that, too. After all, she'd been helping Maddox hide the true accuracy results all along. Now, her life was at stake.

Cecilia peered up at her. "There's something else. I know you won't understand, at least not at first, but whatever you might think of me, it's time to tell you."

Hope wanted to tell her not to bother, that she'd already discovered what Cecilia would say next.

But Cecilia kept going. "I can't explain it all now, although I will soon, I promise... but there's a five percent chance the algorithm's wrong about my prognosis. A one in twenty chance that surgery *would* help me."

If Hope had any remaining doubts about their plan to help Izabella, Cecilia's words erased them. Her skin crawled.

It was true. All of it was true.

She'd wanted to give Cecilia the chance to explain, certain there'd be a justification. All along, she'd been so afraid of disappointing her mentor, of letting her down if she didn't get the faculty position. But it had been Cecilia who'd lied to her. For what? Now she was the one who would pay the price for it.

No. Not only her.

Izabella had been paying the price, too.

And how many others?

Worse, if she and Jacie hadn't discovered the files, Hope would have accepted the label of a non-responder—even about someone she loved.

She'd been so sure Cecilia would tell her it had been all Maddox's fault. But Cecilia had admitted she knew everything. That would make her responsible—that she'd made a deliberate choice to destroy Hope's research.

But now she was ill, and that erased everything. Hope would figure out a way to help her.

Cecilia clasped her hands together in her lap. "I know this will be hard for you to hear, but I've decided it doesn't matter for me. I'm too old to take the five percent chance." Her gaze hardened. "Please, I don't want you to argue with me about this."

Hope couldn't believe what she was hearing. She lowered herself to the edge of the bed, balling the sheet in her fists to hide the shakiness in her limbs. "Old? You're not old—"

Cecilia laid a hand on her arm. "You know what I want. I never want to be on machines. That's not a life. Promise me."

It was cruel of Cecilia to ask this of her. Hope closed her eyes. The pain of reliving her mom's death under the viciousness of Maddox's questioning still blistered inside of her.

To think that, all this time, everything she'd done in her career at PRIMA she'd thought she'd been doing in service to her mom's memory. So no other little girl would go through what she had. But here she was again.

Hope didn't want to make any more doomed promises. But after a moment, she opened her eyes and studied Cecilia's face. From the pain in her eyes, it was clear Cecilia knew what her request would cost Hope. She nodded. "I found the files—the email to Maddox. *You* deleted my research. *I want to know why.*"

Instead of denying it, Cecilia lowered her gaze and gave her a sad smile. "I always expected you would figure it out."

Hope's lungs constricted, making it hard to breathe. She reached for her necklace but came up empty, groping at her bare neck. The call room—she must have lost it when she changed into scrubs. She'd have to go back later. Her hand clutched a fistful of her shirt at chest level instead. "Why? Why the lies? Why the secrets?"

Cecilia rubbed her face. "It's complicated."

Hope wasn't going to let her off that easily. "Try me."

•

"I was trapped." Cecilia inhaled and let out a slow breath.

Hope wouldn't accept that. "There must have been another way."

"Marah did it without my knowledge—"

"But you could have come forward. Afterward."

"I wanted to. God knows, I wanted to." Cecilia's shoulders sagged. "It wasn't that simple. It was my life's work… and I thought I could fix it, adjust the algorithm before they started using it on patients. I worked day and night—"

"But you didn't. Fix it."

"I failed. But I'm close, so close now—"

"This is all your fault." Hope's arm swept out. "Every other person given a prognosis from PRIMA is someone's loved one, too. Child, parent, spouse, brother, sister—"

Cecilia's eyes filled with sorrow. "You think I don't know that?"

"Do you?" Hope fixed her in an unforgiving stare and filled her in on Jacie's sister.

Cecilia started to speak, stopped, and then started again in a slow, careful tone. "That grieves me immensely."

"You should have found a different way. You didn't have to go along with Maddox."

Cecilia took in a deep, pained breath. "I couldn't see a way out and was afraid of what they might do if I left. If no one within the Corporation knew the truth, to keep Marah in check."

She smoothed the bedsheets over her legs before continuing. "I never expected you would forgive me—that's not why I'm telling you. And I *will* fix it—before it's too late." She sat up straighter, squaring her shoulders. "It's taken me years longer than I ever imagined. In the beginning, I thought I could fix it in weeks or months. I never thought years—"

"You never thought it mattered to mention to me I was building my career upon a system of lies?" Heat rose in Hope's chest and head. "Every action I've taken, every patient I've treated, is now in question. You're as bad as... *them*! You've made me just as bad as *them*!"

"Them, who?" The sadness in Cecilia's voice only intensified the pressure in Hope's head.

"Them—the doctors who treated my mom. Gambling her life on statistics." Hope forced herself to inhale through her nose and drop her voice. "Now, you've put Jacie's sister in the same situation. We don't know, can't know, if she's going to survive or—"

She choked on the words.

"You poor girl." Cecilia pulled Hope into her arms. "You thought PRIMA took away all the uncertainties, made you a perfect doctor. But don't you know? There's no such thing."

Hope struggled, but Cecilia's arms locked around her, unexpectedly strong. Something cracked inside her, and a deep well of grief bubbled to the surface. Stifled for so long, the unbearable pressure demanded release, and the words found their escape. She mumbled into Cecilia's shoulder. "I was so sick of visiting her in the hospital. I wanted her to be home for a change."

Cecilia stroked the back of her head. "It's okay. You can let it out now. You're safe."

Maddox had forced Hope to disclose a part of this story. But that had been different—Hope had detached herself from emotion. She'd never told this to someone who cared about her. The full story. "The night before she died, I didn't go see her..."

Cecilia relaxed her arms slightly, and Hope pushed herself back to gulp in a breath.

"You were a child, Hope. A *child*."

It was time to finish telling this—all of it. "The next day... the next time I saw her... the last time..."

"She was gone?"

Hope shook her head. "She was being coded."

But there was more. Something she'd kept back from telling Maddox. Something she'd told no one.

"My dad and this counselor." Fire blazed in Hope's heart. "She had convinced him of this theory she had. She said I wouldn't understand that my mom was dead unless..."

Hope told it all to her. The formaldehyde stench. The frigid air. Her father picking her up and carrying her into the morgue when she refused to go in. Her fingers digging into the doorway. Paint chips under her fingernails. She'd already seen her mom die—she didn't want to see her body again. But they'd forced her to. Brought her to the shape beneath the white sheet on the stainless-steel table. Her dad's hand picked up the corner of the sheet...

And then she'd felt nothing. Numb, empty. She'd channeled it all away, somewhere else, so she wouldn't have to feel the pain. And in its place, something else grew.

Shame.

That she could be so cold, so unfeeling.

It had been a survival mechanism. She'd thought it easier to bury her grief so deep inside she could pretend it didn't exist. To intellectualize it and tell herself the solution was to become a better doctor than her mom's doctors. To blame them and promise she would prevent anyone else from going through what she did.

But she hadn't, had she?

PRIMA was a *lie*.

Sean Medrano floated in her memory and her cold delivery of the prognosis to him and his wife. The way their granddaughter had looked at her when she'd entered the room. Hope's body shook. *What have we done?*

In their attempt to spare those who wouldn't benefit, how many had they denied treatment? Because even though she hadn't known the truth about the accuracy rate, she'd been complicit. So confident the algorithm would protect them from repeating human mistakes. Maddox's twisted rationale came too close to her former beliefs—how else would they keep from over-treating those who would die anyway?

Cecilia squeezed Hope's hand. "You can't escape grief. If you try to run away, you can never leave it behind." She pulled Hope back against her shoulder. "Sooner or later, you must face it, let it in, and accept it. Move through it. You *will* come out the other side. I think it's time, Hope. It's been almost twenty years. It's time to forgive him—and yourself. It was no one's fault. Some questions have no answers. That's part of being human."

Hope was so tired. Worn out from trying to control everything around her but afraid to admit she couldn't.

Cecilia's voice became a near whisper. "If only I never sent that email..."

Hope whispered back. "Why did you?"

Cecilia's voice remained soft and steady, as if Hope a child and Cecilia reciting a bedtime story. "It had been a normal day. I remember that most, how normal the day had started. We were so close to perfecting the algorithm. If it were only that easy—eliminate the data that didn't fit. But then it wouldn't be science, I reminded myself.

"But it gave me an idea. It was only supposed to be a theory. Exploratory. I thought we could work backward to see how we might improve the accuracy. Before heading out that day, I sent the dummy analysis off to Marah. To brainstorm the next steps."

"The email."

Cecilia nodded. "The next day, Marah walked into my office. She had that air of self-satisfaction and told me, 'Congratulations.' I asked her what was happening. She said they had accepted our manuscript for rapid online publication. I asked her what manuscript. The email was exploratory, she must have understood, a dummy data set. I'd made it clear it was only to help us find new ways to perfect the algorithm, not launch the program. She said we'd reached our target accuracy. The publication was already online as a pre-print, and she'd put my name as the first author. *PRIMA: A Prognostic Intelligent Medical Algorithm Model for Healthcare Decision-making.*"

"Why didn't you put a stop to it?"

Cecilia shook her head. "I tried. I told her we couldn't do this. *She* couldn't do this. It wasn't ethical, wasn't right. 'There were no other data sets,' she said to me. 'You perfected the algorithm. End of goddamn story.' I tried to push away from her. My instincts told me to flee, but she wouldn't let me leave. She hissed at me, 'I don't think you heard me. There were no other data sets.' I told her she wouldn't be able to get away with it. But she said the committee had secured support at the highest levels. I didn't know what she meant. She told me to get ready for a press conference. I'll retract it, I thought. I'll contact the editor, retract the paper, and tell them the data was falsified. They would have to pull it."

She gave Hope a sad smile. "Then I got a message from you, congratulating me. I could see the headlines—the scandal. I would be ruined. Marah would accuse me of lying, and I would never work in academics again. Who would ever hire me after admitting to publishing falsified data? And your name was already attached to mine in research circles...

"Marah was already there, and others from the administration I knew only tangentially. Everyone wanted to shake my hand. Marah walked by me to reach the podium and hissed in my ear, 'Be a team player.'"

Hope shivered. She, too, had experienced that hiss in her ear.

Cecilia's gaze became unfocused. "Marah summarized our work—my work—of the past decade. She introduced me, but all I could do was stand there. I had envisioned our success many times, but not that twisted nightmare, assaulted by applause and trapped by the reporters' cameras. I heard Marah talking, announcing the formation of the PRIMA Corporation. Afterward, she grabbed my arm and steered me out of the conference room. I remember her fingers like cold daggers in my flesh."

Her gaze refocused on Hope. "So yes, I was a coward. I thought I didn't have a choice and that I was protecting you. I had thought it the only way."

Hope processed the story, scrambling to understand. Cecilia, blackmailed by Maddox all these years...

She hadn't stopped to consider how extensive the PRIMA organization, how many people invested in its success. People who used their power to manipulate the system without regard for the individual. If Maddox had crushed a world-renowned scientist like Cecilia under her thumb, what chance did Hope have to stop her?

Did this excuse Cecilia's actions? Hope needed more time to process this new information. While Cecilia was telling her story, Hope had almost forgotten why they were here. In this room, on OASIS. Cecilia was a patient. She was ill, a non-responder, and didn't want to fight it...

It was too much. Hope couldn't think about it now, and would come up with a plan after Izabella's surgery. She squeezed Cecilia's hand. "I'll come back later, and we'll talk more about your cancer and what we might do."

An inner light shone in Cecilia's eyes. "It's time, Hope. Time to fix this at last."

A knock at the door, and Abbie stuck her head in. "It's time."

CHAPTER TWENTY–TWO

MONDAY 22 OCTOBER 2035
7:00 PM
OASIS Unit, PRIMA

Hope and Abbie exited from OASIS into unexpected chaos. Several EMTs filled the corridor, surrounding a patient on a stretcher—*Izabella*.

Something must have gone very wrong. Hope's heart froze, then pounded in her ears. Where was Jacie? Behind the EMTs, she spotted a middle-aged couple and recognized Jacie's parents from their family photos. With them stood a white man with gray-black hair and kind eyes, dressed in jeans and a button-down shirt with a polka-dot bow tie and a stethoscope slung around his neck.

Someone tugged on her arm. Jacie, pulling her aside, panic in her eyes. "My parents couldn't get her here because of the storm, so they called our family physician, Dr. Meier." She jerked her head at the man with the stethoscope. "He called an ambulance to get her here."

"You told him the plan?" Hope hissed at Jacie but then fell silent when heads turned their way. The OASIS staff emerged to check on the commotion.

Hope's mind raced. They would have to use this to their advantage.

She beckoned the EMTs onward with an impatient wave, glad she'd changed back into scrubs. "Is this Miss Stone? Get her in here. We've been expecting her."

Jacie grabbed one side of the stretcher and spoke in an undertone to her parents. "It's okay. This is Dr. Kestrel—the one I told you about."

They snuck a few glances at Hope, and she felt her cheeks go warm.

The bedraggled entourage swept into the unit, and Hope grabbed Abbie's arm, speaking in a low voice into her ear, "Change of plan. We need to act like she's a scheduled OASIS admission before taking her to the O.R."

Abbie didn't miss a beat as she became all business, overseeing the transfer of the frail teenager to a hospital bed. They had her hooked up to the monitors in a matter of minutes, started an IV, and drew labs.

One of the other nurses registered her into the system but wrinkled her brow after a minute. "Strange. She's listed as a Patron for OASIS, #7984, but the algorithm's not getting a match for treatment."

Hope's blood drained into her feet, and she and Jacie exchanged a panicked glance.

"Oh, wait," the nurse said. "She's an add-on for the O.R. tonight. 7:00 PM—we better get her processed."

Oxygen returned to Hope's brain. "Let me give you her pre-op orders–"

Dr. Meier, pacing off to the side, rushed to the bedside as if he'd been holding himself back but couldn't stand it any longer. He spoke at the same time as Hope, so they said the words in near unison — "Type and cross two units packed red blood cells, O-positive, and start broad-spectrum antibiotics."

She raised an eyebrow at him.

He held out his hand. "Dr. Noah Meier. I'm her family physician."

Hope ignored the hand, giving him a curt nod in its stead, and swiveled back to the nurse. "What are you waiting for?"

The nurses rushed to carry out the orders, leaving Hope alone at the bedside with Jacie, her parents, and Dr. Meier. Izabella lay in the bed, eyes closed, exhausted. Jacie sank into a chair and let out an audible sigh of relief. Her parents huddled together in the corner, their countenances a mixture of hope and fear. Something about the moment made Hope recall her argument with Jacie after she'd spoken with Sean Medrano and his wife.

"It's just—if they were my parents—I mean... I thought about how I might want them to be told—or how they might want to be told... and I think kindness might be an important part of—"

"You think showing empathy would be better? Trust me. It's not."

The thing was, she did feel empathy for them. Of course she did. It was only the showing of it she found difficult. To drop the barriers and open herself to vulnerability alongside them. She'd always believed it better to hold herself apart as a physician, and the algorithm helped reinforce that.

But Jacie—and Izabella—had shown her the truth. Any unwillingness to show empathy hadn't been for her patients' benefit. It had been for hers. To protect herself.

Maybe she was finally ready to change that.

Hope hesitated, then went over to them. "I promise we'll do everything possible to save your daughter."

Something she'd never said to a patient or their family without the algorithm backing her.

She turned back to Izabella in time to see the first convulsions of her limbs.

•

Izabella's arms and legs jerked in tonic-clonic motions. Her back arched, and Jacie grabbed her shoulders as if she could stop the seizure by force. Their parents tried to help, but Jacie batted them away. Not good. Jacie was giving in to panic.

Hope's instincts took over, and she shouldered them all aside. This girl was ill, she was suffering, and PRIMA had denied her medical treatment. It wasn't right, it was unjust, and Hope was going to do something about it.

She reached inward and found her center, drawing on it to slow her heart rate and clear her mind. First, they needed to prevent Izabella from aspirating her saliva into her lungs. "Rotate her onto her side."

But Jacie wasn't listening, and her grip on her sister remained too tight. Hope swore under her breath. She couldn't stabilize Izabella and deal with a panicking Jacie.

In normal circumstances, she would call for the Rapid Response Team. But that risked the discovery that none of them belonged there, and Izabella losing her chance at the surgery.

But she wasn't alone.

Noah stepped in, placing his hands on Jacie's upper arms. "Dr. Kestrel's right. You have to let go of her."

Jacie blinked and released her grip on her sister, allowing Noah to pull her away from the bed.

Hope rolled Izabella the rest of the way onto her side, and Noah returned to the bedside, helping cushion her head.

Meds. They needed meds. Now. "Damn it. Where's—"

"Right here." Abbie burst in, holding up a syringe. "Valium, five milligrams IV stat?"

A fierce grin erupted on Hope's face. They didn't always need the algorithm. "Give it. Now."

With deft hands, Abbie administered the benzodiazepine. Within thirty seconds, the convulsions slowed and then stopped.

Hope stepped back to allow Jacie and her parents to return to the bedside. She then surveyed the monitor readings. Izabella's vitals were holding. Tachycardic, but that was a normal physiologic response—for the heart to beat more rapidly in response to physical stress. As long as the rhythm remained normal sinus, Hope wasn't worried about the girl's heart.

No, Izabella's heart was young and strong. That wasn't the concern. Hope's stomach tightened, and she swiped the screen to bring up the lab results.

What she saw wasn't a surprise, but she'd hoped she might be wrong. Hope closed her eyes for the space of two breaths. Upon opening them, the first person she saw was Noah, studying her face with grave concern.

They both glanced toward Jacie and her parents, their attention devoted to Izabella. The girl's eyelids fluttered open, but she remained in a post-ictal state—an altered state of consciousness—to be expected after a seizure.

Noah stepped closer to Hope and pitched his voice low. "Renal failure?"

Hope gave a single nod. The lab results had confirmed what she feared. Uremia—a buildup of fluid, electrolytes, and toxins in the blood because of failing kidneys.

Surgery to remove the lung tumors wouldn't do any good if the girl's kidneys weren't working. Hope clenched her fists. This could all end up being futile. Like her mom all over again.

Jacie's eyes lifted to Hope's from across the room.

Hope gritted her teeth. She had to try. She had promised. "Jacie, can you and your parents step out, please? I need to place a central line. Your sister needs dialysis."

Jacie's face fell. She didn't argue but shepherded her parents out, explaining dialysis to them on the way.

Her uncharacteristic acquiescence unnerved Hope, and she caught Jacie's arm, holding her back behind her parents. "Hey, you okay?"

"You said 'please.'" Jacie swallowed. "It must be bad."

Hope hesitated a fraction of a second too long. "A momentary slip. It won't happen again."

Jacie held her gaze for a moment before ducking her head and leaving.

Noah remained, watching her.

Hope crossed her arms. "What?"

"It's okay, you know."

She cocked her head at him, not understanding.

Noah raised an eyebrow. "To care about your patients."

Hope narrowed her eyes, only to let the expression go upon returning her attention to the girl in the bed. She cleared her throat. "Fine. Are you going to just stand there or help me?"

• • •

A short time later, they'd placed the line, and Hope gave Abbie the go-ahead to call the dialysis tech. Noah stepped out and returned with two paper cups, holding one out to her, reminding her of Dalton and that day in the park. His eyes crinkled. "The universal fuel of doctors. Some things haven't changed."

Hope accepted the cup and studied him out of the corner of her eye, deciding he must be in his mid-to-late sixties, which meant he must have been in practice for nearly four decades.

Noah raised his cup toward Izabella. "Something else that hasn't changed, despite all the technology. The principle of dialysis, dating back to the 1960s."

Hope rubbed her forehead, too tired to respond.

"My father was a part of it. Right here in Seattle." He chuckled. "Let me guess, they don't teach about the *Scribner Shunt* at PRIMA?"

She shrugged. "What's the use of learning about obsolete technology?"

Noah studied her for a long moment, and Hope had to stop herself from squirming under his gaze before he continued. "Some things in medicine never change, and we forget our history at our peril. In the early sixties, Scribner established the first outpatient dialysis unit in the world. Only there was a problem. There wasn't enough capacity to treat everyone." He fixed her in a steady stare. "Do you know how they decided?"

Hope didn't.

"By committee. *The God Committee*, it came to be called. It tore my father up inside. I don't think he ever got over it, the ones the committee didn't select."

Hope looked back at Izabella, the girl's frail form nearly swallowed by the bed and the dialysis team surrounding her. "The algorithm didn't select her for treatment...."

She trailed off.

Noah examined her with a sad demeanor. "Is it any different?"

Hope's vision clouded. Who was this man, anyway? To force her to confront the questions she'd already been asking herself. She struggled to find the right words. "You think we need a—what, a—*committee* to vote on it?"

He blew on his coffee. "I don't have the answers. But we should ask ourselves, how will history judge *us* a century from now?"

"I don't—"

Jacie's arrival saved her from having to come up with a response. "Can my parents come back in?"

Hope indicated they could, and Jacie went to fetch them.

Upon their return, Jacie pulled Hope aside. "Does this mean the surgery is off?"

Hope hesitated. "No, but we have to delay it. She should have a full hemodialysis session first."

"How long will that take?"

Hope took another slug of coffee and grimaced. "Four hours."

Jacie sagged against the wall, and Abbie returned to the room.

Hope's head jerked up, remembering something else. "Dalton and Poppy." They'd agreed not to text inside of PRIMA in case their communications were picked up. "Someone needs to go tell them what's going on."

Abbie pursed her lips. "I'll do it."

Hope gave her a grateful nod, and Abbie slipped out the door.

Jacie tilted her head and went out after her, and Hope followed her into the hallway. Jacie stared at the ceiling and blinked rapidly. "Does she still have a chance?"

Hope didn't want to lie, so she chose her words carefully. "I don't know. But I know she's already proven the algorithm wrong by surviving this long and responding to the oral chemotherapy PRIMA denied her."

Jacie nodded and wiped her eyes with the back of her hand.

Memories of the early days of her mom's treatment rose in Hope's mind. Her words came out awkwardly at first, but she couldn't stop them. "With my mom, after her surgery, they told her ninety percent of women in her situation would be cured. I remember thinking, even as a kid, what about the ten percent who won't be? How do we know who they are? But the thing was, no one knew. Doctors had to tell any woman diagnosed with early-stage ovarian cancer that she could be the one in ten destined to have a relapse. So they told my mom, do you want to take chemotherapy for six months, and bring it down by fifty percent, to become a one in twenty chance?"

Jacie's eyes seemed to darken. "So did she?"

"She was the one in twenty who took the chemo and relapsed, anyway."

Jacie reached out a hand as if to touch Hope's arm. "I'm sorry."

Hope took an impatient step backward. "I'm trying to say that when I thought the algorithm could predict who would be that one in twenty, I thought it would be a good thing."

Jacie twisted her mouth. "But would you—your mom, your dad—have wanted to know she would relapse?"

"You don't understand. She was so sick... and if the cancer was destined to metastasize throughout her body, she should have at least been spared all the bad stuff from the chemo."

The sorrow in Jacie's eyes made a pressure throb behind Hope's brow. Because she didn't want Jacie's pity. She needed her to *understand*. Hope blew out a breath and tried again. "A few years after she died, when I was fourteen, I discovered the last chemo she tried had only a ten percent chance of success." She clenched her jaw to keep the quiver out of her voice. *"Ten percent.* That meant they knew there'd be *no* expected benefit for nine out of ten people they treated. They should have said it had a 90 percent chance of *not* working. She could have spent more time with me at home instead of her last days in the hospital, no hair, puking her guts out."

Jacie's eyes searched her face. "I'm sorry your mom wasn't in the ten percent who had a response. But for those ten percent, it wasn't hopeless, and maybe for your mom, it meant something—to try."

Hope shook her head. "I thought Cecilia had perfected the algorithm so no other family would have to go through what mine did. No more false hope. We would know up-front. It would be fully transparent. I thought it would change everything...."

Silence rose between them.

After a moment, Jacie cleared her throat. "Did you find her? Cecilia?"

Hope glanced up the hall. "She's there. Room Seventeen."

"What did she say?"

Hope let out a rueful laugh. "Maddox has been blackmailing her—for years."

"No. I mean—that doesn't surprise me—but why is she here?

Hope stared at the floor. "I didn't want to tell you. She has gastric cancer. She's a non-responder."

Jacie's hand flew to her mouth. She quickly dropped it and spoke in a halting voice. "But that doesn't have the significance we thought—"

"It doesn't matter. She said she doesn't want to try any treatment. That a five percent chance wasn't enough for her, and she's only here for pain control."

"I'm sorry." Jacie bit her lower lip.

"Yeah. Me too." A thickness in her throat kept Hope from saying anything else, and she took another swallow of coffee to cover it up.

"There's something else I have to tell you, too." Jacie dropped her chin to her chest. "I—I lied."

"About why you're here at PRIMA? Yeah, I know." Hope gestured to Izabella. "I think I got it."

"No. I mean, yes, you know all that. But, I mean, there's something else."

Hope gave her a quizzical look. "What?"

"When I told you I heard nothing from inside Maddox's office." Jacie twisted her hands together. "That was a lie."

Hope raised an eyebrow at her.

Jacie's words tumbled out. "I was so certain we'd be caught and lose our only chance to save Izabella—and then I heard it all. *You.* Everything you told Maddox in the hallway." Her gaze met Hope's. "I can't believe you did that. Put yourself on the line to help me."

Hope shrugged one shoulder.

"I'm so sorry for what you went through as a kid." Jacie's expression tightened. "Maddox didn't have the right to force you to re-live all that. I—I thought it would probably kill you to know I'd overheard. So, I lied and said I didn't."

Hope supposed she should be angry, but she wasn't. "Why are you telling me now?"

Jacie's eyes gleamed. "Because I heard what *she* said after that, too. Her plan to use the algorithm to deny people care before they even get outwardly sick. I hid around the corner." She held up her phone. "And I got it on video."

CHAPTER TWENTY-THREE

It was close to midnight now, and OASIS was quiet. The type of quiet that sets doctors on edge, knowing it never lasts.

While the dialysis team unhooked Izabella from the equipment, Hope slipped out into the hallway. She'd spent the past four hours with Jacie and her parents in Izabella's room. So far, no one had challenged her presence back at PRIMA—thanks to Abbie's actions normalizing her presence to the other nurses.

Room Seventeen drew her eyes. What would it hurt to dart in for one more check on Cecilia before they took Izabella to the O.R.? She could tell Cecilia about Jacie's video of Maddox and ask her advice on the best way to leverage it. They could finally turn the tables on Maddox.

Before she could think it through, her feet took her up the hallway. She glanced left and right before slipping inside and shutting the door behind her. It took a second to adjust to the dim light. The bed—empty and neatly made. Empty—as if Cecilia had never been there. Had she been discharged? But why would she leave without telling Hope?

She dashed back to Izabella's room to find Abbie prepping the girl for transport. Hope sidled up to her and spoke in an undertone. "Cecilia's gone."

Abbie sighed. "I know. She insisted on being discharged."

"But—why didn't you tell me?"

"She also insisted on that."

Heat flushed through Hope's body. She didn't understand Cecilia's decisions—any of them.

Abbie capped the IV. "Okay, meds are in. She's ready."

Hope had to focus on Izabella now. After the surgery, she'd track Cecilia down and talk some sense into her.

The new surgery plan entailed Hope and Abbie transporting Izabella to the O.R. while Jacie and Noah retrieved Dalton and Poppy from the lab. Dr. Meier—or Noah, as he insisted they call him—would join them. She almost smiled as she recalled his words. "I'm here to do everything I can to help my patient, Izabella. I don't buy into Marah's algorithm, and don't take this the wrong way, but you're a little understaffed, and I can hold a retractor as well today as I did forty years ago."

Jacie had wanted to join the surgery, but Hope had ruled it out. "You may be an intern, but this is your sister."

Dalton had backed her up. After Jacie used her badge to get them into the O.R., she would thus return to OASIS to wait with her parents.

Hope gave them a curt nod, and Jacie and Noah headed out to get Dalton and Poppy.

•

Hope and Abbie wheeled the unconscious Izabella out of the hospital's freight elevator. Cold sweat trickled down Hope's spine beneath her scrubs, belying the fact that so far, sneaking Izabella down to the O.R. had been almost too easy.

As if reading Hope's mind, Abbie broke the silence. "Don't make me regret this. I'm putting my job on the line because I know you can save her."

Hope swallowed and took in Izzie's sleeping form. Now wasn't the time to doubt her plan—or her surgical skills. She could save her. She *would* save her. Even if PRIMA had designated the girl a non-responder, and even if taking her to the O.R. against the algorithm's recommendation would end Hope's career if they were caught. She didn't care about that anymore. PRIMA wasn't the solution she'd thought it to be, and it meant nothing weighed against the girl's life. But Abbie's belief in her caused her throat to tighten, and she had to choke out a reply. "I got this."

They whisked the stretcher down the deserted hallway, Abbie propelling it from the foot while Hope guided the head, the metal side rail cold and slick under her sweaty palms. They rounded a corner to their destination and spotted Jacie, Noah, Dalton, and Poppy ahead, gathered outside the last O.R. suite at the end of the corridor. She and Abbie brought the stretcher to a hasty stop in front of the group.

Everyone stared at her expectantly. For a moment, she almost wished someone else was in charge, someone else to shoulder this burden. Hope met each of their eyes—the best team she'd ever assembled, even if Noah was a newcomer to them.

Tension shot upward from her rigid shoulders to the back of her head, and she waved an impatient arm at Jacie. "Don't just stand there, do your thing, genius-hacker-intern. Get us inside."

Jacie held her badge up to the security sensor in a confident stance, the red light on the panel reflecting off her purple-rimmed glasses. Her matching-color scarf now tied up her mass of curls, making Hope think again of the coiled spring full of potential energy, waiting to be released.

It took Hope a second to realize nothing had happened. The sensor light remained red.

Hope's heart leaped into her throat. This couldn't be happening. Maybe Hope had been wrong to entrust Jacie with the responsibility. It had been too much to expect of an intern, no matter Jacie's computer science background. But she hadn't any other choice. For once, Hope had admitted to something she couldn't do alone.

Jacie flashed a nervous smile, then wiped the badge on her scrubs and tried again. Same result.

"Why isn't it working?" Dalton hissed at her.

Hope's eyes involuntarily traced his jaw, the stubble of this late hour, and then landed on his lips before tearing her gaze away. She couldn't think about him that way, no matter what had transpired between them earlier. They needed to be colleagues again. Surgical partners, that's all.

Jacie continued to swipe her badge in rapid motions, speaking through gritted teeth. "Have some faith, old man. I know what I'm doing."

Dalton's lips, which Hope's eyes had wandered back to despite herself, quirked upward. "I'm barely in my thirties—"

"She's going to wake up if we don't get her under full anesthesia," Poppy interrupted, her brow creasing above the portable monitors hooked to the side of the stretcher.

Wisps of hair escaping from her long braid framed her flushed face, and Hope recognized the worry in her friend's eyes and voice. The nurse's intuition that any doctor ignored at their peril.

Izabella continued to sleep under the influence of the light sedative they'd given her on the unit, but Poppy was right. They were running out of time.

"Give it to me." Dalton snatched Jacie's badge from her hand, waving it in front of the sensor pad.

Nothing happened.

"Didn't we agree this is my thing?" Jacie wrested the badge back from him, swiping it in increasingly desperate motions. But half a minute later, she sagged backward, and the secured doors to the O.R. remained closed.

Dalton swore and ordered Abbie—the only one with another legitimate PRIMA badge—to use hers instead.

Jacie shook her head in frustration. "I only re-coded mine. There wasn't time to do more."

Hope observed them all as if from a distance. Jacie and Dalton bickering, Poppy's focus riveted on the monitors, and Abbie and Noah hovering off to the side, expressions of uncertainty on their faces. This was all Hope's fault. They were going to fail. She'd be responsible for all of them losing their jobs, and Izabella would lose her only chance at a cure. She should have known it was foolish to go up against PRIMA. But despite herself, she'd dared to believe, even if only for a short—

"We should call it off." Dalton's eyes found Hope's, an intensity in them she tried to ignore, and his voice somber. "It's not going to work."

Jacie snorted. "Like that? You're giving up? I thought you were supposed to be some kind of legend around here. It's no wonder Hope had to replace you as High Resident—"

"Quiet!" Hope slashed her hand in the air. A faint noise from down the hallway had reached her ears. "Someone's coming."

They all fell silent, trading panicked glances. The sound of footsteps became unmistakable, getting louder, coming toward them.

A scream rose in her throat. They had no way to explain what they were doing with a patient outside of a locked O.R., with multiple doctors not on staff, she herself now included in that group. No longer a part of PRIMA, and all of her work, her research, destroyed.

All she'd wanted was to save this one last patient. The girl deserved better than what PRIMA had done to her.

Hope couldn't believe they'd come this close, only to fail. All because of her. Like her mom all over again.

A second later, the aroma of jalapenos and melted cheese reached her nose. *Oh no.*

Leach sauntered around the corner only to halt so quickly upon spotting them he almost tripped.

"Kestrel, what are you doing?" His gaze swept over them, taking in the scene, and stopped to rest on Jacie. "Dr. Stone, I see you're making questionable choices again." His eyes then widened when he noticed Dalton. "Dr. Fall. I don't believe you're welcome here anymore."

Dalton's face remained impassive. "Dr. Leach."

Noah raised his hand. "Dr. Meier."

Everyone turned to stare at him.

"What?" The older man dropped his hand. "I thought we were doing introductions."

For a few seconds, none of them moved. Then Leach placed himself in front of the doors.

Hope's mind spun frantically. They couldn't have come this far only to fail. "Wait, I can—"

Leach held his badge up to the sensor.

The light changed to green.

The double doors opened slowly, like stoic guards reluctant to stand down. Poppy was the first to recover her wits and moved to brace the doors before they locked again. The rest of the team, besides Hope, rushed Izabella inside.

Hope stared at Leach, her mouth opening and closing, but no words coming out.

Leach's expression was unreadable. After a moment, he pinched his bottom lip. "If you walk through those doors, you'll be throwing your career away."

What was he playing at? Leach's presence here, helping them get into the O.R., made no sense. His concern about Hope's career at PRIMA made even less. "Like you care?"

"Think about what you're doing." He held his hands out at his side. "The AI did *not* recommend treatment for her. Don't throw your career away. No matter who she is."

Leach's words gave voice to her inner fears. She'd be operating in the unknown. Untethered and lost, like the balloon at the park.

But he was the resident who still believed in the algorithm. That wasn't her anymore.

If Izabella survived, proving the algorithm wrong, it would also prove everything Hope had believed in had been wrong. Did she have the courage to follow through? What would that mean for Cecilia?

Hope locked gazes with Leach. "There's no other choice."

He gave her a bitter smile. "I thought you might say that."

Hope scrutinized him. "Why are you helping us?"

"You really don't get it." Leach shook his head, and without another word, he whirled around, heading back the way he'd come.

Hope stared at the space where he'd been. She had no time to analyze his behavior, his motives for helping them, and no time to worry if he would still alert Maddox. They had to operate.

She entered the prep area and exchanged a worried glance with Dalton, but he only shrugged, shook his head, and started on his scrub. Abbie and Poppy conversed in low tones over the AAU, initiating the anesthesia protocol. Not only would it regulate the medications and ventilator settings, but activate blood transfusions and vasopressors if needed.

Jacie took one last glance back at Izabella, her eyes moist. She squeezed Hope's arm. "Good luck. I'll see you back upstairs."

She hurried off, shoulders hunched.

There was no going back. This couldn't stop at Izabella. After the surgery, Hope had to stop Marah Maddox for good. Even if it meant sacrificing everything she'd ever worked for.

CHAPTER TWENTY-FOUR

MONDAY 22 OCTOBER 2035
11:55 PM
Marah's office, PRIMA

A knock at her open door interrupted Marah at her desk. Cecilia stood in the doorway, leaning on the frame. Marah's surprise let slip her annoyance at the unexpected intrusion. "What the hell are you doing here? At this hour?"

Cecilia stepped into the room. "It's time, Marah. I've done it."

"Now, what?" Marah set her tablet down and removed her glasses, pinching the bridge of her nose. "It would help if you told me what you're talking about."

Her patience had been tried enough earlier tonight at the meeting. Damn Noah Meier. What a waste of a talented physician—dumping his career into the useless pit of primary care. The last two words sounded in her mind like profanity.

"The algorithm," Cecilia said.

Marah didn't like the resolute expression on her face.

"I have the way to fix it, finally." Cecilia stepped closer and held up a flash drive. "I analyzed for new mutations in the cancer cells from the HEARTH patients' blood samples, using Hope's DNA techniques to account for the epigenetic changes that happen at the very end, as the cancer cells metastasize and take over the body."

"So?"

Cecilia's voice strained with urgency. "We must upload these additional data sets to the machine learner and restore Hope's other data sets. The ones you deleted."

Marah tapped her fingers on the desk. She supposed she had given Cecilia permission to go ahead with this project. She stalled. "I hadn't expected you to have results so soon."

Cecilia crossed the rest of the way to Marah's desk and set the flash drive on it. "All this time, I told myself I didn't have a choice. But I've come to realize that's not an excuse. Not making a choice is in itself a choice. I've been working to fix that for five years. It's time to do the right thing, Marah."

Marah gave her a few slow, deliberate claps. "Well, well. You have a spine, after all."

She picked up the flash drive and twirled it in her fingers. She could destroy it and kick Cecilia out—that would be satisfying. But as much as it annoyed her to admit it, she still needed her.

If she let Cecilia upload this *fix*, it would shut her up and get her out of Marah's hair tonight, so she could see the results of the vote in peace. If this fix of Cecilia's failed, no loss to Marah, she'd remove it, and everything would be the same. If it worked, and the algorithm's accuracy improved, all the better. She made Cecilia wait in silence for a few seconds longer before handing her back the flash drive. "Do it."

Cecilia connected it to the hard drive.

Marah folded her arms across her chest. "How long is this going to take?"

"It shouldn't be long." Cecilia's posture sagged, and her voice contained a new weariness.

Marah gestured to a chair. After all, she wasn't a monster.

Cecilia sank into it and replied with the stiff politeness that had always rubbed Marah the wrong way. "Thank you."

Marah flapped a hand in dismissal and, with the other, stifled a half-yawn. Now she'd have even more leverage to use on Cecilia. Good. She stretched her arms over her head to restore her circulation. God, what time was it? Would the vote ever come in? She checked her tablet again, but still nothing. Leaning back in her chair, she stretched her neck to one side and the other. Patience—everything was coming together.

Cecilia interrupted her thoughts. "I'm done after this. The algorithm will be fixed."

Marah tilted her head. "We'll see."

Cecilia gave her a sad smile. "Why do you do this?"

Marah rose from her chair and placed her hands on the desk, leaning across, her face inches from Cecilia's. "If you don't watch out for yourself, no one else will. If I hadn't done it, someone else would have, only not as well. So, yes, *I* seize power. So I can make sure it's done *right*."

"No matter the cost to the innocent bystander?"

"You've got it all wrong. I'm the one that protects the innocent bystanders." Marah lowered herself back to a seat, smoothing the front of her sweater to calm herself. She didn't need Cecilia here, questioning her. Weak Cecilia. She had only herself to blame for her position.

Still, something made Marah want to explain things tonight to ensure Cecilia would understand. Maybe it was seeing Noah Meier after so many years, or having Hope Kestrel beg for her job back, or knowing the merger vote would be finalized any minute. Whatever the reason, she found herself telling Cecilia something she never talked about. "Years ago, the residency program gave me a choice. Take the blame for an accidental error—to protect the hospital and my higher-ups—and give up my position to transfer to another program. Or protest my innocence, have the blame pinned on me anyway, and have no career left. You can guess which choice I made."

"That is... unfortunate. I'm sorry."

But Cecilia didn't sound sorry. She sounded... judgmental. A flash of heat traveled across Marah's body. "That's reality, Cecilia. Life doesn't give us all roses. What divides us is how we handle the thorns. There are only two choices in life. Profit. Or loss—"

An alert on the monitor caught her attention, and cold fury replaced the heat. "What the fuck is this?"

Cecilia gave her a blank look. "What?"

Marah spun the monitor around to show Cecilia the screen.

VIRUS DETECTED

...

...

...

INITIATING PURGE

Cecilia's mouth dropped open, but she said nothing.

Marah's hands clenched and unclenched. She jabbed a finger in Cecilia's face. "You thought you could upload a virus? In my system? You didn't think I would have precautions in place?" She felt her face twisting in anger and turned it into a sneer. "You're pathetic!"

Cecilia backed away. "It wasn't a virus. I uploaded the new data for the algorithm. I don't know how—"

But Marah had already activated the emergency alert on her phone. Seconds later, Vincent and Sydney burst through the door.

Cecilia gaped at them. "What's happening? I didn't do anything."

It took an extraordinary effort for Marah to keep her voice level. Another alert flashed on her screen. "Take Dr. Li to security and hold her there while I call the FBI. Industrial sabotage."

Podcasts / Algorithm Anarchist Podcast / The Hidden Agenda

Rachael: Hi everyone, I'm Rachael, and this is *Algorithm Anarchist*. Where we remember, the most dangerous lies are the ones that use the truth to sell themselves.

[music]

Today I want to share some thoughts about what's happening behind the scenes at PRIMA and their latest merger attempt.

What's the goal of a merger? Power?—Yes.
But more than that—control.

You all want to know what I think? If this merger goes through, PRIMA will have more bodies under its control. More bodies over which they'll have ultimate—and undisputed—say.

Oh, you have a terminal illness, and you want a second opinion? PRIMA won't pay for that. Do you want to see a doctor outside their network? They won't pay for that either. And with every merger, there'll be fewer and fewer doctors not a part of the PRIMA network. Good luck finding one, and good luck paying out of pocket—since those outside the network have to raise their fees to remain solvent.

It's not hard to see PRIMA's endgame. Healthcare for All. The U.S. government Medicare contract.

If PRIMA gets that, the era of the doctor–patient partnership will be over, replaced by the algorithm–patron dictatorship.

If that happens, who do you think will ultimately control the algorithms? Nope, not PRIMA.

The government.
That's what everyone needs to be talking about.

This merger isn't just about two healthcare corporations. It's PRIMA's stepping stone toward their *ultimate* merger.

One that humanity doesn't want to see happen.

At least, not for those who aren't among the privileged few.

Which means all of us, people...

CHAPTER TWENTY-FIVE

TUESDAY 23 OCTOBER 2035
12:05 AM
O.R. Suite 1, PRIMA

Hope scrubbed in alongside Dalton and Noah, her senses registering everything in ultra-focus. The blazing lights, the sharp antiseptic smell, the low tones from the anesthesia station, Dalton's tense shoulders...

So different from how she remembered him before a case. The O.R. had been his second home. Was this new tenseness because of Leach? Or from what had almost happened between them earlier?

She again gave silent thanks that her phone alert had gone off when it did, stopping them from making what would undoubtedly have been a big mistake. That hadn't been the time or place. But maybe after this was all over...

No, she needed to block everything else out. One step at a time. Izabella's surgery first, then figure out what to do about Maddox afterward. Then go find and help Cecilia. Then, maybe, Dalton....

Step one, Izabella had to pull through this okay. Hope couldn't allow any thoughts otherwise. If anyone could be in the five percent, it would be her. But the logical part of her brain warned against such fantastical thinking, the sort she'd previously belittled. She scraped under her fingernails harder, trying to use the motion to purge those thoughts from her brain. The same ultra-logical brain that insisted on asking how she could forgive Cecilia for betraying her. Sweat beaded on her forehead, and she had to suppress the urge to wipe it away halfway through her scrub.

Cecilia's prognosis hadn't sunk in yet, and Hope didn't want it to. After the surgery, she'd convince Cecilia to get help, too. Just like they were helping Izabella. All she could control was the present. Izabella's surgery. Focus on that.

Dalton let out a low laugh from the sink beside her.

Hope eyed him. "What?"

"Just thinking."

Her mind unhelpfully pictured his lips beneath his mask, and she was glad for her own mask to hide her flushing. "It's good to be back, isn't it?"

Dalton's hands continued their precise movements, and he didn't look at her when he spoke. "You asked me why I left. I didn't think I had a choice."

Hope finished her scrub and donned her gloves, careful not to look at him fully, as if doing so would stop him from talking more about it. She ventured cautiously, "Because of Maddox?"

"At the time, it appeared so unfair. Why would I ever admit to an error I'd never made? Why should I take the blame to protect her precious system? I didn't care that the PRIMA algorithm wasn't perfect—I never expected it to be. No system has the capacity to be perfect." Dalton shook the water from his hands. "But Maddox wanted me to admit to something false. Then, when they realized I wouldn't go along with it, they hinted I could—"

His eyes tightened, and he didn't finish the sentence. "Let's just say they didn't give me a choice. So I left, taking the separation agreement my attorney negotiated for me. Signed the NDA."

They entered the O.R. together, hands up at shoulder level to avoid touching anything. Abbie readied their sterile gloves. Noah lagged behind, not finished with his scrub yet.

Dalton gazed around the sterile room. "There's nothing I've tried since that comes close to this...."

Hope understood. Nothing compared to her love for the O.R. Except, maybe, the man standing across from her. What? No, compartmentalize. She stepped up to the table.

He took the position across from her. "Sometimes, I wonder, would it have been so bad to have signed the forms? Something in my sealed record that few others would know about. To still be here, doing this." His voice dropped. "What would have been so bad about that?"

Standing across from him, the past year dissolved as if he'd never left. His presence in the O.R. made her feel safe, that he had her back, that they were a team again. Could they be even more?

Noah came up behind them to stand at Hope's shoulder, waiting for an order. Abbie positioned the tray of instruments within her reach. Hope's gaze wandered over to Poppy, intent on the AAU, and then back to Abbie at her elbow.

It felt good to be part of a team. Her team. She didn't have to stop Maddox alone. After the surgery, they'd figure out the best strategy. Whether going to the Board of Directors, the medical authorities, or the public, they'd figure it out together.

But thoughts of the Board only reminded her of the merger vote. If it passed, Maddox would have more power on her side. They needed to go to the authorities before the Board announced the results. The minute they finished Izabella's surgery.

Now that she'd decided, the heaviness lifted from her shoulders. She squared them and held out her hand. "Scalpel—"

A loud click cut through the sterile air behind her, and Abbie's hand froze halfway to handing Hope the instrument.

The O.R. door—being unlocked from the outside.

Hope spun as if in slow motion. The doors were opening. No, this couldn't be happening.

Three people marched through them, and Hope leaped to plant herself in front of Izabella.

Maddox in the lead, her private security flanking her like bodyguards. None of them were in scrubs.

"You can't be in here like that!" Hope sputtered. "This is a sterile space."

"It's good that you haven't started yet, then." Maddox flashed a glacial smile beneath even colder eyes. "I don't recall reinstating your privileges as part of our little conversation earlier."

The blood drained from Hope's head. "It was an emergency situation. I did what was in the best interest of the Patron."

"That's always your convenient excuse, isn't it?" Maddox scanned the room, taking in the others. "My, my. Quite a goddamn party you decided to have. And no invitation for me?"

Sweat trickled from under Hope's surgical cap down the back of her neck. She blurted, "I'm the one to blame. They had nothing to do with it."

"How *noble* of you, Dr. Kestrel." Maddox paced the room. When she reached Dalton, she crossed her arms and drummed her nails on her forearm. "Well, well. Dalton Fall..."

Dalton kept his gaze fixed above her head.

Then, Maddox spotted Noah, and naked surprise flashed across her face before she reined in her expression.

"Hello, Marah." Noah gave her a cordial nod. "If only you'd replied to my emails."

Maddox appraised Izabella's still form on the table. "This is the girl?"

"What are you talking about?" Hope had to deflect Maddox's attention back to herself. She had to protect her friends. "Whatever you want, I'll do it. Let the others go."

Maddox swiveled to saunter over to Hope. "Whatever I want? I thought that's what you already promised."

Hope knew what she had to do. The only action Maddox would accept. "I'll leave. For good, if that's what it takes." She lifted her chin. "But Izabella gets to stay, and the surgery gets rescheduled, with someone else, the right way, the full AR and everything — and whatever other treatment she needs."

"And why would I agree to that?"

Tears burned behind Hope's eyelids, but she held them back. She had no way of controlling this situation, but she could sacrifice herself and her knowledge. It was all she had to bargain with to save Izabella. "I won't tell anyone what I found. About the accuracy rate and Cecilia's files. The destruction of my data sets."

"You thought you could hold *that* over my head?" Marah scoffed. "Like I didn't trace an unauthorized access to the tablet of a certain intern of yours—"

"It wasn't her fault. It was all me." Hope had a hunch that, ultimately, Maddox mostly wanted to see her give up. To win the power struggle. Hope would do it if it would save Izabella, but her friends shouldn't have to suffer for it. "But Poppy and Abbie get to keep their jobs. They didn't really know what I was asking them to do."

Maddox cackled, the sound echoing in the sterile space. "You think you're in a position to bargain with me? You're a cog in the wheel."

Hope stood her ground. "*And* you hire Dalton back as High Resident."

"No, Hope—" Dalton started.

"This is where you belong, Dalton." Hope cut him off. "If I have to leave, there's no one else I'd rather know is here."

"*There's no one else I'd rather know is here.*" Maddox mocked Hope, rolling her eyes. "You're lucky I'm in a rather generous mood. Seeing as how one of your colleagues was good enough to inform me about your plan."

One of her colleagues?

Leach. He'd been a traitor, after all. Hope's vision clouded. She should have known he would never have helped them without an ulterior motive. He'd let them in, only to go running to report them to Maddox.

Dalton stepped forward.

For a split second, Hope thought he would strike Maddox. "No, Dalton, don't do anything stupid!"

He halted and spun around to face Hope, standing shoulder to shoulder with Maddox. His gaze fixed now over Hope's head, not meeting her eyes.

Maddox put a possessive hand on his elbow.

A horrible understanding crept over Hope. Her voice sounded like it came from somewhere far away when she spoke. "I thought we were a team."

Dalton gestured around the O.R. "This. It's what you said."

Hope couldn't speak.

That yearning filled his eyes again as he lowered them to meet hers. "This is what I was meant to do, what I was born to do."

Hope's mouth filled with a bitter taste. To think she'd almost allowed herself to care about him again.

Dalton gave her an imploring gaze. "I'll make sure Izabella's surgery gets rescheduled—"

"You needn't worry. Dr. Fall will return with full privileges." Maddox cut him off, smirking. "In return for his show of good faith, alerting me to your little plan here tonight. And seeing as we have a sudden vacancy in the High Resident position."

The image of Dalton standing beside Maddox made the finality of it all hit home. Hope should have seen this coming. How could she have been so blind? The bitter taste in her mouth escalated to nausea. Earlier tonight, she'd let him distract and confuse her with that near-kiss. Wait, had he done that on purpose?

She wouldn't let herself show how much he'd hurt her. She kept her chin up, eyes dry. It wasn't all for nothing. Izabella would receive treatment, and that was all that mattered now.

If her career would be the price, then so be it.

But she wanted to know why. He at least owed her that. She swallowed hard and found her voice. "Why'd you pretend to go through with it if you planned to betray us?"

Dalton stared at her, and his eyes showed a fleeting glimpse of anguish. "It's not—"

Maddox cut him off again, stepping in front of Hope. "To think of all the wasted resources invested in you. The opportunities you've had that you took for granted. You've had it *easy*. Your floor was my fucking ceiling. And this is how you repay me?"

Spittle sprayed from the corners of her mouth, landing on Hope's scrubs. Some of it hit Hope's bare skin, and she had to brace herself from recoiling.

Maddox waved at Abbie and Poppy. "Your friends can keep their jobs, but they'll all be signing NDA's." She pivoted to face Noah. "As for you, if you speak one word of this elsewhere, PRIMA will press charges against you for practicing in our facility without privileges. I trust you understand what that would mean." Her gaze swiveled back to Hope. "Funnily enough, I believe you'll stay quiet in trade for this girl's care. Take her back to OASIS. I'll allow you the professional courtesy to see her stabilized. After that, you will not be returning. Ever."

She spun on her heel, leaving Hope staring into Dalton's eyes. For a moment, she thought he would say something more. To fix this, to make it right. Instead, he broke off his gaze with a pained expression and followed Maddox out the doors, the guards flanking them through the exit.

The wave of betrayal washed over Hope.

The fortress that had been her career, her shield against grief, disintegrated. She'd lost everything.

No, not everything. Izabella would receive treatment. Hope would hold on to that.

In the silence, the ventilator released a muffled hiss every three seconds. Hope was grateful when Abbie, Noah, and Poppy said nothing.

CHAPTER TWENTY–SIX

"Don't act so miserable. You did the right thing."

Marah leaned back in her chair, addressing Dalton from behind her oversized desk. God, she was more tired than she wanted to admit. And where were the goddamn merger results? She wanted them before she took care of the matter of Cecilia.

The dark floor-to-ceiling windows of her corner office reflected Dalton's image in multiple. The triple-paned glass muffled the clamor of the storm still raging outside, and an inward glow of satisfaction warmed Marah's chest as if amplified by the wind. She stretched out an arm toward the chair in front of her desk. "Please, sit."

Dalton ignored her invitation.

Marah sighed. Must he insist on making things difficult? She leaned forward, resting her chin on her hands. "You're a gifted surgeon. Think of all the people you'll help by returning to PRIMA. This is where you belong. I'm surprised it took you this long to realize it."

The muscles at the angle of his jaw tensed. "I'm here, aren't I?"

Marah pushed back from her chair and strolled out from behind the desk. She couldn't allow him to let Hope Kestrel get under his skin. "Poor Dr. Fall, I know what you need. To forget the shock and betrayal in her eyes? She doesn't know, does she? But perhaps after some time, you'll make her understand how you passed on our offer to pin the blame on her a year ago.

Maybe your attempt to help in that girl's surgery will be enough for her to forgive you one day."

Dalton shook his head and stepped back from her. "I can't believe I used to think you and Hope had a lot in common."

Marah's lip curled at the unexpected comparison. "Oh?"

His arms hung at his sides. "Both of you want to believe the system's perfect, incapable of mistakes. But I'm more of a pragmatist. I understand there's no such thing as a perfect system." His eyes drifted to the statue on her desk. "But she's not like you or me. Hope believed in the system she thought would perfect healthcare because she thought it would help real people, like her mother. Whereas people like us embrace the bigger picture. We convince ourselves we're accepting the sacrifice of the few to benefit the many."

Marah picked up the statue and turned it in her hands. "You may be right. But you know what Virchow said? *'Medicine is a social science, and politics is nothing else but medicine on a large scale.'* Conversely, to succeed in medicine means to master the politics. I think you're getting that now."

Dalton cocked his head. "Didn't Virchow oppose the theory of evolution? Only history will prove us right or wrong. No system, not even PRIMA, is perfect. Mistakes happen."

Marah slammed the statue back down on her desk. "Not mistakes, Dalton. *Exceptions.*"

She pressed her hands together, getting herself back in control, and swiveled to stare out into the storm, her back to him. "Don't do anything too hasty. You're a true asset—we don't want to lose you. Again."

Marah pasted on a smile, turning around. But he'd gone. No matter, he was back in her fold now. Dalton Fall was a talented surgeon, an asset to PRIMA, and Marah almost regretted how events had played out last year. But having him back now proved she'd handled it the right way.

She'd known he would eventually make the right choice. The choice that she'd made all those years ago. The day everything had changed for her. When she'd lost the rose-colored glasses...

She'd been a senior resident. More years ago than she cared to admit now. God, she'd been so young—twenty-eight years old...

The chief of the surgery department, Dr. Rankel, had appeared at the team room asking to see her. The rotation had been going well, and she'd been enjoying her increased responsibility as a senior resident. True, the hours were brutal, and she remained at the mercy of the attendings, but mostly, the camaraderie and O.R. time made up for it.

The rest of the team had filed out of the physicians' workroom, sneaking a few glances back at her, no doubt wondering what she'd done to deserve the attention of the department chair. She became acutely aware it was only now the two of them on the mismatched sofa and chairs, the bank of computers behind them, food wrappers and empty coffee cups strewn about.

Marah reassured herself the nursing station was right outside the door, and he'd left her alone since that incident in the auditorium. There was nothing to worry about.

Rankel cleared his throat. "Dr. Maddox, ahh, it seems there's a matter that's been brought to my attention."

His serious expression, and the fact he addressed her as "Dr. Maddox" rather than his usual informal use of her first name, put her on guard. But she couldn't have anticipated what he would say next.

"It appears there's been a medication error, and, ahh, there's no easy way to say it, an adverse event."

"What?" Her mind ran through her patients over the past month. She couldn't recall any problems.

"When you entered discharge medication orders last week on Mrs. Bogdana, you prescribed an, ahh, incorrect dose of her anticoagulant."

Marah's shoulders drew up. She couldn't have done that. She would never screw up like that. Besides, she remembered clearly—she hadn't written for the discharge meds. He had. All she'd done was sign for them because he'd walked off and ordered her to.

Rankel clasped his chin with his hand. "It was a mistake anyone could have made while overtaxed and overtired. Which, I'm afraid, is still how you residents are made to practice in this, ahh, training culture."

Marah's hands had gone clammy, and she jammed them under her arms at her sides, biting her tongue against what she wanted to say. You wrote the order. This is your mistake. *Instead, in a small voice she hated, she asked, "Is she okay?"*

"*She came into the ER with a GI bleed, and they initially stabilized her. That's when they figured out the issue with the dose. Unfortunately, her son is a physician himself and realized the, ahh, prescription error.*"

Rankel smoothed the front of his white coat with deliberate motions. "There's no easy way to say this. Even though her condition initially stabilized, the next night, she bled again. Intracranial bleed. There was, ahh, nothing that could be done."

Marah's posture went rigid. The scents of stale coffee and stagnant upholstery made her gag. Her voice came out brittle. "But why didn't the pharmacy catch the error?"

Rankel shook his head. "You know that's not how it works. It will flag dangerous interactions, but it can't know if you, ahh, ordered the wrong dose altogether."

He ordered the wrong dose altogether—but she couldn't accuse him of that. She understood how the power structure worked. Her thoughts cast desperately for another way out of this. "What about the nurse? When she reviewed the discharge medications with the patient, shouldn't she have noticed the change and checked with me?"

Rankel pressed his lips together in a tight line. "To be honest, many a nurse has saved me from a mistake. But with the pressure to discharge patients so quickly, the nurses aren't able to give the same, ahh, attention to the discharge medications."

Marah let herself slump a little.

But his next words made her go lightheaded. "I'm afraid ultimately the responsibility falls on the discharging physician, Marah."

She couldn't breathe. "But, I'm only the resident...."

"*Yes, but you are a fully licensed medical doctor, and you, ahh, signed the orders."*

Marah bit her lip so the pain would keep her from saying anything else.

She clenched her fists, her nails biting into her palms. Her words ground out from between her teeth. "Why doesn't someone fix the goddamn system so it would recognize if the wrong dose is ordered?"

Rankel let the profanity go. "That would be quite a system. But, of course, that's why we go to, ahh, medical school."

He attempted to soften the last sentence with a smile, but it came across as his usual leer. His continued pretense of being a fatherly figure had made her want to vomit, and her career had flashed before her eyes.

Marah had made herself go cold inside, numb. She'd wanted to get it over with. "What happens now?"

"The Quality Assurance team is here to meet with you. They have some, ahh, options to go over with you."

Options.

Like what she'd offered Dalton...

Marah blinked back to the present, taking in the panoramic view, inhaling and exhaling until her heart rate returned to normal. She'd been almost sorry to have put Dalton through the same thing, but tonight proved she'd made the right choice.

The residents needed her to watch over them the way no one had for her.

She stretched her legs and kicked her heels off. PRIMA now did what she'd needed in a system all those years ago. If an occasional exception to the system's accuracy occurred, the vast number of people the system benefitted far outweighed it.

It wouldn't do to allow any perception of a *mistake* in the system. That was simply not acceptable. Dalton saw that now, too.

Too bad Hope Kestrel hadn't been able to. But Marah couldn't save them all.

Now, to take care of the Cecilia problem.

• • • •

"I didn't—" Cecilia's voice emerged tentatively in the dim light of the security office. "I told you, I know nothing about that computer virus."

Marah paced while Sydney guarded the entrance. "The FBI is on their way."

Cecilia stepped back, glancing around as if searching for answers.

Marah pressed her. "You think you're so goddamn smart, don't you? But you didn't know about my security software."

Cecilia shook her head and sank into the chair. "I told you, I don't know what you're talking about—"

Marah clenched her fists, the pen in her right hand snapping in two. She hurled it to the floor, her muscles tensing so hard they were shaking. "Do you see? This is why I can't trust *anyone*."

Cecilia held up her hands, palms toward Marah. "But it wasn't me. I don't know anything about a virus."

"Then, who? Are you saying someone else had access to your program?"

"No one." Cecilia's gaze clouded, going distant. "Unless..."

Marah's blood pounded in her ears. After everything she'd done for Cecilia, guiding her career, steering her research in the right direction, and this was how the woman repaid her? But it only proved Marah had been right to arrange for the private cybersecurity. She was the only one with the vision and guts.

The adrenaline rushing through her body made it hard to focus, and her mind took a few seconds to process Cecilia's words but then seized on them. "Unless?"

Cecilia averted her gaze.

Marah gripped her arm, forcing Cecilia to look up at her. Her voice dropped to a hiss. "Who was it, Cecilia?"

Sweat beaded on Cecilia's brow, and she slumped in Marah's grasp.

Marah gave her arm a shake. "Oh, don't be so dramatic."

But Cecilia's eyes rolled back in her head, and her slack body weight pulled her down out of Marah's hands.

"*Fuck.*" Marah lunged just in time to keep Cecilia's head from banging into the floor.

She shook Cecilia's shoulder and called her name. No response. She checked for a radial pulse, then a carotid. Nothing. "You've got to be goddamn kidding me."

Marah kneeled beside Cecilia and started chest compressions, yelling up at Sydney. "Don't just stand there. Call a fucking code!"

CHAPTER TWENTY-SEVEN

TUESDAY 23 OCTOBER 2035
12:15 AM
Main Campus, PRIMA

When the OASIS nurses didn't question Izabella's premature return from the O.R., Hope decided she didn't want to know what lies Maddox must have told them.

Maddox's guards had whisked Abbie, Poppy, and Noah away to sign their NDA's, and Hope had transported Izabella back to OASIS alone. She surrendered Izabella into the nurses' capable hands, remaining in the corridor. She couldn't bring herself yet to find Jacie to tell her and her parents what had happened.

At some point, the snow had transformed into freezing rain. The precipitation clattered on the glass like skeletal fingers tapping in the night. A shiver passed through her, and she reached for her necklace out of habit, only to have her bare neck remind her again it was lost.

The voice of Osler came over the intercom, jolting her to attention. *There is a Code Blue in Security, Basement Level. Repeat. There is a Code Blue in Security, Basement Level...*

Hope's body reacted in instinctual alarm, her heart racing. A Code Blue was no longer her duty, but these were her last moments in PRIMA. Something compelled her to go. One last chance to help as a physician and make up for her failure. To do this one last thing before facing Jacie and her parents.

Without thinking it through, she sprinted for the stairwell. Her feet flew, carrying her down to the bottom level. She raced up the hall and skidded to a halt in front of the Security office, nearly colliding with one of Maddox's private guards—the man.

Hope braced for him to block her, but he stepped aside, pointing her through the door. "In there. Hurry."

She recovered from her surprise and charged in, only to freeze mid-stride.

No, this couldn't be right.

Hope's brain couldn't process the scene before her. Cecilia on the floor, and Maddox, performing chest compressions.

But Cecilia shouldn't be down here. This couldn't be happening.

Then, the next moment, Leach was there, pushing past her. A nurse followed with the Code Cart.

Hope remained frozen, motionless, her breath coming in quick gasps. Icy fingers of dread wrapped around her heart and squeezed it bloodless.

Please, no.

The rest of the Code team rushed in, spilling into the hallway. The scene transported her back to that day outside her mom's hospital room, eleven years old...

No. This couldn't be happening again.

Hope's mind snapped back to the present. Leach, about to intubate.

"Stop!" Her voice came out as a strangled cry.

She stepped forward and lifted an arm to stop him, but her body had become so heavy, like moving underwater. But she had to—she had promised. She collapsed to her knees and put an arm between Leach and Cecilia.

Leach cursed.

Hope pleaded with him. "You have to stop. You don't understand. She made me promise her—"

Leach tried to reach around her.

A nurse had relieved Maddox on chest compressions, and Cecilia's body jerked with each thrust.

Her mom's body flashed before Hope's eyes. The things the doctors had done. She couldn't bring herself to look at Cecilia's slack face.

Instead, she took one of Cecilia's limp hands in hers, bending down to rest her forehead on it.

It was so cold.

Leach pulled back, confusion on his face.

Another nurse began hooking up the leads to the defibrillator.

Hope remembered her mom's body convulsing, back arching. The way her body had become a lifeless puppet from the shocks. She couldn't let that happen again. She forced herself to stand, putting herself between the Code team and Cecilia's body. Her voice rose. "She's a DNR. She didn't want this!"

Leach shook his head in grim determination and called out. "*Osler*, what is Dr. Cecilia Li's code status?"

There is no code status on file.

Leach resumed preparations to intubate. "Get back. You shouldn't be here. You're in the way."

The nurses pushed past Hope and finished connecting the defibrillator leads to Cecilia's body.

The machine's impersonal voice filled the room. *Shocking in three, two...*

Hope threw herself over Cecilia's body.

"Damn it, Hope!" Leach yanked one of the defibrillator wires to disconnect it.

Hope pressed her ear to Cecilia's chest. Nothing.

The loudest nothing in the world.

She raised her head to spot Maddox standing against the wall, a sheen of sweat on her cheeks and forehead, her blouse untucked and in disarray. The first time Hope had seen her appear not in control of a room, her guards flanking her.

But Maddox could stop all this.

"She didn't want this. You know she didn't want this. She made me promise her." The room narrowed to her and Maddox. "She said if it came to this to please let her go... Please."

Hope laid her head back on Cecilia's chest. No movement. No heartbeat.

Gentle hands touched her back. "Dr. Kestrel is right. It's not what Dr. Li would have wanted."

Hope raised her head in surprise to find Maddox's face a mirror of her own. Grief and loss and shock and pain reflected back to her. It was too much. Maddox had no right to those same feelings.

Something ripped open inside of Hope.

"Are you happy now?" The harsh voice that tore out of her throat belonged to a stranger. "She didn't tell me until it was too late. Because the algorithm told her she was a non-responder. This is never what I wanted—all of this... *futile*—"

Hope's voice broke on the last word.

A silence followed, and the members of the code response team stared at the floor.

Cecilia's lifeless hand slipped from Hope's fingers.

Maddox was the one to speak into the silence. "Call it."

Leach's eyes went from Maddox to Hope to Cecilia's still body. The argument left them. "Time of death, 12:25 AM."

The staff filed out with still-downcast eyes.

Hope had been too late. All her work had been for nothing. Her belief in the algorithm, in Cecilia's work, in their work together, in PRIMA—this is where it had led her.

To failure.

Loss.

Her vow to never again see a loved one suffer from failed medical treatment had meant nothing.

Cecilia was gone.

Hope spoke the words she should have said to Cecilia long ago. *"I love you."*

But she had waited too long.

CHAPTER TWENTY-EIGHT

TUESDAY 23 OCTOBER 2035
12:45 AM
Marah's office, PRIMA

What a goddamn disaster.

Marah allowed herself to sink back into her chair and close her eyes. Cecilia—dead. She had to admit she hadn't seen that coming.

Immediately afterward, she'd had to head off the FBI, which hadn't brought her any closer to determining if Cecilia had been telling the truth. It didn't matter, though. Her cybersecurity had taken care of the computer virus, and Cecilia, well, if she had created it, she wouldn't be a problem any longer.

Marah didn't need Cecilia's "fix." The only others who knew about the error rate—Hope Kestrel and her friends—were taken care of.

To think Cecilia had been a patient on OASIS earlier tonight. Apparently, the woman had checked herself out and came directly to Marah's office. Why would she have done that? If Marah had known, she wouldn't have put her down in Security. Why hadn't Cecilia said anything? Typical.

At least, she'd been wise enough to accept what the algorithm had told her about her case. But they should have admitted her to HEARTH. Instead, another death within PRIMA. Hadn't Cecilia known the paperwork nightmare this would cause Marah?

She was glad now she'd allowed Cecilia to have the blood samples she wanted. Maybe it had given her some sense of closure, even though it obviously hadn't worked out as Cecilia had intended.

And Marah owed Cecilia for the idea. The one that would allow her and the Corporation to carry out the algorithm's logical next phase. All without Cecilia ever having known.

Once they won the vote from Seattle Healthcare Associates, it would give them another 300,000 patients to draw from. Marah gave an impatient tap at her screen. It didn't change, and she resigned herself to waiting, loosening a button at her collar.

The action triggered another memory. One she hadn't allowed herself to think of in many years...

Her senior year of residency. Grand Rounds. Months before the day Rankel had come to the workroom to end her career. Back when she thought if she only worked hard enough and impressed him and the other senior surgeons, she'd be assured of her place amongst them.

Marah had taken her place at the podium. Rankel's hands had startled her, pinning the microphone to the lapel of her white coat. She'd reached up to do it herself, but his fingers had been firm on her collarbone. She tried to nudge them off, but he didn't move them aside.

"Ahh, there you go, Marah, all set." Rankel spoke as usual in what he probably imagined a fatherly tone. But also, as usual, his gaze strayed to her chest.

Marah's cheeks burned, and she clenched her teeth.

Whatever, let him pin the microphone. She couldn't make a scene in front of the entire department. She pressed her lips into a tight smile.

"One more thing." Rankel pitched his voice low for her ears only. He shifted in front of her, his back to the audience, blocking their view of her.

His fingers trailed down her sternum. What the hell?

To Marah's horror, he unbuttoned the top buttons of her blouse.

"That's better." He gave her chest a lingering pat.

Marah's shocked gaze rose to meet his eyes. She could have slapped him, but she only stood there. He was the chief of the goddamn department. So she stood there like a stupid mannequin. Like the useless object he thought her to be.

Hadn't the audience noticed? Why hadn't anyone said something? But he'd made sure no one had seen.

Marah cast a wild glance around the auditorium, struggling to control her breathing. Roughly split, the surgical department included about eighty-five percent men and fifteen percent women. Right at the national average, she'd looked it up—a whopping increase from the two percent of female surgical residents in 1980.

Somehow, by the 1990s, she'd expected more progress.

But even though the audience held a smattering of female colleagues, women weren't in the positions that mattered—the leadership positions.

What Rankel had just done had happened in front of the entire department, but it didn't matter. No one there saw her. *She wasn't anyone that mattered.*

Not yet.

I am not someone who matters—yet.

But I will be.

Marah didn't reach up to re-fasten the buttons, not wanting to draw more attention to her cleavage. Nor to give Rankel the satisfaction of knowing he'd unnerved her.

She launched into her talk on auto-pilot. Somehow, she made it through and answered questions coherently at the end.

Afterward, Marah stalked off before Rankel could corner her. She should have been basking in accomplishment. Instead, she wallowed in disgust, and somehow, instead of directing it all at Rankel, the one who deserved it, she focused a deep loathing on herself. All she wanted was to get to her call room and shower.

Once under the cold stream, the shame gave way to anger.

Marah pounded the wall with her fists. The spray hit her face. She drove out the doubting thoughts until everything distilled down to a single conviction. Someday, I will be the one that matters. *She would protect others from having this kind of thing happen to them.*

She pushed the pain down, deep inside, vowing to rise above it all and not end up one of the failures, not like the resident she'd heard had committed suicide. She was a survivor. Since medical school, she'd been building a shell around herself, and now she reinforced it, adding more layers, making it indestructible.

Marah was goddamned sick to death of being underestimated because of how she looked. She'd made a vow. I will never censor myself again...

The chime of her tablet brought her back to the present, and she banished the unpleasant memory. It must have been the trauma of Cecilia's death, allowing that memory to sneak to the surface.

But here she was. She *had* made sure of it.

Marah opened her tablet, and at the message on the screen, a delectable coolness spread through her veins.

The vote. They'd done it. *She* had done it.

She twisted her lips in a grin of ferocious satisfaction.

Seattle Healthcare Associates had become PRIMA's latest acquisition. PRIMA now controlled the Seattle healthcare market.

From here, the rest of the state. Then the West Coast, and then the nation.

Marah envisioned a giant fist reaching back in time to crush Rankel, squeezing and squeezing and squeezing until the arrogance vanished from his face. She wished she could also reach back to tell her former self not to worry, that in the end, she would rise to the top.

Cecilia's words to her echoed in her mind. *Why do you do this?*

Her breath hitched, and the giant fist now squeezed inside her chest. For a fleeting moment, she pressed her hands to her face.

Oh, my old friend, I'm sorry. It shouldn't have been you.

Then she lowered her hands. Cleared her throat. Gave a slight shake of her head.

The algorithm had been right, after all. Cecilia Li's case had been terminal.

PART THREE: *TREATMENT*

I now apply myself to my profession. Support me in this great task so that it may benefit mankind.
— The Prayer of Maimonides

CHAPTER TWENTY-NINE

TUESDAY 23 OCTOBER 2035
1:15 AM
Main Campus, PRIMA

Cecilia was gone.

It was a cruel reminder of Hope's childhood lesson. Believing in *hopefulness* would only betray her.

Hope paced the narrow width of her old call room, the same one she'd changed in earlier. With nowhere else to go, she'd retreated to it, sure she'd never get back inside if she left the building. After the code, she'd slipped back upstairs. Despite everything, she wasn't ready to leave yet.

She stopped pacing and let herself sink to the ground, her back against the bed, her leg brushing up against her bag.

The room's precision and order she used to find so comforting now appeared cold and hostile, white sheets tucked in tight at perfect angles to the wall. The quiet from the noise-dampeners made her thoughts all the more deafening.

Cecilia was gone.

Hope leaned into the bed, her white scrubs blending into it, wanting to dissolve into that whiteness, for it to swallow her up. Tilting her head, she focused on the cool sensation of the sheets on the back of her neck.

The stringent scent of bleach stung her eyes. *White for knowledge, white for illumination, white for cure, white for perfection.* The oath the interns recited during the swearing-in ceremony and awarding of the white scrubs. Hope had helped write it.

Maddox had wanted a new oath. *None of that antiquated Hippocratic nonsense.*

Had Hope been that naïve? To believe in the promise of perfection?

She didn't want to feel this. Shattered and unprotected and so hatefully weak. She had nothing left. No family. No career. Cecilia had left her, just like her mom. Dalton had betrayed her, and Marah Maddox had won.

Her limbs went numb, as if they didn't belong to her. Heat burned behind her eyelids, but no tears would come.

A sliver of light shone under the door but did nothing to warm her. She dragged a blanket off the bed and curled it around herself.

Cecilia's voice somehow filled her mind. *You're the strongest person I know. You always were. I don't believe you're giving up. Don't you dare.*

Hope spoke aloud. "Don't *I* dare? How dare *you*? You're not even here anymore—"

What was she doing? She needed to stop this. Imagining a conversation with Cecilia.

I'll always be with you.

Hope put her hands over her ears. She was suffering from some kind of delusion, that's all. Her mind doing this to cope with the grief. She yelled into the empty call room. "You're both gone! You both left me—"

A sob lodged in her chest.

You mustn't quit, Hope. Everything you need is within you. It always has been.

But she *wasn't* strong enough. She'd only been pretending. So no one would ever see how deeply she'd been hurt. She slumped down and pressed her cheek on the cold floor.

She'd thought PRIMA offered the solution that would make up for everything and heal the wound deep inside her. She'd thought she'd made the right choice—the one that meant she could control the outcomes. But she couldn't control any of it.

Hope let the blanket fall off her shoulders and clambered to her feet.

But Cecilia's voice had gone. The ongoing silence a reproach.

An irrational impulse seized her. She had to see Cecilia one more time, even understanding it wasn't her, only her body. Maybe then she'd hear her voice one more time, so Hope could tell her she was sorry.

But it wouldn't be like how she'd been forced to view her mom's body. This time, it would be different. This time, it was her decision. Her choice—and it wouldn't involve the morgue.

• • •

PRIMA didn't even have a morgue of its own. On the rare occasion, when necessary, they used the morgue at HEARTH, across the city. But with no indications for an autopsy for Cecilia, PRIMA would release her body directly to the funeral home.

As High Resident, Hope knew about the area in pathology where Cecilia's body would be held until the funeral home collected it. Not wanting to second-guess her decision, she would go immediately. Cracking the door, she peeked out to ensure the coast was clear, wincing at the brightness of the hallway lighting. Shouldering her bag, she slunk down the deserted corridor, her destination clear in her mind.

A part of her wondered what she was doing. Another part answered—denial. She was in denial. The first stage of grief. It was normal.

But somehow, she couldn't let go of the belief that if she could be in the presence of Cecilia's body, she could say what she needed.

And what was that? That she'd loved her like a mother? That she'd been wrong to doubt her? And she was sorry—

With each heavy step down the stairwell, she pushed those thoughts away. The numbness in her body spread to her mind, and she welcomed it. She came to an abrupt halt outside the door to the holding area. There was only one problem. She no longer had a badge.

Hope's hands trembled. This was all *her* fault—Maddox. She'd taken away all of Hope's control. It was Maddox's fault Cecilia was dead, and it was because of Maddox that Hope was powerless. *Again.*

Her mind replayed the encounter outside Maddox's office. When she'd allowed Maddox to humiliate her and force her to talk about her mom. *It was my fault... I broke my promise...*

It had all been for nothing. She'd allowed Maddox to play her for a fool—*for nothing*. She pressed her palms into her eyes.

Damn you, Cecilia, for making me promise you—

The door swung open, and a lab tech stood in the doorway. Hope had only the impression of gray scrubs and thinning hair. He stopped short, startled to find her there, and took in her white scrubs. "Can I help you, Doctor?"

Hope steeled herself to edge past him. "I'm here to examine the body brought down earlier tonight."

His hand gripped her forearm. "You can't."

Hope glared at the spot where his hand touched her. "Yes, I can. Move."

The tech blanched and released her arm, but didn't step aside.

She broke out in a sweat. Why wouldn't he let her pass? Surely few others in the hospital could know about her termination.

He offered a nervous smile that quickly faded. "You can't see the body because it's not here."

Hope cursed under her breath. The funeral home must have already collected Cecilia's body. It wasn't the tech's fault, but she wanted to scream at him, strike him. She crossed her arms and pressed them into her diaphragm to prevent herself from doing either, then spoke through clenched teeth. "Which funeral home—"

Osler's voice overhead cut her off. *Attention, dialysis team, to OASIS Unit, STAT. Attention, dialysis team—*

Dialysis team?

Hope stared at the tech, but no longer saw him.

Izabella.

She sprinted back toward OASIS.

CHAPTER THIRTY

TUESDAY 23 OCTOBER 2035
1:30 AM
OASIS Unit, PRIMA

Hope barreled through the double doors of OASIS, her eyes scanning for catastrophe, her body bracing to arrive on the scene of another Code Blue. But instead of chaos, all was eerily quiet.

She rushed to the nurses' station, her feet stumbling. Was she too late? But Izabella's bio-readings were stable. Better than stable—improved. Hope's knees buckled, and she collapsed into a chair.

"Dr. K?"

Hope spun around at the sound of Abbie's voice.

"Dr. K, you shouldn't be here. Not after—"

"Where's the dialysis team?" Hope's heart hadn't stopped pounding. "I heard the STAT page—"

Abbie placed a hand on the chair. "We thought her line had clotted, but it's fine now. We didn't end up needing them."

Hope nodded as if convincing herself Abbie's words were true. Then looked at Abbie as if seeing her for the first time. "You're back. But where's Poppy?"

Abbie's hand fell away. "I found her an empty room to get some sleep. After—"

"They made you sign the NDA."

Abbie's shoulders slumped. "I'm sorry, Dr. K. I need this job—"

Hope rose to her feet and gripped Abbie's shoulders. "Never apologize for that."

The adrenaline had receded, and her body had returned to its new state of numbness. She released Abbie and headed down the hall to see Izabella for herself.

Hope reached the doorway and paused. Izabella appeared to be sleeping comfortably, her color improved. Jacie and her parents sprawled in the bedside chairs, leaning into each other, eyes closed. To Hope's surprise, Noah had stayed, too, and snoozed in a chair in the opposite corner.

Her blood rushed to her heart, and a sudden warmth filled her chest. *Izabella was okay.*

One thing tonight she'd done right.

Even if she hadn't accomplished the surgery, she'd gotten her the dialysis. And Dalton had promised to get her the operation soon. Despite everything, Hope believed he meant it. He might have betrayed her, but he'd never betray a patient.

Her head tipped back, and she let her body sag against the doorframe. If something had happened to Izabella, she couldn't—

The momentary surge of fierce joy upon finding Izabella safe receded, and the raw grief of losing Cecilia clawed its way back to the surface. She wished only for the numbness back.

At some point, she realized Jacie's eyes were open, watching her. She lurched away, not ready to face Jacie and her family yet.

But Jacie's voice followed her up the hallway. "Hope, wait. Is it true? About Dr. Li... I'm so sorry—"

Hope halted but didn't turn around.

From the opposite direction, Abbie took a few steps toward her from the nurses' station, twisting her hands.

A nerve by Hope's right eye twitched. She expected what Abbie would say and didn't want to hear it. She couldn't bear it.

Abbie glanced at the doorway to Room Seventeen. "We all are, Dr. K. We're terribly sorry for your loss."

Hope held back the tears. She understood they needed to give their condolences. She remembered that same unendurable time after her mom died. But she didn't want their sympathy. She didn't want to be in that vulnerable space. There was only one thing she wanted right now. To locate Cecilia's body.

She swung around to face Jacie. "I need you to help me with something. I know you don't owe me anything anymore, especially since I was unable to perform the surgery tonight, but—"

"It's okay." Jacie gently cut her off. "Noah explained to me what you did—"

"I'm sorry. I failed. I let you and your family down—"

"Hey." Jacie stepped closer. "She's here, isn't she? You did that."

"No." Hope shook her head. "You did. By never giving up."

"How about we did it together? Or is that too much for the great Dr. Hope Kestrel?" She softened her words with a smile. "No one said you have to be everyone's savior, you know."

Hope swallowed and waited for the tightness in her chest to lessen. She cleared her throat. "It's about Cecilia—"

She explained how Cecilia's body was gone from the holding area and asked if Jacie could find out which funeral home had taken custody.

Jacie whipped out her tablet. "On it."

A wave of dizziness passed over her. Noah, who'd emerged from the room while they'd been talking, held out his hand to her like a wary handler approaching a caged mountain lion. "Why don't you come sit down, Dr. Kestrel?"

Hope allowed Noah to lead her into an empty patient room and lowered herself onto the edge of the bed. Noah closed the door behind him and then took the bedside chair. She'd never been in one of these rooms without an actual patient occupying the bed, and the quietness struck her. Noah didn't break the silence, and she was grateful.

Her body shook, and she found herself unable to stop it.

Noah leaned forward and took her hand.

Only then did the tears finally come. Somehow, it was easier to cry in front of a near stranger.

After a moment, Noah released her hand, retrieving a box of tissues.

She took one and swiped furiously at her eyes. "I'm fine."

"I know," Noah said. "But you don't have to be."

What did he know? Suddenly, she wanted to be alone. "How are you even still here?"

"The family asked me to stay."

"And Maddox allowed that?"

"It surprised me, too, at first. But Marah and I, we... it's hard to explain."

Hope's eyebrows shot up, wanting to know more despite herself.

"We trained together, as residents. It was a long time ago. But she wasn't always the person she is now." He sighed. "She still made me sign the NDA, though. It was that or face prison charges. Part of me wanted to let them imprison me—for the principle of it—but what would happen to all my patients if I were in prison?"

Hope said nothing. She didn't want to talk about Maddox.

Noah waited a long moment. "It wasn't your fault your mentor died."

But it *was* her fault. Hope wished she could go back and change everything. She clenched her hands in her hair. "I was a part of PRIMA. If *they* hadn't designated her a non-responder, she would have wanted to try—"

Noah interrupted in a gentle voice. "Each of us looks at risk through a different lens. Whether someone chooses to try medical treatments despite long odds will be influenced by their unique life experiences. It's not our job to choose for them."

She released her head and tilted it back to stare at the ceiling. "Maybe I wish she *hadn't* had a choice. I wanted her to stay. With me. I don't care if that's selfish."

"It was an act of love to let her go. With dignity, as she had wanted."

Hope glared at him. "So why did you help Jacie and her sister then?"

Noah leaned back in his chair. "Izabella deserved to have that same choice. I'm her family physician, her advocate. We're not just gatekeepers. We help ensure our patients are getting the right resources and care about what happens to them in the hands of other specialists—and systems."

Something about the way he said it gave her pause. "You knew—about the algorithm. Didn't you? About Maddox covering up the actual accuracy rate."

"I didn't know the exact details, but, yes, I suspected something like that."

Hope couldn't speak through the thickness in her throat. The desire to stop Maddox overwhelmed her. But how?

Maddox had taken everything from her. Hope had been too arrogant, and Maddox had manipulated her. Hope had traded away her only leverage to guarantee Izabella's care, and she'd do it again in a heartbeat. But it couldn't end like this. "We have to do *something*. Go public, the news media—"

"We won't get any traction." Noah's voice contained a new sorrow, and he turned his tablet toward her. "The merger vote went in PRIMA's favor. They control too much of the city now. They'd bury the story."

Hope fell silent. *The merger.*

But it couldn't be too late. She had to stop PRIMA from hurting any more innocent people like Izabella. All these years, she'd thought they were building a system that would give meaning to her grief. She wouldn't let Cecilia's death be in vain as well. As soon as Jacie told her the location of Cecilia's body, she'd go after Maddox. No matter what it took. She'd find another way. "Forget the media then. Go online, post it ourselves, social media—"

"They'd only discredit you. Bury the story. Algorithms play a role in more than just healthcare." Noah gave his head a tired shake. "In the end, I fear it still wouldn't be enough to stop Marah."

Hope hated knowing he was right. Cecilia was dead and couldn't testify against Maddox. Their only evidence was now hostage to Izabella's life. And even if Hope somehow found a way, PRIMA would delegitimize it. No one would believe her now that Maddox had ended her career.

Noah continued. "I suppose it's no surprise the merger went through. Most of my colleagues will grasp at anything that promises to make things better. Even if the promises are false." He let out a soft snort. "I guess, technically, this means I work for PRIMA now, too. One day soon, physicians like me won't exist anymore. I'll be obsolete."

Hope's head throbbed. "How have you done it? Without algorithms?"

He offered a bemused smile. "There've always been algorithms. They weren't computerized, but they've always been part of medical practice. The differential diagnosis, for example."

Noah shook his head at the blank expression Hope gave him. "Part of medical training for over a century, and your algorithm threw it out the window in under a decade. The practice of beginning with a broad mindset for all conditions that could cause the patient's symptoms. Then narrowing it down in a stepwise fashion, taking a detailed history, doing a physical examination, and running tests. Then synthesizing all the findings into the best fit for a diagnosis. The *doctor* does this. Not the computer."

He sounded like a teacher who enjoyed his topic.

Hope chewed on her bottom lip. "But what if you're wrong?"

"It's always a risk, but that's why one doesn't practice in a vacuum." He hooked one arm over the back of his chair. "You have colleagues, conferences, tumor boards, ways to come together to use the collective minds and experiences to benefit the patient—"

"But aren't you afraid of not knowing enough?"

Noah gave her a patient smile. "Always."

Hope struggled to integrate Noah's approach with the way PRIMA had trained her to think about practicing medicine.

Noah leaned back and crossed one ankle over the opposite knee. "I often observed over the years the best doctors listen to their gut. Clinical instinct was something one either had or didn't—it couldn't be taught."

Hope bristled. "But if that's true, then AI algorithms are even more necessary. We shouldn't rely on human instinct for pattern recognition to practice medicine. There would be huge variance between doctors."

Noah spread his arms. "I agree with you. I don't think AI algorithms are going away. The problem with PRIMA is Marah Maddox. She took shortcuts and implemented it before it was ready, without disclosing the limitations and the real error rates. The algorithm could be a useful tool. But we should teach doctors it's only that—a tool. A tool they need to wield with caution and thought before making a final decision about patient care."

He continued in a softer voice. "Human beings are remarkable organisms. Despite the best computerized predictions, what unfolds in the body may still defy expectations, in both good ways and bad. We must not forget that, and we must disclose the risk to our patients, whatever the error rate, be it one in twenty, one in a thousand, or one in ten thousand. Let them decide what that risk of error means to them. If we do that, it's still an excellent tool."

"Like Cecilia did," Hope said in a small voice.

"Any tool can become a weapon in the wrong hands," Jacie said.

Hope wondered how long Jacie'd been standing in the doorway.

She lifted her eyes to Jacie's. All she wanted was for Jacie to tell her which funeral home had Cecilia's body. But something about Jacie's expression made Hope's hands go cold. "What is it?"

Jacie's face had gone ashen. "I don't know how to tell you this."

The coldness spread into Hope's chest, and she rose to her feet.

"Cecilia's body isn't in a funeral home." A sheen of sweat glinted on Jacie's brow. "It's at—she's at—the morgue. At HEARTH."

No, not the morgue. Hope's words faltered. "But—bodies are only transferred to the morgue for autopsy—and I didn't give permission. It isn't something Cecilia had wanted."

Her vision went black around the edges. Only one person could have diverted Cecilia's body to the morgue.

Hope clenched her jaw. *"Marah Maddox."*

CHAPTER THIRTY-ONE

Hope leaned forward, bracing her hands on her knees and lowering her head until the room stopped spinning. When she straightened back up, Jacie promptly handed her a glass of water.

Hope stared. Jacie—the only person to stick by her since the night Maddox first threw her out. Jacie—who'd taken the risk of hacking Maddox's computer to help save her sister. And Jacie, *who'd then taken a video of Maddox outside her office.* Hope grabbed Jacie's arm with her other hand. "The video. Your phone."

A pained expression crossed Jacie's face. "They took it—Maddox's guards. They told us what'd happened and made it clear what I had to do to allow her surgery to be rescheduled." She averted her gaze. "I'm sorry, I never would have signed the NDA and let them take my phone if it wasn't for Izabella—"

"Don't." Hope gave her forearm a gentle squeeze before releasing it. "You did the only thing you could."

"But—" Jacie's eyes darted to Noah.

Noah gave Jacie a cryptic nod. "Maybe it's time to tell her."

Hope's gaze ping-ponged from one to the other. "Tell me what?"

Jacie shifted on her feet. "So, it's possible I had a backup plan. Only, I'm not sure if it worked."

When nothing more was forthcoming, Hope raised her eyebrows in impatience. "And? What was it?"

"I uploaded a latent computer virus into PRIMA."

Hope sank back onto the edge of the bed. She downed the rest of the water and set the glass carefully on the bedside table. "Explain."

"Infected emails, sent to all employees. In a large organization, it only takes one inattentive person to click, and the malicious software gets introduced. Then, in Maddox's office, I might not have told you the whole truth..."

"About?"

"About why it took me so long to get her password."

Hope struggled to find the right words. "I suppose none of this should surprise me—"

"I used the first few minutes to upload the second phase of the virus."

Hope glanced at Noah and then back to Jacie. "So why don't you two seem happy about this?"

"It must not have worked." Jacie rubbed the back of her neck. "I don't know how, but Maddox must have stopped it."

Hope remained silent for a few moments, processing. "What was it supposed to do?"

"I'd hoped it would replicate fast enough to cause them to take the algorithm off-line. To give us a window to help Izabella."

Hope's body tensed. "Are you serious? Do you know what kind of trouble you would've been in if they'd caught you?" She wheeled on Noah. "And you knew about this? Of course you did. You helped her because you might not be so *obsolete* if this virus succeeded."

Noah held up his hands in a placating gesture. "No, this wasn't about me. It was about helping Izabella. About righting a great wrong."

"But if it succeeded, how would that have helped? We already had a plan. I told you I would—"

Hope broke off, and Jacie lowered her gaze.

The painful tightness in Hope's throat constricted further. Her voice came out flat. "You didn't trust me to follow through."

Jacie's cheeks flushed. "I do *now*."

THE ALGORITHM WILL SEE YOU NOW | 217

Noah's eyes cut toward Jacie, but he addressed Hope. "It didn't hurt to have a backup plan. Marah Maddox has always had a way of remaining one step ahead of everyone else."

One step ahead of everyone else. With Noah's words, a terrible realization filled Hope, and with each heartbeat, the dread escalated.

No, Maddox couldn't be.

It was too horrible a thought. But Hope had to follow it to the conclusion, no matter where it led.

Her breaths came too fast, and she jumped up, grabbing Jacie's arm again. "We have to stop her. You heard her, too, in the hallway." She used her other hand to grab Noah's elbow as the words tumbled out. "She told me. But I didn't pay attention. The next step. Sequencing DNA after death. To identify new cancer mutations. To provide data for the algorithm."

Noah's expression became tight. "To improve the accuracy?"

Hope couldn't get the words out fast enough. "To identify the incurable before disease even manifests. How did she put it? *To weed them out of the healthcare system.*"

Noah grimaced, rubbing his hand over his mouth.

Jacie's eyes widened, and she stumbled back a step, her arm falling out of Hope's grasp. "The HEARTH delivery..."

Hope grabbed Noah's arm tighter, not letting him go. "Don't you see? I think she's already been doing it. To all the patients who've died at HEARTH. The non-responders."

Jacie pulled at her scarf, her voice halting at first, then picking up speed. "I wondered about that Virchow statue on her desk, how she even made his name her password, so I cyber-stalked her background. Maddox was a surgical resident early in her career, but in her last year of residency, she made an abrupt switch to pathology. But ultimately, she went into administration. It's strange—she's using PRIMA to make her former specialty obsolete. But *Virchow* was her password."

Hope released Noah, and out of habit, her hand reached for her necklace, forgetting it wasn't there. She pinched her skin instead, and the words tumbled out of her. "HEARTH made all the nurses draw blood samples on their patients right before death. They were told the families signed consent, but Poppy had concerns. They buried it in the admission paperwork, and most families likely didn't even understand what they were signing."

Jacie's eyebrows squished together. "But then, what was Cecilia doing with the samples?"

Hope's hand fell to her side, and she clenched both fists. "She must have been trying to *fix* the algorithm. Of course. How could I ever have doubted her? Cecilia never intended for my data sets to be omitted from the neural network. It was all Maddox. She told me—earlier tonight—before..." Hope swallowed, pausing until she got control of her voice again. "Maddox had been blackmailing her. But Cecilia had been trying to fix it. She must have been using my epigenetic techniques on the *final draw* samples. Analyzing the DNA from circulating tumor cells from patients near the end of life. To create better data sets for the machine learner."

Her brain abruptly remembered something else. That day at HEARTH, with Poppy—that faintly familiar scent. Maddox's perfume. She must have been there that day. *Because the morgue was there.*

Hope had finally connected the dots. "Maddox is taking it one step further. Amplifying DNA from *postmortem* tissue."

An expression of horror passed over Jacie's face. "Virchow... the father of pathology... *and autopsy...*"

"She's doing it herself." A crawling sensation spread over Hope's skin. Maddox had admitted in the hallway she had far more sinister plans for the algorithm's future. But Hope hadn't suspected she'd been *using autopsy tissue without permission* to obtain the DNA data to implement it. "She's collecting data to feed to the machine learner to adjust the algorithm. That's why she took Cecilia's body. To harvest her DNA."

Noah's eyes had become dark. "But not intending to improve treatments for all. Rather, to exclude those who'd be a cost to the system—"

Jacie finished the sentence. "To pre-emptively deny treatment to thousands... millions... to take away the choice before it was given... just like Izzie..."

Like what Hope used to think—using the algorithm for absolute decision-making was better than individual choice.

A choking sensation seized her. *She had behaved no better.*

She'd wanted control, but control is only an illusion. To deny choice and the capacity to hope doesn't give one any additional measure of control. But to allow it would mean to allow uncertainty. Imperfection.

Hope had never been brave enough to risk that. But what else had she denied herself? Her ability to love? To allow friendship? To let herself believe she didn't have to always be alone?

Now, she realized it was the one thing she *could* control. Her choices. Even if it meant opening herself up to grief and pain.

But choosing one meant accepting the other. No matter how much it might hurt. Was she strong enough to choose?

"Oh! I just remembered." Jacie dug in the pocket of her scrubs. "Here."

Hope stared at Jacie's outstretched hand, at what it held.

"I found it outside the lab." Jacie shrugged one shoulder. "I've noticed it's important to you."

Hope reached out and accepted the necklace.

Jacie's words returned to her from the night she'd told Hope about her sister. *It's funny—for someone named Hope, you sure don't know much about the concept.*

She'd been right. Hope clutched the recovered necklace in her fist. A tingling sensation spread from her fist to her arm to her chest. She couldn't give up. They could still stop Marah Maddox. They had to. *She* had to. Because to hope *is* to choose. Choice makes us human.

Hope fastened the chain back around her neck, then held herself still as the relief of its familiar presence sank in. It wasn't the existence of choice that had led to her mom's death. The existence of choice had allowed her mom to retain hope. Even when—

Even when Hope had given up. She could see that now.

Then, when she'd thought she might hope again—because of Izabella—she'd lost Cecilia. But Cecilia would never have wanted her death to cause Hope to give up.

If she gave up, she'd be no better than Maddox, who believed the system shouldn't allow *any* choice.

All the confrontations with Maddox replayed in Hope's mind. How she'd expounded on her insane ideas in the hallway. The spittle at the corner of her lips. The pleasure she'd evinced at holding her power over Hope in the O.R. The spittle that had sprayed Hope while she ranted.

The spittle...

Hope stared down. She was still wearing the same scrubs. The ones Maddox had sprayed with spittle.

Saliva.

She rushed to the door. "I have to go."

Jacie gave her a blank look. "Go? Where?"

"To the lab."

CHAPTER THIRTY-TWO

"Wait, at least let me go with you." Jacie dogged Hope's heels down the corridor.

But Izabella's voice floated out to them, stopping Jacie in her tracks. "Jacie?"

"I'm right here, Izzie!" Jacie stretched one arm back toward Izabella's room.

Hope shooed her back. "Stay with your sister. You've done enough. Already put yourself at enough risk."

Noah caught up to them. "Then I'll come."

Hope shook her head. "Stay here. Keep an eye on Izabella for me."

And Jacie, she didn't say out loud. Just in case Maddox had ideas about circling back for her.

Noah met her eyes and gave her a solemn nod.

Jacie held out her badge to Hope. "Take this, then. You'll need to get past the security checkpoint to the research wing."

"Thanks, Jacie." Hope twisted her mouth. She hadn't been sure before, but now that Jacie had told her of her secret backup plan, she had a pretty good idea her suspicion was correct. "Or, should I say... *Rachael.*"

Jacie opened and closed her mouth. "What—How? I mean, I'm not—"

"I saw your podcasting setup." Hope folded her arms. "That day at your house."

"It's not—"

Hope cut her off by pulling her into a brief hug.

Jacie stiffened. "Uh, what's happening here?"

Hope let her go just as abruptly.

Jacie was still sputtering when Hope plucked the badge from her startled hand and strode away.

Only a lone security guard staffed the checkpoint to the research wing at this hour. Unfortunately, it wasn't Kyle. That luck had used itself up.

Hope recognized the guard but didn't know her name. Perhaps mid-fifties, a middle-aged white woman who, from her fit physique, worked out regularly. A bead of sweat trailed between Hope's shoulder blades. She'd passed this security guard for years. She should have taken the time to learn her name.

Holding Jacie's badge up to the scanner, she shielded the picture from the guard's view with her hand. She took a step through, but the guard stopped her.

The light had remained red.

Hope's heart pounded in her ears. Maddox must have deactivated Jacie's access to the research wing. But if she couldn't pass the checkpoint, she couldn't get to the lab and carry out her plan.

She shoved the badge in her pocket before the guard asked to check it manually and tried talking her way through. "I think I spilled coffee on my badge earlier tonight. But you know me, of course. Everyone knows me here. Dr. Kestrel—I'm the High Resident?"

The guard narrowed her eyes. "Rules are rules. Sorry."

"But—"

"Perhaps I can help." A male voice came from behind her.

Hope uttered a soft curse. Of all the worst luck. *Again?*

She slowly turned and locked eyes with Leach. Her stomach plummeted. It was over. She finally understood what to do, and it would be too late.

What was he even doing here? His sudden appearance too convenient—like it had been outside the O.R. He must have only pretended to help and afterward gone and reported everything to Maddox. Now, he'd report her presence again, and Hope would never set foot in her lab. Her plan would never happen.

Maybe she should just go for it and bolt through the checkpoint. Then she spotted the taser on the security guard's belt and realized that would be a bad idea.

Hope's gaze returned to Leach.

The corners of his mouth twisted upward.

She braced herself to run for it, anyway. She had no other choice.

Leach reached for his badge. "Here. I'll vouch for Dr. Kestrel."

Wait, what?

Hope almost toppled over as her leg muscles let go of their tension.

It must be a trick. Maddox *must* have sent him.

Leach held his badge over the sensor in a confident stance.

Red. The light remained red.

Hope frowned.

Leach turned the badge over with a perplexed expression, then shrugged at the guard. "That's strange, Emmeline. What do you think?"

The guard—Emmeline, apparently—pressed her lips into a flat line.

He continued to address Emmeline and flashed his trademark smile. "Something's different. Don't tell me."

Hope's mouth parted in disbelief.

Emmeline raised her arm. Hope tensed. She was going for her taser. But no, she patted her hair. "It's a little darker. I wasn't sure at first, but I let my hairdresser talk me into it."

"The right decision." Leach's smile was so sincere even Hope believed it. "How's that grandson?"

Emmeline beamed. "Cuter every day."

Hope rubbed her brow, dumbfounded. Was *this* how he acted around Maddox?

"You look way too young to have a grandkid." Leach strolled through the checkpoint. "You have a fantastic night now."

Hope stared after him, then shifted her gaze to Emmeline's face.

Emmeline took out her tablet and waved Hope through, patting her hair and humming to herself.

Hope's feet shuffled a few steps. Her body wouldn't respond to her mind's command to *move*.

The guard cleared her throat.

Time snapped back to normal, and Hope chased after Leach. She called back over her shoulder, "Thanks... Emmeline!"

She caught up with Leach and came around his side.

He stopped and stared straight ahead, his face stony. The charm he'd brought out for Emmeline had vanished.

Hope wasn't buying it. "You happened to arrive exactly when I needed to get through security, is that it? Like you just happened upon us outside the O.R.?"

Leach pinched his lips together. "You know what? You've been through a lot—last night and... before. So I'm going to excuse your rude behavior." His voice dropped, and he held himself stiffly. "I'm sorry for your loss."

Hope's mouth fell open for a second time, with no words. Leach was *sorry*?

But it hadn't been Leach who'd betrayed their presence in the O.R. to Maddox—it had been Dalton. Leach had, in fact, helped them. Maybe he hadn't gone to Maddox at all.

Hope swallowed past the dryness in her throat.

"Okay, you're right. You didn't have to do that. Back there, and... the O.R." She couldn't believe what she was about to say. "Thank you."

Leach's nostrils flared. "I have a name."

Hope narrowed her eyes, not understanding.

He gave her a long, pained look before breaking eye contact to stare at the ceiling. "A first name."

When Hope said nothing, Leach made a noise of disgust, stepping away, but she stopped him with a hand on his arm. He wasn't her enemy, and she shouldn't treat him like one. It was this place that made them believe they were enemies. But she was done letting PRIMA tell her what to do. What to think, who to trust.

"Thank you... Caleb." She gave his arm a squeeze. "You're a good doctor, Cal."

His eyes betrayed a glint of something Hope thought might have been...
gratitude.

"Just put a stop to Maddox." He glanced away. "Because I can't."

"Can't?" Hope crossed her arms. "Or won't?"

The muscles in his neck corded. "At first, I believed. In her vision, in
everything she told me. That she was the only one who could watch out for
us. The residents. That her way was the only way to safeguard our futures in
healthcare."

Hope hesitated. "And then?"

A bitter expression came over his face. "Let's just say, now it is more a
matter of *can't* than won't."

Leach moved away, and she didn't stop him this time. The full
understanding of his words didn't dawn on her until he'd disappeared
around the corner.

Maddox controlled him. He must be on a Performance Improvement
Plan, too. Maddox had him on her leash, and if he wanted to keep his job,
he had to follow her bidding. Like what she'd tried to do to Dalton.

Hope *could* understand—the desire to remain at PRIMA, no matter the
cost. Before learning the truth, she would have done the same thing.

How many others had Maddox trapped? How many more would fall
victim? Doctors *and* patients...

Hope twisted her necklace, gripping the pendant tight. She couldn't let
Maddox use Cecilia's body to further her twisted scheme.

Not with so much at stake. Leach was right, she had to stop Maddox.
Failure wasn't an option.

Hope hurried in the opposite direction. To the lab.

CHAPTER THIRTY-THREE

TUESDAY 23 OCTOBER 2035
7:00 AM
Cecilia's lab, PRIMA

Five hours later, Hope had finished. She blinked around the lab as if only now realizing her location. She only had to hold it together for a little while longer. Only until she stopped Maddox, and then she'd allow herself to grieve. She promised herself she *would* mourn this time. This time would be different.

One last step. She retrieved the report from the DNA sequencer and sealed it in an envelope. There. Now, she just had to deliver it to Maddox.

She used Jacie's badge to let herself out an emergency exit in the stairwell to avoid going back through security. Thankfully, it worked, and no alarm sounded. But as soon as she stepped outside, another obstacle confronted her. The storm. She'd forgotten about the damn snow. The lab had no windows.

The sky had the beginnings of daylight, but the streets remained as vacant as 3:00 AM. Any other time, Hope might have marveled at the crystal-covered trees and icicle-coated buildings, but now, all this frozen water was nothing but another barrier keeping her from her destination.

She'd planned to use a ride service. But as she checked apps on her phone, they all had the same emergency alert—*drivers and vehicles out of service due to inclement weather.*

Hope shivered from more than the cold temperatures. Her need to stop Maddox went beyond Cecilia now. So much more beyond. If she didn't stop her, more and more clinics like Noah's would eagerly join PRIMA, putting more and more patients at risk.

Maddox clearly believed the layers of corruption she'd built to surround herself were impenetrable, and maybe they were. But *she* was only human—and she had underestimated Hope.

But first, Hope had to *get* to HEARTH. She scanned the empty street. With no cars out, she could walk up I-5 in under two hours. Would it be fast enough?

There was no other choice.

She shuffled toward Yesler Way, pulling her jacket tight across her body. But she'd taken only ten steps when her feet flew out from under her, landing her on her right hip.

As if that wasn't bad enough, she crumpled to the ground in pain when she attempted to stand. Stupid clogs. She'd turned her ankle. Panting, she flopped back. She couldn't walk several miles in the snow on a sprained ankle.

Hope crawled over to a signpost and used it to haul herself up, the frozen metal so cold it burned her gloveless fingers. She snatched her hand back, but not fast enough. A layer of skin pulled off her fingertips, adhering to the metal.

She blew onto her hands and then shoved them into her sleeves before bracing herself to try her ankle again. She took several rapid breaths, balancing her weight on her right leg, her hip protesting, before testing her left foot again.

Tendrils of fire snaked up from her ankle to her knee. She groaned, collapsing to the ground and yanking her left sock down to inspect her ankle, swearing at what she saw. Immediate tissue swelling, inability to bear weight—all signs of a severe sprain.

Hope sprawled onto her back, her breaths coming fast. The snow underneath her had melted enough to seep into her clothes, and the coldness took her breath away.

"Is this the best time to be making snow angels?"

Hope jerked up to a sitting position. She knew that voice.

The rumbling of an engine preceded a mirage appearing in the desert of snow—Jake's truck. Hope blinked. With Poppy in the driver's seat.

Poppy hung out the window and grinned. "Need a ride?"

Hope no longer felt the cold. She scrambled to get up, but her ankle gave way again.

Poppy's face fell, and she dashed out of the truck to Hope's side.

Hope waved her off. "We can't have *you* falling."

Poppy tugged at Hope's arm. "Together, then."

Hope put some of her weight on Poppy and found she could hobble. They crossed the short distance back to the truck with their arms around each other, a grin erupting on Hope's face despite the pain. "Where'd you come from?"

"I stayed the night in one of the call rooms because of the storm. Abbie helped me find one." Poppy assisted Hope into the passenger seat before going to the driver's side. A gust of wind blew her door shut a half-second after hopping in.

Hope buckled her seatbelt and turned sideways to prop her throbbing ankle up on the seat.

Poppy reached out a hand and placed it gently on Hope's knee. "Abbie told me about Cecilia. I'm so sorry."

Hope looked away. "There's no time. We need to go."

She couldn't indulge in emotion. Not until she stopped Maddox.

"Hey." Poppy's voice was soft but insistent. "You were there for me. Let me be here for you."

Hope hesitated, then placed a hand over Poppy's, intending to give it a quick squeeze so they could get going. But Poppy turned hers upward, gripping Hope's before she could pull it away. Hope panicked. She was too vulnerable, too exposed. But Poppy squeezed harder, not letting her hand go.

After a moment, Hope stopped fighting and let her hand go limp. Her shoulders slumped. She could trust Poppy—she knew that. But to trust someone else enough to show the imperfect person behind her defensive walls? The one Cecilia had seen and somehow loved, anyway?

She made a half-laugh, half-sob sound and wiped her eyes with her other hand. "This is nice and all, but you need to drive."

Poppy released her hand with one last squeeze and put the truck in gear. "Where to?"

Hope instructed Poppy to head for HEARTH, filling her in on the rest as she drove. All of Maddox's twisted plans.

The color drained from Poppy's cheeks.

Then, Hope told Poppy about *her* plan.

CHAPTER THIRTY-FOUR

TUESDAY 23 OCTOBER 2035

7:15 AM

HEARTH, Wallingford neighborhood, Seattle

Hope swiped Poppy's ID badge over the sensor pad at HEARTH's employee entrance. It seemed she was making a habit of collecting her friends' badges these days.

Poppy had been livid when Hope had informed her she'd be doing this alone. But she'd reminded Poppy of the NDA she'd signed and that she couldn't risk losing her job—not with the pregnancy and Jake still unemployed. Besides that, Hope needed to confront Maddox by herself, one on one. They had unfinished business.

Before departing, Poppy had used her scarf to wrap Hope's ankle. It was enough for Hope to bear partial weight on her left side.

The door buzzed open, and she limped inside and through the lobby, where the reception desk stood empty, evidence of the early hour or the storm delaying the staff.

The formaldehyde odor alerted her when she reached the basement if there was any doubt of the morgue's location. But another faint scent reached her nostrils, too, layered underneath. *Power, with a capital P.* There was no doubt. Maddox was here.

The double doors leading into the morgue reminded Hope of the doors to the O.R., another pair of silent sentinels to pass. The old fear crept in, immobilizing her, and her limbs wouldn't obey. She couldn't face Maddox here—not the morgue, the scene of her childhood nightmares.

An unwanted image of Cecilia's body laid out on an autopsy table flashed through her mind. What if she was too late? She remembered what Noah had said. *Marah Maddox has always had a way of remaining one step ahead of everyone else.* Maybe this all was hopeless.

But Maddox had *abducted* Cecilia's body. The thought rang in Hope's mind, chasing away the doubts. Death had taken Cecilia from her, but that didn't mean Maddox had the right to play God.

Hope took a painful step through the doors, squinting at the fluorescent light gleaming off the stainless-steel surfaces. Then she saw it. A body on the table. Covered in a white sheet.

She froze.

But Cecilia's voice didn't come to her.

Of course it didn't. This wasn't Cecilia, but only an empty shell. Cecilia was gone. Forever. Hope had to suppress the sudden desire to run away and never stop running.

A grating screech of metal on metal emitted from the far wall, and Hope tore her gaze from the white sheet. There, Maddox swiveled on an industrial stool, a tray of instruments at her elbow.

"How many times must I kick you out?" Maddox's tone patronizing, as if Hope's presence hardly worth acknowledging. As if she hadn't *stolen Cecilia's body* for unauthorized autopsy and DNA harvesting.

Hope clasped her hands across her body to steady herself, regaining control. She wasn't eleven years old anymore. That day was in the past, where it would stay.

A cold fury flowed through her and annihilated any more thoughts of running.

Hope hobbled toward Maddox, ignoring the pain in her ankle, her gaze averted from Cecilia's body. She had a plan—she only needed to stick to it. She *did* have the strength to succeed, and she wouldn't forget again. "I'm not letting you do this. Not to Cecilia's body. Or to *anyone* else."

Maddox's voice was laced with exasperation. "But how will you stop me? We won the merger vote, and you gave up your so-called *evidence*. Or don't you remember? Besides, do you think the public really wants to know about the five percent error in the algorithm? To twist themselves in knots, trying in retrospect to determine who were the five percent over the past five years? An impossible equation to solve."

Heat flushed through Hope's body. "But it's the *chance*, don't you see? The *chance* that PRIMA was wrong. That's what you took away from all those people. No matter how small it might have appeared to you."

The chance, no matter how small. Understanding flooded her veins. *I get it now, Mom. It's what you thought you had to do... for me.*

Hope had never understood before. She'd always thought it unfair the doctors had offered treatments to her mom that, in retrospect, had been futile.

Noah's words. *It's not our job to choose for them.*

Even though the chance might have been slight, her mom had wanted to take it. It had been *her* choice.

It wasn't false hope. Because there's no such thing. *Hope* exists inside us, and it doesn't depend on outside factors.

A revelation flooded her. *If it doesn't depend on outside factors, no one else can take it away.*

Like Cecilia had said, it was time to let go. To move forward—to not let the past paralyze her.

Time to stop being a False Hope.

Maddox pinched her brow. *"I* am not the villain here. I don't know why you're making me out to be. I only deal in facts and reality."

"But you're trying to deal in the future." Hope shifted her weight away from her left side and took a hitching step closer. "The funny thing is, I get it. I get you. Because I used to think like you. That people shouldn't be given a choice, that the *choice* led to suffering. That *we* knew better, and PRIMA made us better. To replace the previous generation of doctors who allowed for too many uncertainties. But there was only one problem. You built the system on *lies.*"

Maddox rose from the stool. "You and me, we don't get to the top by following rules. *Their* rules. We have to make our own. We *are* better. You can still succeed, Hope. Work with me. I can help you—I see your potential. You can have your position as High Resident back. We can do great things together. You only have to let those few percentage points go."

Hope recoiled as if the words had physically slapped her.

Sean Medrano, Poppy, Izabella, Cecilia, her mom...

She drew herself up and glared at Maddox. "They're *people*—not percentage points."

Maddox responded with a cruel laugh. "Where are all your people now? Looks to me you're here all alone."

"I'm here by myself. That's not the same as being alone." Hope wouldn't let Maddox's words distract her from her purpose. "I'll never go back to working for you."

"You have to admit, we'd be a formidable team. You're not the witless little idealist you pretend to be, are you?" Maddox flashed one of her chilling smiles. "You only need a better mentor. Cecilia's influence did you no good. I'll offer you one more chance—join me, return to PRIMA, where you belong."

"Why?"

Maddox dropped her voice, but her eyes remained fixed on Hope's. "We'll use the algorithm to reform the healthcare system. No more ineffective treatments. You know I'm right. It's inevitable. *Be a part of it.* Or be left behind."

Hope locked eyes with her. For the briefest moment, she saw a vision of herself giving in to join Maddox, rising to heights of power, surpassing even what Maddox must dream of. She saw what might be.

But she had never wanted power. She only wanted justice. To help people, to prevent them from suffering as her mom had.

Hope closed her eyes and took the envelope out of her pocket. The envelope that contained the lab data she'd generated. For a second, she almost hesitated. Inside this envelope, she had the power to change things. But at what cost?

She turned it over in her hands, opening her eyes to raise them to Maddox's. "Say you're a fifty-five-year-old woman. A tiny number of your cells are harboring a mutation. A time bomb. In ten years, those cells will grow into a tumor. PRIMA will identify you a decade before you ever get sick."

Maddox's face went a shade paler.

"Only wait a minute. You're not a fifty-five-year-old woman. Those ten years have already elapsed. You're a sixty-five-year-old woman."

Maddox's eyes bored into hers. "What are you saying?"

Hope met her stare. She almost felt sorry for her. Almost. "Only the mutation's not a responsive one. I guess we can weed you out of the healthcare system. Saving resources all around."

Maddox snatched the envelope. "This is *my* predictive genetic report? You're bluffing. This phase isn't even available yet. You don't have what it takes to do this." A shadow of doubt passed across her eyes. "How did you get this?"

Hope lifted her chin. Emotions warred within her body. Anger flared, and with it, unleashed the grief. She sought the numbness, but it had retreated. She gave in and held fast to the rage.

Then she remembered what her mom had said about the mama duck. *I think she's very sad. But I think she knows she needs to be strong.*

All this time, she'd been playing the wrong game. Not any more.

Hope fixed Maddox in an unblinking gaze, her voice as steady as her hand wielding a scalpel. "Did you think, as the High Resident, I wouldn't know what happens in my hospital the moment it happens?"

Maddox's knuckles turned white as she gripped the envelope. "Is this a goddamn joke?"

Hope's stance remained unmoving. "This is your report."

Maddox sniffed in disdain. "I never gave a fucking blood sample."

Hope spoke the word deliberately. "Saliva."

Maddox went still.

The pain in Hope's ankle faded to a distant part of her mind. "I'm sure you're familiar with my award-winning research on extracting DNA from trace amounts of bodily fluids. It's why PRIMA first recruited me, after all. It seems quite a bit of your saliva ended up on the front of my scrubs in the O.R.—I didn't even need as much as you were so generous to provide."

Maddox gave a snort of dismissive laughter. "Even if you collected some of my *spit*, that doesn't mean this report is real."

Hope had thought she would enjoy seeing Maddox on the defensive, but she'd been wrong. No joy existed in this moment. No matter how horrible a person or what had made her this way, the algorithm had handed Maddox a death sentence. One Hope had delivered. And if that didn't affect her, she was no different from Maddox.

So instead of trying to shut the emotions out, she accepted them. She allowed the empathy—even for someone like Marah Maddox. Because Maddox had been wrong—having empathy didn't make her weaker. It made her stronger. She spoke in a soft voice. "It's not a fake. The report belongs to you. It's your DNA data. From your saliva."

"Blackmail? That's beneath you, Dr. Kestrel." Maddox drummed her fingers on the tray. Her gaze probed Hope's. "If it's real, why hide it in an envelope?"

"Because I'm giving you a *choice*. To open it, or not." Even Marah Maddox deserved a choice, and giving it to her was what separated Hope from Marah. "More than you gave all the others."

Hope took in the PRIMA logo covering the wall behind Maddox's head—the snake wrapped around the staff. She cocked her head. "Do you know the story of the rod of Asclepius? Zeus killed Asclepius after he went one step too far as a physician—raising patients from the dead. Zeus couldn't have anyone appearing more powerful than himself."

She allowed her gaze to wander back to the shape under the white sheet on the table. Cecilia's body. *Maddox will not touch her.* Hope couldn't remember now why she had ever been afraid. "Some people confuse the rod with the caduceus, the staff of Hermes—the trickster. You see, Zeus and the other Olympian gods used Hermes to do their dirty work."

The corners of Maddox's mouth drew in. "What are you babbling on about? Why are you telling me this?"

"Because I've been wondering which one is more like you. At first, I thought Hermes. Perhaps it hadn't been all your fault, and the Corporation had been using you to do their dirty work." Hope stood straight, her shoulders back. "But you're not Hermes. You're Zeus—the one who can't stand to allow others to come close to the same level of power."

Maybe Hope couldn't take down Olympus. No mere mortal could. But if she took down Zeus, maybe, just maybe, the resulting chaos would be enough.

For the mortals to win.

She couldn't control Maddox's actions, but she didn't need to. She was certain Maddox would open the envelope. Zeus, after all, wouldn't be able to ignore any potential threat.

Hope allowed her gaze to linger on Cecilia's body one last time. She didn't need to peer under the sheet to know she was gone, nor see her body to know she would hear Cecilia's voice forever in her heart.

"It's time for you to leave." Hope had to force the words past the ache in her throat, but her voice held steady. It wouldn't break. "I'm going to call the funeral home orderlies. If I find out you touched one cell of her body, *one cell*, the entire Board of Directors will receive a copy of your DNA report. You won't be able to get care anywhere." The exact thing they'd done to Izabella. Maddox's DNA report would precede her everywhere. "But if you go now, you'll take the only copy. You have my word."

Maddox's fist clenched, crumpling the envelope. Then, without another word, she whirled away and stalked out of the morgue.

The heavy steel doors shut behind her, leaving Hope in thunderous silence. She limped to the autopsy table and whispered. "I did it. We did it."

But the tears wouldn't come. She sank onto a stool, then stayed with Cecilia's body until the orderlies came.

Afterward, she headed to the stairwell. With each halting step she took, she expected to become lighter and lighter. After all, she'd won. She'd stopped Maddox.

Instead, it was as if the layers of a burden she hadn't even known she carried condensed to become heavier and heavier.

Maybe being a doctor meant never shedding that burden, but accepting it, even when it was too heavy to bear. Embracing the understanding it would never get easier because it wasn't supposed to. She was human.

CHAPTER THIRTY-FIVE

TUESDAY 06 NOVEMBER 2035
5:45 PM
Ocean Shores, Washington

Two weeks after Maddox had disappeared, Hope stood with her bare feet in the water. The waves crested in their endless cycles, the astonishing cold of the ocean an anesthetic to her healing ankle. It was all insignificant next to this, a power as beautiful as it could be terrible.

Her mind imagined what would happen if the wave didn't crest and break but kept coming. Would she try to outrun it? Or would she stay and face it, knowing there'd be no escape?

After the storm two weeks ago, an unusually mild weather spell had followed, drawing atypical crowds for the season to the Washington Coast. The scattered families dotting the beach fascinated Hope, the parents letting their small children play near the waves. Something with such latent power, the unthinkable possibilities that could manifest. A dark part of her mind wondered if people would obey the instructions to walk to high ground. Or would they all rush to their cars, panic taking over, clogging the narrow roadways, and dooming all?

The fog rolled in, and the surrounding people became fewer and fewer. She found a hollow in the sand nestled beside a piece of dry driftwood, providing partial shelter from the wind, and she curled herself into it. The air carried the smell of fish and crab.

Only then did she open her bag and pull out the letter. It was time.

Hope stared at the words on the outside of the folded piece of paper. *For Hope. To be opened on the occasion of your thirtieth birthday.*

When her mom found out she was dying, she wrote a series of letters to Hope. One for each birthday until age eighteen, one for twenty-one, and then twenty-five, which Hope had believed to be the last letter. Nine letters.

Hope had read each letter a single time and then buried them away. They were all contained in the bottom dresser drawer in her bedroom. What good would re-reading them do? It would only dredge up things she didn't want. Things she wanted to put behind her.

That's why, when Cecilia had delivered this one, she'd decided not to open it. An unexpected tenth letter her dad must have held onto and mailed for her upcoming birthday. It felt like Cecilia had given it to her years ago rather than weeks.

She blinked furiously. She shouldn't have taken Cecilia for granted. She should have known how abruptly everything could change. So now, she should read the letter—in case she never got another chance. She took a deep breath and unfolded the single hand-written page.

Dearest Hope,

When you read this, you will be old enough to understand. As I write this, I know the treatments aren't working, and my time is short. But I would rather have had the shortened life I was given than lived into old age if it meant having you. And even if the treatments give me only one more day with you, that's a choice I make each day out of love and not fear.

Remember, the truth in your heart will never fail you.

I love you.

Mom

Hope clutched the letter to her chest. Her breaths came easier. At some point, she noticed the sun setting. The fog hid the golden orb's final descent, but the orange and purple streaks that filled the sky were even more brilliant for it. She tugged her sweater closer around herself. The sky gradually darkened, and the tide came in. It would be so easy to stay here. To never go back.

Who was she to think she could reverse an ocean? Power was no different in any other form. It swept over those who got in its way.

And yet...

There was Izabella.

Poppy and her unborn baby.

They were alive, weren't they? Hope had done that, hadn't she?

She recalled Dalton's words. *No system has the capacity to be perfect.* Had she truly believed PRIMA could be?

A seagull swooped down to land on the flat expanse before her, and a smaller bird alit beside it. Hope squinted, and her body rose from the sand. The bill, the markings, the wings—*it couldn't be*. Her body tingled all over. A Pacific Swallow.

The bird didn't appear to know it didn't belong this far north. It hopped closer and cocked its head, staring right at her. She held her breath, and something indescribable passed through her. She sank back to her knees.

Mom?

The bird bobbed its head before taking to the air, soaring into the dying light. Hope's eyes tracked it until it vanished from sight.

In the remaining space, a lone figure approached. The silhouette came closer until it became recognizable. She clambered back to her feet, brushing the sand from her legs.

A gray wool beanie pulled down low over his ears, his clean-shaven face accentuating the sharp angles of his jaw—Dalton.

He came to stand beside her, facing the waves. She stiffened. He spoke first. "You gave up on doctoring, is that it?"

Like he had the right to ask her anything. Hope planted her feet wide in the sand, refusing to look at him. "What are you doing here? How'd you find me?"

"You told me. Remember?" Dalton picked up a shell and tossed it into the waves, waiting for it to disappear before speaking again. "Maddox is gone, disappeared without a trace. But you know that. What'd you say to her?"

The next wave crashed at their feet, the mist from the cold spray reaching Hope's face. She didn't owe Dalton anything. "I gave her a choice."

Hope sensed him scrutinizing her, and several more cycles of waves crashed to the shore before he spoke again. "I see."

"Do you?" She whirled to face him.

Dalton held his hands out to his sides. "It's not like you think—"

A bitter laugh escaped Hope's lips. "Isn't it, though?"

"It's not black and white." The expression around Dalton's eyes tightened. "Haven't you figured that out yet?"

Despite the cold spray, heat rose in her face and chest. Who did he think he was? Coming here. It had seemed pretty clear to her in the O.R. that all he'd wanted was his job back. "I've figured out enough."

Hope counted seven waves before Dalton spoke again, his voice strained. "The Board asked me to step in."

What did he want her to say? She knew, of course. She'd seen it on her newsfeed—PRIMA had hired him as the new interim Director. After the *mysterious resignation* of Dr. Marah Maddox.

She shifted her weight to the right. Her left ankle still throbbed a little, like something else that pestered her. Something about the sequence of events she still didn't understand. She didn't want to ask him—or talk to him at all—but she couldn't let it go. "The dates and initials you gave me on the coffee cup. One set was your personnel file, where you knew I'd find the record of the performance improvement plan. But the second set... how'd you know about Maddox's email to Cecilia?"

Dalton gave a short laugh. "Maddox told me about it herself when she made me sign the NDA. Couldn't resist bragging about everything she'd done, as if she thought it would help convince me. I figured Cecilia would've saved a copy, that she must have been as trapped as I was. That day you contacted me, it felt like fate." He fell silent and bent to select a smooth stone. He rose, turning it in his hand. "It isn't like you, Hope, to walk away. To take the easy way out."

"Is that what you think I'm doing?" Hope clenched and unclenched her hands. "And you took the hard way, is that it? Staying to... what? Pretend you're building a better system? What about what you did last year? Leaving and signing that NDA?"

Dalton hurled the stone beyond the breaking waves, his shoulders set in tension. "There are things you still don't understand."

Hope flashed a stiff smile. "Please, enlighten me."

"Now that Maddox is gone, I can tell you the whole story. I *want* to tell you. Everything." Dalton swiveled to face her fully. "Last year, the choice she gave me... if I had chosen to stay, they would have pinned the error on someone else."

Hope stared into his piercing eyes, seeing the truth in them. She gasped. "Me."

"When you came to me, I had to get back into the system the only way I knew how. By making Maddox believe I would finally throw you under the bus for the sake of my own career."

"But... you made me believe it, too." Hope hated how small her voice sounded.

He reached forward and took her hands. "I know, and I'm sorry."

Hope jerked them away. "So that makes it all okay? Because you're *sorry*?"

"No, Hope, that's not what I—" Dalton broke off with a groan, grabbing her hands again. "There wasn't another way to save the girl. I knew from the moment you called me."

The warmth of his hands enclosed hers. She didn't know what to say. He'd done it all to protect her? To protect her and help Izabella?

Dalton's gaze bored into hers. "We're making things right. Cecilia's fix for the algorithm worked. It turns out the computer virus Jacie tried to deploy is what prevented it from activating correctly at first. Jacie's been able to recreate Cecilia's work."

Hope became hyperaware of her hands in his, and he squeezed harder, as if he knew what she was thinking. She swallowed. "And Izabella?"

She hadn't heard from Jacie and had been afraid to contact her. Fearful of what Jacie must think of her for leaving.

Dalton gave her a gentle smile. "The surgery was successful. Only time will tell, of course. But for now, she's okay, back home with her family, recovering."

Hope nodded, not trusting herself to speak.

He released her hands and picked up another stone. "PRIMA isn't going away, but we can make it more transparent. Because if people like us *don't* stay, it won't be long before another Marah Maddox comes along."

Hope balled her hands into fists at her sides, recalling her words to Maddox. *They're people, not percentage points.*

Dalton flung the stone, then reached an arm toward her, palm up, and their eyes met and held. "Come back. Help me. We can do it together."

Her heart rate sped up. But something inside her made her swat his arm aside. Anger flared in her chest. "You—it's not that simple! You don't get to ask me that!"

Dalton didn't defend himself, his voice tinged with sorrow. "I'm so sorry about all you went through. About Cecilia."

"You don't get to say that either!" She was yelling now. "You let me think you—"

Hope bit off the words. *Betrayed me.* A painful tightness squeezed her throat. She wouldn't let him know how much he'd hurt her. Even if it had been to protect her, finding out didn't erase the confusion. It wasn't that easy to decide she could trust him, even if she wanted to. Now he wanted her to come back? To work with him? Or something more?

The sun had dropped below the horizon, and they were the only ones remaining on this stretch of beach.

She bit down on her bottom lip. "How do you know you won't become her? Maddox?"

Dalton raised his eyebrows and offered her a questioning gaze. "You'll have to come back. To make sure I don't."

Hope dropped her eyes and dug her toes in the sand to stop herself from stepping closer to him. "It shouldn't ever be up to one person."

Could she go back? Now that Maddox was gone? She wasn't ready to answer that, nor so naïve to think PRIMA would have simply dissolved without its leader. But could she count on Dalton to hold PRIMA to a more ethical course? Even with the pressures to turn healthcare into profit? Did she even want to be a part of healthcare anymore? But what else would she do? It was all she'd wanted since age eleven—since she'd seen her mom die.

Would she let Maddox take from her the deathbed promise she'd made to her mom, too?

The smoke from a bonfire up the beach hit her nostrils, and the scent triggered a flood of childhood memories. With them, the last memories of her mom arose from their submerged depths. This time, she allowed them. And this time, instead of seeing it through her eleven-year-old eyes, she saw the scene from afar.

Her mom's body.

Her father on his knees, his elbows on the bed, head folded down in grief next to hers.

Hope's brain then flashed to herself as she'd been beside Cecilia at the end.

Flash. Back to her mom's hospital room. The doctors and nurses exchanging glances of sorrow, their faces decimated by grief.

Hope saw herself as she was then—a child, scared and lost, trembling at the doorway.

Come, she whispered to that child. *This is not all that it was.*

She folded her child self in an embrace. *Remember...*

Gripping the pendant on the chain around her neck, she lifted her eyes to the darkened sky, allowing herself to experience the memory of how her mom used to smile at her. It hurt still, and a part of it always would, but something else existed there now, too. A sliver of comfort in the memories. They didn't have to be only about pain.

Hope had thought she needed to fix the system to make her mom's death have meaning. But doing so wouldn't bring her mom back. Nothing would. It was time to let her mom go.

Cecilia's loss, too, remained an open wound. But instead of burying her grief in a deep hole and covering it up, as she'd done for so many years after her mom's death, Hope had forced herself to grieve her. To *feel*, to remember. No matter how much it hurt. It was the least she owed her. And bit by bit, the open wound was healing. For now, only around the edges, but enough to make her see that one day, she would recover.

But not without a scar.

It wasn't disloyal or a betrayal. It was part of being human. What Cecilia would have wanted for her.

A wave surged past her knees and brought her back to the moment. The current tugged at her lower legs when it receded, but she kept them firmly entrenched in the sand. She faced Dalton and said the words she'd been afraid to speak. "How do I know *I* won't become her?"

Because if power reveals our true selves, how could she be sure she didn't have an inner Marah Maddox inside of her?

Dalton took her hand once more. "If the people who can run things the right way all walk away, aren't they equally to blame?"

Hope shook her head and stepped back, her hand slipping away from his. "As long as the system allows for unequal distribution of power, others will manipulate it. In the wrong ways."

Why could some people harness power in a way that carried everyone else along? Even when the ones being borne along *knew* it was wrong? Could Marah Maddox truly be single-handedly responsible for everything PRIMA had done? What about all the others who hadn't stopped her?

Dalton was right. Things weren't as black and white as she'd wanted to believe. Her mom *had* understood her choices. She hadn't been a passive victim. Hope had wanted to blame her mom's doctors, but she recognized now how misplaced that blame had been. Her mom's doctors had given her mom choices, and her mom had made them. Even if it might not be what Hope would have chosen for her.

And how could she know? What it had been like, faced with the choice of chemotherapy. A young mother, only a few years older than Hope's age now.

All Hope had to be responsible for was herself.

But was that truly the extent of her responsibility?

Maddox had twisted her purpose for her own ugly goals, but that didn't mean Hope had to let her destroy it.

There was no question what her mom would want her to do. And Cecilia. They would want her to go back and fight. Fight to make things better, even if they would never be perfect. But what did *she* want? Dalton was right—algorithms weren't going away, and PRIMA would continue. If it didn't, another would take its place. Maybe she *could* make a difference, only not in the way she had always thought.

Dalton broke the silence. "I hired Noah."

Hope snorted, a laugh escaping despite herself. "To do what?"

"Head up our new AI ethics oversight committee."

She couldn't help the slow smile that formed on her lips. "Maybe there *is* hope for you."

Dalton shrugged. "I left him debating with *Osler.*"

The laugh built into something more, and Dalton joined her. Then he sobered. "There's something else I need to show you."

He brought out his phone, opened a video, and pressed play.

Hope took the phone from him with a trembling hand. On the screen appeared Maddox—*and her*. The video Jacie had taken.

"So we could treat those people before they ever manifest full-blown cancer?"

"In some cases, yes. For those who have a responsive mutation."

"And for the others?"

"We can weed them out from the healthcare system. Saving resources all around."

The video ended, and Hope handed the phone back to him. "I don't understand. I thought they confiscated Jacie's phone."

Dalton shook his head and grinned. "They took her sister's. She'd grabbed the wrong one earlier that night and didn't notice until the next day. By then, Maddox had gone. Jacie didn't know what to do with it, so she waited. She only showed it to me yesterday."

He tapped the screen. A second later, Hope's phone chimed with an incoming message. "There, I've sent it to you." He turned his screen so she could see. "Now, I'm deleting my copy. Jacie already deleted hers."

Hope gaped at him. "What? Why?"

"It's what Jacie and I decided together. You should be the one to choose." He pocketed his phone.

"Jacie stayed?" Hope had thought she might have quit internship after achieving her sister's care.

The corners of Dalton's mouth twitched. "She stayed."

Hope stared at her phone. She didn't want this responsibility. She shifted her gaze to the darkening horizon, and the waves broke on the shore in their endless cycle. Some things would always carry on.

The tide was coming in, and the next wave surged higher than the rest. Dalton hurried backward, but Hope didn't shy away. The wave crested above her waist. The cold spread through her, cleansing her. Patients had died at PRIMA, but it hadn't been her fault. She had to accept it had been out of her control.

Maybe, in the end, what mattered most was what action we each chose when faced with a power greater than ourselves. A doctor's role wasn't to stop death, or pick and choose only those one could save. Some will always die of illness despite all doctors do. Such is the human condition.

But the choosing, to be a doctor anyway—perhaps even more so because of it, the knowing of it—that's why she would go back.

But on her terms.

Her mom had been right. The truth in her heart wouldn't fail her. It had just taken her some time to find it.

Dalton's words from the park came back to her. *When you figure out the answer to that question, let me know.*

Hope headed toward the dry sand. As she passed Dalton, she said, "I know what I have to do."

•   •   •

Podcasts / Algorithm Anarchist Podcast / Upsets, Transparency, and Truth

Rachael: Hi everyone, I'm Rachael, and this is *Algorithm Anarchist*. Where we remember, the most dangerous lies are those that use the truth to sell themselves.

[music]

Not to worry, people, I didn't abandon you. I had to go dark for a while, yeah. But I'm still here.

You've been clamoring to know my take on the sudden change in leadership at PRIMA? Well, strap in and try to keep up.

Yes, the merger happened. PRIMA subsumed the large multispecialty group formerly known as Seattle Healthcare Associates. This means PRIMA now controls most of our regional healthcare market. But who exactly controls *PRIMA* now?

Not Marah Maddox. The one-woman powerhouse of PRIMA for the past decade has disappeared. Do I know where she went? And more importantly, why she vanished?

Those are the questions you all are *asking*. But they're not the questions that matter. The ones you *should* be asking.

Such as, if algorithms are here to stay, how do we ensure healthcare justice?

Let's review some recent history about pivotal changes in healthcare in the U.S.:

In the 1990s: the rise of the HMO.

In the 2000s: the healthcare MBAs started their climb to power, replacing MDs in hospital administration, effectively rendering physicians voiceless.

In the 2010s: the insurance companies dominated by implementing their mandatory "prior authorizations."

In the late 2020s: the algorithms.

It's not enough to move forward. It's not *possible* to move forward without reconciling with the past. The past isn't something to be buried. No matter how painful. Someone recently taught me that.

The world deserves the truth.

All of you, listeners. You deserve more.

So demand more. Transparency. Truth.

Hope only dies if we choose to let it.

Make your choice. I've made mine...

EPILOGUE

In the sufferer let me see only the human being.
—The prayer of Maimonides

Nine Months Later
MONDAY 04 AUGUST 2036
08:30 AM
HEARTH, Wallingford neighborhood, Seattle

The patient had an estimated prognosis of four to seven days and had explicitly asked for admission to Seattle's HEARTH. Would Hope be comfortable accepting her? As the director of HEARTH, she had the final decision-making power. She'd studied the e-chart in silence and then said yes.

Now, she couldn't put it off any longer. She finished checking her social notifications. Brayden's parents had posted a pic of him at a Mariner's game, new hair clearly visible. Jacie's latest posts were a mix of her bemoaning the second-year residency workload while celebrating Izabella's ongoing remission.

Hope allowed herself an inner smile, then closed her tablet and pushed back from her desk. "Come on, Gaia. Time to work."

The German shepherd sprang up from the corner at the sound of her voice.

Hope had contacted Kyle and taken one puppy, after all. They'd already named her, and Hope had kept it. Gaia—the ancestral mother of all life—now had a doggie bed in Hope's apartment *and* office, having passed her certification as a hospice therapy animal.

The dog padded over, yawning, and Hope scratched behind Gaia's ears. The details of the patient's chart replayed in her mind, and she blew out a long exhale. "On second thought, this visit might not be a good one for you."

She settled Gaia back on her cushion with a treat and headed to the patient's room alone, the rain pattering on the hallway windows the only accompaniment to her footsteps. The gray sky afforded a glimpse of her reflection in the glass, and she ran a hand over her head. She still wasn't used to her lighter hair color after so many years of dyeing it. Somehow, losing the dye had made her feel lighter inside, too.

Hope approached the closed door and raised her hand, but the door swung open before her knuckles could deliver the soft knock she had planned. She took a step back to allow the passage of the person exiting.

Noah didn't speak but nodded at Hope with a somber gaze. His eyes held a faraway expression, sorrowful yet somehow at peace.

She waited a long moment, watching him disappear down the hall, before clearing her throat and entering the room.

The emaciated woman lay on her side, half-hidden under the stark white bedsheets, her back to Hope. A few wisps of white hair clung to her mostly bald head.

The patient's chart had informed Hope she'd traveled Europe seeking different experimental treatments for months before returning to admit herself to hospice care. Hope wouldn't have recognized her without the name attached to the records.

Hope cleared her throat a second time. "Hello, Dr. Maddox."

The woman raised her head to look at Hope over her shoulder. "For fuck's sake, call me Marah."

Hope fought against a desire to walk back out. Why had Maddox asked for her? Why had she come here? She could have gone to any hospice facility.

Marah attempted to sit up and fell back with a grimace.

Hope approached to help prop her up, adjusting the surrounding pillows.

Marah fluttered her hands toward the bedside chair, waving away Hope's ministrations. "Have a goddamn seat already."

Hope grit her teeth and slowly lowered herself into the chair. The rasping sounds of Marah's breaths gradually became steadier.

Marah bared her teeth in a macabre smile. Her skin pulled so tight from the weight loss of the cancer, she resembled a grinning skull. "How's the baby?"

"What?" Hope startled, then realized Marah must mean Poppy's daughter. The daughter who'd been born no thanks to this woman in front of her.

This dying woman in front of her.

Hope unclenched her jaw and reminded herself of her responsibilities as the hospice director. She took in Marah's skeletal-thin form, and the heat in her head faded. Whatever Marah said to her wouldn't change the fact that Hope would go home afterward, and Marah would not. Ever again. Hope would do her duty as a physician, no matter who the patient. She could detach her emotions and do her job.

She replied in an even voice, "The baby's beautiful. Healthy. Three weeks old." She hesitated before adding, "They named her Hope, if you can believe that."

Marah cackled, and it morphed into another coughing spell. Hope offered water, but Marah waved it off. Exhaustion saturated her face. "Children always seemed like too much trouble to me."

Hope studied her. "And now? Do you regret it?"

A pained look crossed Marah's face. "Hardly. This way, I'm not leaving anyone behind."

The empty room drew Hope's glance. No flowers. No cards. And no drawings from grandchildren. She knew from the staff there'd been no visitors.

Except for the one she'd just seen leaving—Noah.

Hope's eyes returned to Marah's face, and she realized Marah had been tracking her gaze around the bare room.

Marah arched a sparse eyebrow. "What the hell happened around here? You, the goddamn hospice director?"

The heat returned to Hope's cheeks and spread to the back of her neck, but she didn't rise to Marah's baiting.

Marah gave off a low chuckle laced with her former arrogance. "His betrayal cut too deep, didn't it? You should ask him the full story."

"How do you know he didn't already tell me?" Hope would not let Marah provoke her. Besides, her and Dalton's relationship was none of Marah's business. Hope was still figuring it out herself, and they were taking it slow.

A flash of the old predator gleam lit up Marah's eyes. "I wasn't sure you'd agree to admit me."

Hope uncrossed and crossed her legs to regain her composure. What kind of sick game was Marah playing? Hope didn't know if she could remain objective. Marah may now be a hospice patient, but that didn't mean Hope could forget everything she'd done. She spoke in a low voice. "Why? Why did you want to come here? For one more chance to torment me?"

Marah's eyes were feverish, over-bright, and she stared so long Hope worried she might be on the cusp of a partial seizure.

"You taught me something—" Marah's body doubled over in another coughing fit. She closed her eyes, her breath coming in short pants until she regained enough air to speak again. "Sometimes... a five percent chance is worth... taking. Worth more than... everything else in this whole... goddamn world—"

Another spasm cut off her words and racked her body.

Hope had the morphine ready.

The drug did its job. Marah's body quieted.

Marah opened her eyes and stared at the ceiling. Her voice dropped. "It's more than I deserve, you must think."

Hope leaned forward and tucked the bedding in around Marah with brisk movements. "You deserve not to suffer, the same as anyone else."

Because no one should die alone—not even Marah Maddox.

Hope kept her tone professional. "Is there someone... anyone you'd like us to call?"

Marah's left arm snaked out, her fingers clasping Hope's right wrist.

"There was somebody... once." Her eyes drifted past Hope toward the closed door. "But that was a fucking long time ago."

Hope suppressed the urge to wrench her arm away from Marah's icy grasp. She spoke in a quiet voice. "You never thought you were doing anything wrong, did you?"

Marah sighed and released Hope's arm. "I did what had to be done."

She slid her hands under the sheets, but not fast enough to hide their trembling.

A part of Hope wanted to hold on to her disgust at Marah's actions, but somehow, she couldn't. "And now?"

Marah sighed and stared up at the ceiling. "All I have to do is look in the goddamn mirror to know the algorithm was right. It predicted I would die, and here I am, dying. Just like Cecilia."

Hope dug her nails into her palms. Marah had no right to say her name.

Marah's voice cracked and became a whisper. "What do I do now? What do I goddamn do?"

Hope studied Marah with a clinical gaze. Sunken cheeks, sallow skin, patchy scalp. But her eyes... Marah's eyes had not given in yet—they emitted a fragile light from deep within, dim but not gone.

An abrupt clarity hit Hope, why fate had brought them back together. Why it had to be her at Marah's deathbed.

She didn't think about whether Marah deserved it. The words simply came. She didn't know who they amazed more—Marah or herself.

"I forgive you, Marah."

Forgiveness was a gift, and might or might not be earned. In the giving of it, Hope let her burden go. She could forgive, even though she would never forget.

Marah shifted her eyes, but not before Hope saw in them a confirmation. It *was* what Marah had come for.

A startling realization came after. If she could forgive Marah Maddox, she could forgive *herself*.

Why hadn't she already?

The answer arose within her with a bodily force that took her breath away. Because for too long, it had been easier to hold on to the anger.

Hope had thought she'd let it go and finally allowed herself to process the grief over her mom's death, but she'd only gone halfway. She'd shied away from finishing the inner journey.

The memory of her last conversation with Cecilia played in her mind. *It was no one's fault... Some questions have no answers. That's part of being human.*

That day on the beach, when Dalton had found her, she'd *remembered*. Her younger self. Who she'd been—before. And for a moment, she'd embraced that part of herself—but later, she'd pushed her away again. Because she'd thought to be strong and move forward, she had to leave that part of herself behind. She hadn't wanted to bring her along, finding it easier to go back to the anger.

She knew now she'd been wrong. If we choose to leave parts of ourselves behind, we can never be whole. Abandoning the damaged parts of ourselves only gives us the illusion of protection from the pain. But the pain still exists inside us, hidden away, slowly poisoning from within. To be free of the pain, we have to not only embrace those messed-up parts but welcome them—love them, forgive them. Only then can we integrate the pain. Not run from it.

Her mom's death wasn't her fault, nor Cecilia's death. She didn't have to hold on to the anger anymore. She didn't have to hate a part of herself. It was human to grieve, and it was *okay*.

It was okay to be human, like everyone else.

For the first time in all those years since her mom's death, she didn't feel the hollowness inside. For the first time she could remember, she felt... whole.

What an unexpected gift Marah Maddox had given her in the end—the capacity to forgive. A reminder that the truth in her heart would never fail her.

Marah's eyes had closed again. She extended her right arm to the side, her palm toward the ceiling. "Go ahead. I've signed the consent." She gave a low laugh. "Who would have thought to ask the patients to fucking consent themselves to give their blood sample at the end? Goddamn transparency.

Dalton Fall has proven me wrong. *To continually improve the algorithm for the benefit of others.* Who knew?"

Her eyes flew open, and her gaze sought Hope's. It appeared lighter, weightless, reminding Hope of how she'd felt gazing at her reflection in the hallway. "My tissue, too, once I'm gone. I've signed for it all."

"You're not..."

Hope couldn't finish the sentence.

"Come, come, Dr. Kestrel. We aren't people who mince words. I'm close enough. Do it."

Hope wordlessly collected the tubes and drew the blood. She did it herself rather than calling for the nurse. Professional courtesy.

Afterward, Marah's eyes remained closed. Her breathing raspy but even. Hope squeezed her hand.

She might have imagined it. A small squeeze in return. The barest of pressures.

Hope held Marah's cold hand until sure she'd fallen into a morphine-induced sleep, and for some time after.

With her other hand, she brought out her phone and opened the video. In the end, she'd kept it to herself. After all, Marah had disappeared. It had been unnecessary to distribute the video, and Jacie and Dalton had never asked.

She cradled the phone in her hand.

After a moment, she pressed the delete button.

Hope used to think that doctors should—and could—be perfect if they only had the right technology. But now, she knew, technology didn't make a doctor who she was. A doctor had to see beyond.

It wasn't only about predicting cure. It was about nurturing hope. Even at the end. Especially at the end.

Some things in life couldn't be predicted by algorithms. And never would be. There was no algorithm for forgiveness—or the complexity of the human heart and the choices it makes.

Most likely, Marah could no longer hear her. But she murmured the words, anyway. "Call me Hope."

AUTHOR'S NOTE

Thank you for reading *The Algorithm Will See You Now*. I hope you enjoyed it. Below are a few notes I want to share on the resources I drew upon to write this novel.

But first, if you enjoyed this book, I'd be grateful if you would consider rating it on Amazon (or the platform of your choice). Reader ratings and reviews can be instrumental in the success of a novel. You can also spread the word by recommending it to friends and family and posting about it on social media.

In my day job, I'm a hematologist and medical oncologist (a.k.a. doctor of blood and cancer medicine), and I drew on my experience to write the medical portions of this book. I am not a computer scientist, and this book is not, nor intended to be, a treatise on machine learning but a fictional exploration of the risks of the intersection of AI and the corporatization of medicine. I relied heavily on the following sources in writing those portions of this book:

- The Master Algorithm: How the Quest for the Ultimate Learning Machine Will Remake Our World, by Pedro Domingos
- Machine Platform Crowd: Harnessing our Digital Future, by Andrew McAfee and Erik Brynjolfsson
- Life 3.0: Being Human in the Age of Artificial Intelligence, by Max Tegmark
- Weapons of Math Destruction: How Big Data Increases Inequality and Threatens Democracy, by Cathy O'Neill

As an oncologist, I was familiar with the hype about IBM's Watson and its potential role in cancer care in the mid-2010s, only for it to seem to fade away with no fanfare. The following articles, accessed online, were helpful to me in researching why Watson didn't pan out for cancer care, and you may find them of interest as well:

- How IBM Watson Overpromised and Underdelivered on AI Health Care (https://news.mit.edu/2022/artificial-intelligence-predicts-patients-race-from-medical-images-0520)
- Confronting the Criticisms Facing Watson for Oncology (https://ascopost.com/issues/september-10-2019/confronting-the-criticisms-facing-watson-for-oncology/)
- IBM's Watson supercomputer recommended 'unsafe and incorrect' cancer treatments, internal documents show (https://www.statnews.com/2018/07/25/ibm-watson-recommended-unsafe-incorrect-treatments/)
- The University of Texas System Administration Special Review of Procurement Procedures Related to the MD Anderson Cancer Center Oncology Expert Advisor Project (no longer accessible to the public online)
- IBM Watson and Quest Diagnostics Launch Genomic Sequencing Service Using Data from MSK (https://www.mskcc.org/ibm-watson-and-quest-diagnostics-launch-genomic-sequencing-service-using-data-msk)
- The Hype of Watson: Why Hasn't AI Taken Over Oncology? (https://www.technologynetworks.com/informatics/articles/the-hype-of-watson-why-hasnt-ai-taken-over-oncology-333571)
- Novartis announces ground-breaking collaboration with IBM Watson Health on outcomes-based care in advanced breast cancer (https://www.novartis.com/news/media-releases/novartis-announces-ground-breaking-collaboration-ibm-watson-health-outcomes-based-care-advanced-breast-cancer)
- The Shaming of Watson (https://www.futurehealth.live/blog/2018/9/26/the-shaming-of-watson)

- IBM Has a Watson Dilemma (https://www.wsj.com/articles/ibm-bet-billions-that-watson-could-improve-cancer-treatment-it-hasnt-worked-1533961147)

Many articles highlight the dangers of inherent bias in AI, especially regarding race. Here are a few for reference and further reading:

- Artificial intelligence predicts patients' race from their medical images (https://news.mit.edu/2022/artificial-intelligence-predicts-patients-race-from-medical-images-0520)
- Racial Bias in Health Care Artificial Intelligence (https://nihcm.org/publications/artificial-intelligences-racial-bias-in-health-care)
- Even artificial intelligence can acquire biases against race and gender (https://www.science.org/content/article/even-artificial-intelligence-can-acquire-biases-against-race-and-gender)
- How Artificial Intelligence Can Deepen Racial and Economic Inequities (https://www.aclu.org/news/privacy-technology/how-artificial-intelligence-can-deepen-racial-and-economic-inequities)

For more reading on racial injustice in healthcare, I highly recommend Medical Apartheid: The Dark History of Medical Experimentation on Black Americans from Colonial Times to the Present by Harriet A. Washington. In fact, if you read one thing out of these resources, make it this.

For further reading on the evolution of cancer treatments, I recommend The Gene and The Emperor of All Maladies: A Biography of Cancer, both by Siddhartha Mukherjee.

As so happens in books and elsewhere, life imitates art. I had no sooner come up with my plot twist when I received a mailer at my medical office advertising postmortem genetic testing. Please note that I do not believe the concept to be inherently harmful, as long as done with informed consent and with the intent of gaining knowledge to help the individual or collective humanity. Not for the sake of profit (which, you may have noticed, is one theme of my book).

The book's "mis-pregnancy" subplot is based on my own experiences with multiple miscarriages. I started writing this book at the end of 2016, well before the 2022 Supreme Court *Dobbs* decision. I never imagined that by the time this book would be published, the landmark *Roe v. Wade* decision would be reversed, endangering the lives of pregnant women and girls in many parts of our nation.

For further reading on the prevalence of sexual harassment in medicine, I refer you to this 2018 article in the *New England Journal of Medicine*, Sexual Harassment in Medicine — #MeToo. (https://www.nejm.org/doi/full/10.1056/NEJMp1715962)

In this article, the author writes of a woman physician who experienced "a senior male leader in her field unzip the front zipper of her dress at a conference social event," which was the inspiration for the scene where my character Marah Maddox's senior male leader undoes the buttons on her blouse at a medical conference.

The section header quotations are from *The Oath and Prayer of Maimonides*, which is often used for medical school graduation ceremonies in place of the Hippocratic Oath. It can be read in its entirety here. (https://dal.ca.libguides.com/c.php?g=256990&p=1717827#:~:text=Th e%20Oath%20of%20Maimonides&text=May%20the%20love%20for%2 0my,doing%20good%20to%20Thy%20children.)

In fact, my original working title for the manuscript was "The Frailty of Matter," which is from the following quotation from the Prayer of Maimonides:

*Yet, when **the frailty of matter** or the unbridling of passions deranges this order or interrupts this accord, then forces clash and the body crumbles into the primal dust from which it came. Thou sendest to man diseases as beneficent messengers to foretell approaching danger and to urge him to avert it.*

I love hearing from readers, so please don't hesitate to reach out! I try to respond to all messages. The best way to contact me is via my website, https://jenniferlycette.com, or my Facebook Author Page. https://www.facebook.com/Author.JL.Lycette.

ACKNOWLEDGMENTS

Authors often speak of the "book of their heart." This book was a labor of love that took over six years, from the first story idea to the time of publication. I couldn't have done it without the help of the following people:

Stef Magister, who in 2019 selected an early version of the manuscript for the Pitch Wars mentoring competition. I was writing in isolation, unsure of what I was doing, only that I had this story idea burning inside me. Her selection of my manuscript helped me get through the darkest times of doubt. Whenever I wanted to shelve it, I would remember she saw something in it worthy of polishing. She has since become a trusted editor, critique partner, and friend.

Critique partners and writing friends Christine Daigle, Mario Aliberto III, Melissa Poettcker, and Manju Soni, whose ongoing friendship, support, feedback, and humor during endless rejections, kept me inspired. I'm a better writer because of you all. Christine and Mario, I owe you so many thanks for your revision tips and willingness to always re-look at a chapter or a page. Melissa, your suggestions for revising the first chapter, and pushing me to put more romance on the page in the subplot between Hope and Dalton, were invaluable. Manju, your ideas on restructuring the book, especially regarding narrowing down the POV characters and consolidating subplots, were genius.

Additional writing friends and beta readers, authors Karyn Riddle and Heather Levy, and fellow physician-writer Denise, whose time and thoughtful feedback strengthened the story and the manuscript.

Sensitivity reader Kashinda Robinson from Writing Diversely, who provided an excellent review and feedback.

My original beta readers, Steve and Kim, who read a very early and absolutely awful draft and still provided kind words of encouragement that bolstered me to keep going.

The Fearscapes writing workshop, and especially author Ed Aymer, who I thank for your insights and feedback, especially on reworking the book's opening.

The Pitch Wars mentoring program, especially our class of 2019. All the Pitch Wars authors continue to inspire me, and it was an honor to be a part of PW 2019!

Anyone not mentioned here, you know who you are and how much I appreciate you.

Black Rose Writing, who I thank for seeing something in this book when so many others didn't.

My sister for sharing her knowledge of Pacific Northwest trees and my brother for sharing his meteorologic expertise.

My kids (who aren't all kids anymore), who I thank for putting up with Mom always on the laptop. Books have the power to open our minds and change our futures. I write to help preserve the future you deserve.

And my husband, Jason, who read and re-read endless drafts (really, I promise, this is the final version!), who has unwaveringly supported me, first through my years of medical training and now through this crazy writing journey, whose real-life duckling rescue skills inspired the flashback scene with Hope's mom, and who's been the most supportive and steadfast partner, this book would never exist without you.

ABOUT THE AUTHOR

JL Lycette is a novelist, award-winning essayist, rural physician, wife, and mother. She has a degree in biochemistry from the University of San Francisco and attained her medical degree at the University of Washington. Mid-career, she discovered narrative medicine in her path back from physician burnout and has been writing ever since.

Her essays can be found in Intima, NEJM, JAMA and other journals; at Doximity and Medscape; and her website https://jenniferlycette.com.

She is an alumna of the 2019 Pitch Wars Mentoring program. Her other published speculative fiction can be found in the anthology And If That Mockingbird Don't Sing: Parenting Stories Gone Speculative (Alternating Current Press). *The Algorithm Will See You Now* is her first novel. Connect with her on Twitter @JL_Lycette.

NOTE FROM THE PUBLISHER

Word-of-mouth is crucial for any author to succeed. If you enjoyed *The Algorithm Will See You Now*, please leave a review online—anywhere you are able. Even if it's just a sentence or two. It would make all the difference and would be very much appreciated. Thanks!

We hope you enjoyed reading this title from:

BLACK ROSE
writing™

Subscribe to our mailing list – *The Rosevine* – and receive **FREE** books, daily deals, and stay current with news about upcoming releases and our hottest authors.
Scan the QR code below to sign up.

Already a subscriber? Please accept a sincere thank you for being a fan of Black Rose Writing authors.

View other Black Rose Writing titles at
www.blackrosewriting.com/books and use promo code
PRINT to receive a **20% discount** when purchasing.